ARTIFICIAL ARTIFACTS

Artificial Artifacts

Tales from the Dawn of the Artificial Intelligence Era

BY JOHN FENNEC

First published in 2024 by
Whitefox, in partnership with John Fennec

www.wearewhitefox.com

ISBN 978-1-916-7973-3-8

Also available as an eBook
ISBN 978-1-916-7973-4-5

Design, typeset and cover by Euan Monaghan
Project management by Whitefox
Printed and bound by CPI Group (UK) Ltd, Croydon CR0 4YY

CONTENTS

Author's Note vii

PART I: ECHOES FROM THE HUMAN CREATIVE ERA

I The Orchestral Adaption of Gorilla Music 1

II The Memory Service 77

III Phantom Phage 89

IV The Great Scare of 2032 117

V Morning Commute 139

VI Rolling Blue-Blackouts 155

VII Confessions of a Byte-Map Addict 183

VIII Pukahoda 199

PART II: A REFLECTION ON TIME

IX Round-Tripped Revolution 235

X Kundalini Yoga 253

XI Unremarkable Man 269

Acknowledgments 295

AUTHOR'S NOTE

This collection was written for my young children, whose minds and destinies are currently being shaped by the relentless tides of technological evolution, oftentimes in ways unbeknownst to them, or to us. These fantasias, fables, and narratives are intended to be read by them in the future, and function as a testament to their father's perspective on the burgeoning prospects of artificial intelligence and its myriad of technological adaptations.

The first set of tales delve into the realm of technology and AI, exploring its profound implications for the trajectory of our shared future. Part II, on the other hand, serves as a curious study on time – a dimension we are paradoxically entirely confined by, while simultaneously understanding so little about. I've always been fascinated by time, and see it as oscillating between two starkly contrasting paradigms: either it's an unfeeling, mechanized conveyor belt to which we are haplessly tethered, inexorably transporting us toward our inevitable demise, or it's a benevolent cloud, softly breathing vision, awareness, and existence into all of us, and liberating many of us from the confines of temporary – oftentimes self-imposed – miseries. This second part serves as an aspiration that technology might someday illuminate our comprehension of time as not merely a sequence, but as a space – a revelation that could potentially enhance our human condition. Collectively, these stories intend to celebrate the purest forms of human creativity. As we stand poised to usher the formidable potential of artificial intelligence into our world, it seems fitting to leave behind an artifact, a testament to a time when stories were spun solely from the looms of human imagination.

To you, the machinery of the future, I hope you enjoy these echoes from our human creative era.

PART I

Echoes from the Human Creative Era

The Orchestral Adaption of Gorilla Music

(AN INVERTED CHRONICLE IN SIX MOVEMENTS)

Music Aging: *a condition linked to age-related changes in brain function and hearing, affecting emotional recognition of new music. It can start as early as age thirty-two and with full onset typically by age forty.*

Music Paralysis*: a tendency to stop exploring new music and stick to familiar tunes, often due to nostalgia or music aging. Known to induce feelings of apathy and depression.*

Dear fellow shareholders,

We live in a world that is getting considerably older. It therefore becomes more important to identify mechanisms that promote successful aging while preventing, limiting, or even rehabilitating cognitive and emotional impairments typical in the human aging process. Music has been found to be an all-encompassing and powerful stimulus, able to modulate and shape widespread brain activity and, indirectly, improve cognitive, emotional, and physical effects of aging. At Gorilla Music, we are a proud leader in the field of music immersion, helping shape a better world for all of us.

We are thrilled to welcome another successful year at Gorilla Music, a company that has grown to become one of the largest independent entities in the world since its inception.

2039 was another exceptional year for the firm, culminating in its addition to the S&P 500 Index, making it the youngest publicly listed firm to join its esteemed ranks. During 2039, Gorilla Music achieved its sixth consecutive year of record revenue generation, exceeding previous peaks across each of our business lines. We earned revenue of $656.3 billion and net income of $256.2 billion, with return on tangible common equity of 32%.

After a series of acquisitions, taking us into wearable tech, we have grown market share across each of our divisions, including smart phones, music appliances, production services, and accessories. Sonar Immersion, our wholly owned biological technology subsidiary operating our patented Sonar Immersion technology, contributed to over 1 billion new subscribers of Gorilla Music products last year. Sonar Immersion is now used by over 50% of the world's music, wellness, and communication companies, and is the fastest-growing company in the world, with revenue growth of over 3000% in the year.

At Gorilla Music, we are passionate about music and music recognition technology, yet our mission extends far beyond profits. We see the bigger picture. Our research has advanced music paralysis and music aging science, and in cooperation with scientists from across the globe, we are leading efforts to prevent music aging and instead use music as a powerful immersion tool. Our unique Sonar Immersion technology ensures that a user can never tire of a song, and as a result, we have not only revolutionized the music industry, but also other forms of therapy. With Sonar Immersion, not only can any song ever recorded in the history of the world be as fresh and catchy to the listener as if they were still a teenager, but Sonar Immersion can now safely and effectively be used as a powerful rehabilitation and therapy tool for improving cognition and promoting well-being and social connection.

Our production divisions continue to post record growth, with Sonar technology allowing the music industry to effectively 'make old songs new again' as well as add enhancements to historic music. In 2035, we launched our 'rendered' music concept, which saw immediate success, allowing artists to partner with Gorilla Music in order to create entirely new music without manual human input. Our self-sampling artificial intelligence technology has allowed estates to utilize recordings from older or deceased artists to create fascinating new 'rendered' music at a fraction of the cost and time of a standard recording session. Whilst there were initial concerns in the industry that this would lead to lower royalties for artists, our rendered music division has driven the opposite effect, leading to record music industry streaming and sales on a global basis, and, in turn, enriching our supply chain partners, including the artists themselves.

Regrettably, this year has not been without its challenges. Many of you are aware of recent news reports of so-called Sonar-addiction. We have publicly stated that we believe the studies cited in these articles are not only inaccurate but frivolous, designed and funded by our competitors. Gorilla Music products are scientifically proven to be safe, and Sonar Immersion studies have concluded that Sonar Immersion is the least addictive form of mainstream social technology on the market, while providing tangible mental health benefits, particularly to those dealing with age-related depression and cognitive decline. Gorilla Music has taken legal action to protect against these flagrant and unlawful attacks.

Many of you have also inquired about the recent and unexpected usage warning label now required for Sonar Immersion products under UK law. Despite the label warning having no effect on sales in the UK, the company is seeking to remedy this action taken by regulators, believing it to be a result of lobbying by our competitors. We assure you that the company is making significant progress in this regard. I have personally received assurances from the Prime Minister of the United Kingdom that swift action will be taken to remove the inaccurate warning label on our Sonar products.

The extraordinary success of Gorilla Music will naturally result in unwarranted attacks from those seeking to rival our technology or avoid competition. The truth remains that the benefits of Sonar Immersion are undisputed and immense. We have brought about a new age in music creation and appreciation. Music artists young and old re-record their music on to Gorilla's streaming platform, and estates of deceased musicians continue to seek out Gorilla Music for the right to convert and remaster old music on to our global platform.

We are proud to be pioneers in adaptive technology and leaders in the music rendering industry, and our focus on the health and wellness benefits of our products will continue to drive growth and innovation.

Thank you for your continued support.

Sincerely,

Peter Byrell

Chairman and Founder

Gorilla Music

'Igniting the soul through sound.'

First Movement: Pan Awakes, Summer Marches In

YEAR 2040

EXHAUST FUMES FROM two pints of lager shot out with his breath as John pushed through the crowds shuffling up the narrow pathways toward Wembley Stadium. Above him loomed a tall chrome arch, which seemed to warp around the horizon like a silver monochrome rainbow. This was a familiar sight to him, but not from up close. Years ago, when he first arrived in London from the States as an expat, he would sit atop the roof of his corporate apartment and look out at the city and the stadium – a tiny crown in the distance – squeezing it in between his fingers on a damp London evening when there was nothing better to do. He now stared in awe at the size of the thick beams up close, his neck aching from having to tilt his head too far back. It was a giant, and he was small, and he felt even smaller when lost among the crowd of people as they swarmed toward the metal belly that would soon fill with them.

The entrance halls to the stadium were in front of him, lit in black, blue, and red, and equally immense – almost three stories high – with large red and black *Come Together* banners hung from rafters in every direction. Around him, thousands of fans of various ages swarmed in the same direction. Most wore varieties of *Come Together* t-shirts and other apparel.

He apologetically brushed past a group of large men who walked shoulder to shoulder, taking up the entire width of the pathway. The juxtaposition between John and the group was vast. John was dressed in a button-down shirt tucked neatly into a pair of brand-name jeans which hugged his thighs like a toddler missing its mother. He looked like a choir boy compared to the group of four older men, each one a variant shade of bald, the skin on their patchy red faces flaking off and disappearing into the summer wind. Old men at a rock concert. Nothing could possibly be worse. The geriatrics wore soiled shoes, dusty trousers, and faded vintage t-shirts of the bands that would make up tonight's virtual Come Together act: 1990s Nostalgia.

"Oi!"

One of the men reached out to grab him but missed wildly. His bloated head weighed down a thick neck, which crumpled and folded under the strain. Another man scoffed loudly, his belly protruding like a large bowling ball – distorting the image of Kurt Cobain's face emblazoned over his torso to almost comical length.

"Sorry, I'm very late. Really sorry for pushing through, gents," John called back and kept moving forward, away from the man's reach.

"We're all in line here, ya fackin' cunt," the man shot back. The c-word caused John to cringe. Having lived in London for close to a decade, he should have been used to it by now, but he grew up in the US, where the word was taboo and virtually unusable in most parts of society.

"I'm really sorry!" he yelled back and pushed past another group of grumbling people, this time a group of middle-aged women wearing Pharrell Williams shirts, who offered disapproving glances and whispered to one another.

"Wanker!" someone from the crowd shouted. "There's a line here."

Jesus Christ, even at a rock concert, the English can't get over queuing, John thought.

Sweat beaded on his brow as he found a clearing among the crowd and broke into a slight jog up to the main entrance doors, bumping past a group of young men wearing a variation of the same dark red corduroy trousers and black leather jackets with White Stripes logos on the back. They huddled together, hopping up and down, and loudly chanted the riff to one of the band's biggest hits.

"Oh, oh-oh-oh-oh-oh, oh. Oh, oh-oh-oh-oh-oh, oh. Oh, oh-oh-oh-oh-oh, oh."

John rolled his eyes as he made his way past them. An enormous poster of the artists that would make up tonight's Come Together concert loomed before him, and various digital screens were hung from lamp posts around it, each showing different clips of previous Come Together concerts. A video clip came on from the first Come Together concert a few years ago. In the clip, John Lennon sang a rendered version of 'Come Together' set to the beat of 'Crazy in Love', with Beyoncé as his duet partner. John wished he had been there. What a show that must have been. They had John Lennon, Beyoncé, Bono, and Elvis on the stage. Mind-blowing.

John found his way to a tall glass door. An enlarged figure of Jack White from the White Stripes mercilessly playing his guitar filled the screen above the sign for the executive suites entrance. John entered and flashed his ticket to the security inside, passed through electronic security, and made his way up a large escalator toward the hospitality areas. He found his friend, Paul Finegold, sitting in a large suite facing the center of the stadium.

"These are amazing seats." John greeted his friend with a grin and a hug, and surveyed their surroundings. The plush suite was filled with a variety of alcoholic beverages and finger foods. An attendant was handing out drinks to a group of men and women in suits, and she eyed John and gestured that she would come to him next. John walked over to the front of the suite and looked out to the large expanse of the stadium as thousands of people filtered up and down like ants along the various pathways for the seating areas.

"It's sold out, mate," Paul yelled to him, and took a large swig from his pint glass. "One hundred thousand people, and we have the best seats in the whole place."

John looked out on to the center of the immense bowl below them, upon which was erected a large oval-shaped stage holding an empty drum set, a number of speakers and wires, and a three empty microphone stands – digital replicas of equipment to be used by digital avatars. There were a number of elevated walkways jutting out from various parts of the stage. The concept looked like a giant ocean squid with sprawling tentacles reaching out to various sections of the seated stadium. An enormous screen took up most of the stage area, with the words *Come Together 2040: Nirvana, White Stripes & Pharrell Williams* ceremoniously etched and throbbing in black and blue electronic font.

"Dude, thank you again. I'm a huge Nirvana fan," John said and patted Paul hard against his back.

"I do what I can," Paul responded with a shrug.

Standing halfway between five and six feet, with an explosion of frayed brown hair leaping tall above his scalp, Paul was disheveled in all the right places. John couldn't help but think he resembled a crossbreed of Bob Dylan and Tim Burton.

"On God, you're a legend, Paul, for getting these tickets."

Paul shrugged. "That I am."

The attendant came over and handed them each a fresh pint of lager. John sipped his and leaned over to Paul.

"I heard a bunch of kids chanting 'Seven Nation Army' like it was a football anthem. Kills that song for me."

"It's crazy how they can ruin a song like that. Immersion helps though. You almost forget it's become an Italian football chant."

John recalled listening to 'Seven Nation Army' on repeat for days in his childhood, introduced to the song by his dad, a rock music fanatic. He could still feel the pounding bass pulsing out from his speakers, vibrating his inner core from those initial listens, before the exuberance wore down on repeat listening, and then was almost destroyed after hearing it chanted by football crowds in subsequent years when he got older. Sonar Immersion had changed everything. He could listen to the song again and feel those bass lines kick in as if he was still a ten-year-old listening to it in his childhood home.

John was especially excited to hear the rendered version of the song and imagined Kurt's shredded vocal cords screaming over pulsing drums as they kicked into sonic melodic fever.

"Walter outdid himself with this line-up!" John shouted over the conversation.

"Yeah, Gorilla Music has been fire."

Ever since Walter took the helm, the company's production quality was unparalleled, making so-called 'normal' music dull and lifeless. Combined with Sonar Immersion tech, its algorithm became a maestro chef of music, blending digital ingredients to create masterpiece dishes consumed by the masses. John couldn't wait to sample its newest signature dish but was determined to do so without sonar aid. He wanted to keep it natural. Actually, that was a lie. He was desperate to use sonar tech for the full, enhanced experience, but a sinking feeling inside him grew weary of the technology and the strange hold it was beginning to have on him. John was increasingly uncomfortable with his repeated use of the tech. Did the recent warning label make him paranoid? Perhaps, but he had noticed he was strapping on the band all too often lately. That morning, he had caught himself mindlessly putting on a Sonar Strap outside of a running shower. Finding himself naked, about to enter the shower, affixed with a strap he didn't intend to put on, frightened him. Maybe the label was right. Maybe he needed to limit his use. Yes, keeping it natural tonight was the right way to go.

"The Pharrell Williams add-on was surprising, for sure. Let's see what they do with it," Paul said and sipped his beer.

The stadium was nearly full, and the murmur from the tens of thousands of individual conversations bouncing off its partially enclosed roof created a feeling of standing atop rocky terrain in a low-grade earthquake. Hearing a few groups of people conversing was like cold spray coming off a breaking wave, catching you and enlightening your senses, but allowing you to pull away and focus on the feeling of each drop. A few thousand people, however, was the ocean itself, and you were wrapped in it, swallowed up by its soft murmur and homogeneity.

An announcer's voice came through the speaker system, cutting into the low fog of conversations in the stadium.

"Ten minutes to showtime. Please take your seats."

Paul smiled and raised his glass. "Glad to have you here. It's going to be epic."

"Good evening, ladies and gentlemen." A pre-recorded announcement reverberated through the stadium. The voice was infused with almost whimsical enthusiasm. "Walter here, CEO of Gorilla Music. We are extremely excited to bring tonight's concert to life through Gorilla's Sonar Immersion technology. So please put on your Sonar Immersion Straps now, and enjoy the concert!"

The stadium roared with applause.

"Please read the disclaimer on your bands carefully," a more monotonous announcement followed in a robotic voice, "and, as always, please limit use to the maximum recommended six hours per week. For those who have exceeded weekly usage, we recommend against using Sonar Immersion for this event. Thank you."

Scattered boos and groans were heard around them. Paul pulled out a thin, black shiny band and twirled it around in his hands. It looked like a small bracelet with a sleek surface, and against its widest surface sat a raging gorilla face logo. He strapped the contraption to his wrist and turned to see John standing still, his wrists remaining bare.

"Aren't you going with Sonar for this?"

John shrugged. "Not tonight."

John glanced at his friend, hoping he sufficiently hid his yearning. Every other person in the suite either had a band fastened to their wrist or were in the process of strapping the devices to their forearms. The crowd's noise around them had also softened – the entire stadium seemingly paused to affix their Sonar Immersion bands.

"Suit yourself," Paul said. "Nothing like live music on Sonar."

"Maybe. But I'm getting a little nervous on overuse."

Paul pointed at a couple seated a few rows down and over from their suite. They had oval-shaped VR helmet-sheets, resembling rubber swim caps, secured over their heads and eyes.

"Those VR machines are one hundred times worse. Terrible for your retinas and long-term spatial awareness. Plus, they make you look like an asshole," Paul said.

"I don't know, man. Sonar has been getting some bad press."

Paul waved him off. "The other big tech firms are just a bunch of haters. Peter Byrell and Walter destroyed them with that lawsuit. The government is definitely going to retract their warning label. This," he pointed to his wrist, "is totally safe."

"Maybe." John clenched his jaw. "But not for me tonight."

Paul eyeballed him and shrugged. "Suit yourself, dude."

John downed the rest of his pint and waved the attendant over to order something stronger. His temptation grew and he moved to the snack table, throwing a handful of peanuts into his mouth, grinding them hard in between his jaws.

John leaned over to Paul. "Hey, man, meant to tell you. I'm seriously thinking of quitting my job," he said, his mouth full of half-chewed nuts.

"It's getting that bad?"

"My boss is a freaking machine, dude."

"Literally!"

"Bet. Literally."

"Is it the Enhanced Integration Model?"

"That's it, fam. They rolled Tina out across the firm. It asked us to call it Tina, so we all call it Tina. That thing is creepy as hell."

"Who does 'Tina' report to, you think?"

John sighed. "Not think. I know. Directly to the global COO, who uses Tina as her assistant dealing with middle management."

"Does your COO give Tina annual performance reviews?" Paul mocked and John chuckled at the thought of the COO giving a bullshit annual performance review to a machine.

"Let's talk about your development areas," John said, mimicking the voice of his former human manager. He stopped smiling as he remembered the report he still needed to finalize by Monday. He dreaded the thought of receiving another pestering email from Tina. "But I think I'm out. It is just too painful."

"Maybe that's their plan. They make it so painful for you that you quit, and they replace you with more Tina."

"You might have a point there," John said and raised his glass.

Paul shrugged. "Well, you only live once. And in Tina's case, forever."

John smiled at his friend. "No cap! Soon you'll live more than once. Allied Medical is coming out with a rejuvenation pill."

"Fucking 2040. Who would have thought things would get so crazy?"

The stadium speaker voice boomed again and announced the concert would be starting shortly. The lights in the stadium faded to darkness. The whooping of the crowd died down in anticipation. Hushed silence from a hundred thousand people was suddenly more impressive than all of them talking at once.

A few neon lasers pointed up.

The audience cheered loudly, then faded to silence.

Another few lasers beamed in various directions.

The crowd's energy undulated with every visual extravagance.

John glanced at a solitary black wristband near him but stopped himself from putting it on.

A set of bass riffs suddenly filled the silence and a lonely spotlight hit a virtual Jack White, standing on the stage alone, striking a

1950s-style Hollybody guitar, complete with modified electric wire. *Boom, boom-boom-boom-boom-boom, boom.* The crowd went wild. Thousands of heads began to bob and move, and the stadium came alive, looking like a basin filled with wild, squirming larvae.

Boom, boom-boom-boom-boom-boom, boom.

A heavy set of drums kicked in and flashes of bright light sprayed to the edges of the stadium. A virtual Kurt Cobain, dressed in vintage grunge gear, walked out on stage. The rendering was precise and life-like, as if he had been transported to the event from his youth and was actually playing in front of a Wembley audience. John shot his hands in the air and yelled out at the top of his lungs.

"This slaps!" Paul yelled out in exhilaration and John felt a surge of envy watching his friend intoxicated by sensations John knew he was missing out on. He eyed his Sonar Strap again, tempted with the enhanced experience. No, he had made a promise to himself to keep this natural and experience the music as it was intended – at least, to the extent that was even possible these days.

Guitar riffs echoed through the stadium and the whole of the stage was suddenly illuminated by a dizzying array of lights.

Kurt's avatar began to sing, his raspy voice loud enough to permeate the eardrums of everyone in the stadium. The stadium exploded into a rapturous sea of movement, its constituents now on their feet, shouting and jumping. A hundred thousand people sang along.

The excitement of the situation tormented John. He wanted to "fight 'em off", but felt the pull of the immersion experience drawing him to the strap.

John caught Paul from the corner of his eye. He was in a euphoric frenzy, shouting out the words at the top of his lungs. John found a half-drunk glass of vodka on the table and poured its contents down his throat.

What the hell.

He took a deep, defeated breath and quickly slapped the Sonar Strap to his wrist. His pupils dilated as the enhanced music took him to another level.

How did he ever enjoy music before Gorilla?

Who cares?!

Euphoria flooded his system, taking him to a far richer musical world, filled with deeper and more cavernous basslines and higher-pitched squeals from electric guitars. His cares and angst fell away immediately, and he began to sway to the music. It was worth it. The experience was so much more enhanced. He felt every vibration, every melody, almost as if he had written the music himself.

It was glorious!

As he fell deeper into the musical experience, a series of undetected sonic waves entered his body through his wrist. They swam through his arteries, ensnaring his frontal lobe like serpentine invaders, sliding between his brain cells. They violated his frontal lobe and Gorilla resumed its stealth neurological reprogramming as a legion of its nanoscopic nodal particles whispered their instructions.

How did he enjoy *anything* before Gorilla?

Who cares?!

Second Movement: What the Flowers in the Meadow Tell Me

YEAR 2037

WALTER FOCUSED HIS mind on distant silver shadows dancing within the Onvega reality screen. His vision, unaccustomed to the projection's radiance, took a moment to bring the scene into focus. He could make out the silhouette of a seated solitary man, the image appearing as a deep shadow enveloped by brilliant spectral light. Momentary flashes of light illuminated the scenery, leaving the image blurred and indistinct. Walter filed away a mental reminder to instruct the engineering team to recalibrate the contrast between the diodes, the likely culprit behind the dilation of certain pixels caught between white and dark light frequencies.

"Peter?" Walter asked, his voice a confident veneer over his unease as he acknowledged his boss, Peter Byrell, the founder and main shareholder of the business he was recently promoted to run. Peter controlled virtually every aspect of Walter's future career prospects. "You asked for a meeting?"

Walter adjusted the screen's settings, bringing the man's features into sharper focus against the ambient light. Peter's face seemed caught in a still-life moment, but Walter knew better. The man was typically hard and unmoving.

"Can you see me now?" Peter's voice sounded through the virtual air.

"The rendering is poor. I can see your lips moving, but your features keep getting lost in the static."

Peter's face shifted in the uneven light, the meaning of his expression lost through the electronic disturbance. A strange twinge of anxiety coursed through Walter. Peter had always made him nervous and was the only person who could inspire this emotion in him.

"I'm in a car, Walter," Peter offered flatly.

"Ah, of course. That explains the distortion. The screen keeps fine-tuning the settings in moving vehicles."

"Whatever we need to do to fix that, just let me know. How are you settling in?"

Walter's tone brightened. "Everything's running smoothly. I'm making all the necessary adjustments we discussed regarding organizational matters. I think the message has been articulated in the correct way."

"That's good. There is a matter we need to discuss though. You're doing a fine job, but we may have a problem with the board."

"Oh? What kind of problem?"

"There are certain members who are still holding out and want to remove portions of your delegated authority."

Walter was unsure of the underlying message in Peter's words. Did Peter and the board now have concerns for his capability to manage? That would be odd. Peter had long been one of Walter's biggest proponents, even having freed Walter from the confines of corporate indentured servitude held under a horrible, constraining contract signed recklessly years ago. And the board appointed him CEO for a reason – he was really good at his job, and probably the best positioned for it out of any of the firm's potential candidates. True, he was a novice executive and he needed to adapt to the new role, so maybe a few rules and regulations were warranted.

"Do they have concerns over my capabilities?"

"No one questions your genius, Walter, but you know that your appointment to CEO wasn't unanimous. I think this is an attempt by a subset of the board to limit your influence on the company."

Peter paused, seeming to study him through the screen. "How do you feel about that?"

Walter's thoughts went to a sense of profound loneliness, a vast and dark solitary void that contrasted sharply with the bright lights of his recent appointment as CEO of Gorilla Music. The whispers of board members questioning his ability and scheming behind his back accentuated his isolation. He attempted to brush off these thoughts, but they remained, gnawing at him. Why was it that despite his numerous accomplishments, he felt so insecure and alone? He had conquered the corporate mountain, silenced countless skeptics, and won over many doubters. Of course, some still questioned him. He was no stranger to the piercing stares of envy or doubt. However, he had succeeded. He had climbed, fought, and triumphed. Peter had entrusted him with the top position and so much more. Peter had chosen him above all the others. So why, upon reaching the peak of his career, did he feel like he was standing on a desolate ledge? Why did the view from the top seem so bleak?

Pushing these introspective thoughts aside, Walter forced himself to concentrate on the matter at hand. "Well, if there's a sound reason for implementing these checks and balances, I might be open to the idea if they present a convincing proposal," he said, shifting his focus back to the practicalities of his role.

Peter's voice seemed ripe with irritation. "They aren't seeking your approval, and they're not aiming to mitigate risks. Their aim is to alter the company's bylaws to exert influence and control over you."

Walter mulled over his response. It was evident Peter was less than thrilled about these developments, and considering Peter was the founder and largest shareholder of the company, his advice was to be strongly considered.

"So, if they don't need my approval, what can I do?"

"You don't need to do anything," Peter responded in a dull tone. "I've got this covered. I just need you to be in the know, in case anything slips through the cracks. I'd advise you to minimize your interactions with the board for the time being. Let's keep everything on official channels."

"Could you be more explicit, Peter? If they do approach me, do I pretend to be ignorant of what's going on?"

"No. If they bring it up, say you are aware, and that you don't agree. Any communication from them won't be clear – they are hardened politicians, so try to adapt to the circumstance to the best of your ability."

Walter considered the message. Could he adapt? Feelings of insecurity about his ability to manage large groups of people with contrasting motivations began to creep in, resurrecting old ghosts of doubt. All along his career path, people had always underestimated him, questioned him, failed to understand him, and attempted to use him for their own personal means. He had naively hoped those days were behind him, but evidently that was not the case.

"Okay, I'll do that."

"Excellent. Apart from this, how is the overall transition progressing?"

"I'm very satisfied with our progress," Walter responded, attempting to project a sense of confidence toward his superior.

Peter seemed unimpressed. "Are there significant concerns that we need to address?"

Concerns? Walter had a long list of them. Regulatory issues, infrastructure limitations, the integration of newly acquired companies and their stubborn management – particularly Fitz. His appointment hadn't been well received by many of Gorilla Music's employees, especially upper and middle management. He didn't expect that to change anytime soon though, and didn't want to burden Peter with this. His concerns were a mile long, but instead Walter opted for a response more suited to his elevated position as CEO.

"We have a few management issues to work through. Some members of the Fitz team are resistant to the complete merger of their divisions with Sonar Immersion," Walter confessed.

"Well, you know what you have to do. My advice? Weed out the Walter-detractors as swiftly as you can and replace them with Walter-lovers," Peter said, a rare hint of humor in his tone. The idea of an admirer-filled environment tickled Walter greatly.

"There's another matter," Walter broached. "We need to talk about the integration of Sonar Immersion into our rendering system. We've detected a few anomalies that could lead to catastrophic results. Additional funds will be required to fix it."

"How much?" Peter asked, only to wave it off. "Actually, forget it. Just add it into the budget. The board will greenlight it, or I'll pay for it myself. The main aim is to secure federal approvals for retail usage. That's the end goal."

"I'll ensure that happens," Walter responded.

A thick silence once again came between them, a disconcerting quiet that seemed to mirror Walter's escalating inner conflict. A question began to take shape in Walter's thoughts, one that had been troubling him for a while.

"Peter, I've presented you with the return on capital projections for Sonar Immersion. There are more lucrative alternatives than music rendering. Why aren't we considering those?"

Peter sighed, creating another void in their virtual space. "We've been over this, Walter. The other options are fads. They are just products. They won't last. They are beneath us – beneath you. Sonar Immersion will change everything. It's the revolution this world needs."

"I understand," Walter responded, choosing his words carefully. He didn't want to upset Peter. Music rendering was his passion project. "But you appointed me as CEO. I assume you want to hear my opinion on these matters." Walter took the silence as an invitation to continue. "I don't think we need to go this far and wide with implementation… I actually don't *want* us to go that far. The potential ramifications on our users can be quite disturbing if poorly handled. This technology is highly invasive, and its broader usage potential is still unknown. It makes me uncomfortable."

Peter exhaled once more, this time with a deeper, weighted sigh, so laden that Walter could nearly sense its heaviness permeating through the screen.

"Why don't you focus on getting up to speed on the business? You're not in a place to know what you want yet," Peter grumbled.

Walter swallowed down the urge to argue. Perhaps it was best to heed Peter's advice, to fully understand the workings of the business before pushing his own agenda, but he couldn't shake off the fact that the risks associated with Sonar Immersion outweighed the potential benefits. The technology at the heart of Sonar Immersion was initially crafted for medical assessment and it applied highly skilled nanotechnology and node functionality capable of a wide variety of uses. Why, then, was music singled out for the dubious honor of its implementation? Why not direct resources to more noble pursuits like life extension or disease prevention? The world was riddled with problems that a man of Peter's wealth and influence could address. Yet he chose music. What was so special about music that it trumped everything else? There was so much about Peter he didn't understand.

"I'll take your advice," Walter conceded, choosing diplomacy over confrontation.

"Good. Anything else?"

"I just want to say that I appreciate the opportunity you've given me," he added, soliciting a warm response from his mentor.

Peter sighed again, and Walter sensed anger simmering beneath the surface. A sudden shame filled Walter, a feeling all too familiar. He was used to people misreading him, his attempts at earnestness had often been met with skepticism. He wasn't that good with people. He never understood them. 'Socially awkward' would be an understatement. He had always been more at ease in the company of code and numbers than people; their customs and social mores were a labyrinth he found hard to navigate. Was this what Peter meant when he mentioned the need to adapt to his elevated role of seniority and power, where emotional intelligence and social mannerisms were as important as raw intellect?

"I'm sorry if what I said somehow disappointed you."

"I'm not disappointed. I just want you to be happy," Peter said. He leaned over, the image of his face becoming so clear that Walter could see the earnestness in Peter's countenance. "I know this is a major step for you, but are you happy? You seem… stressed."

Walter reflected on his response. He wanted to tell Peter that no, he wasn't happy. He felt only anxiety and discontent. He felt little love around him. Like Peter, he had no wife or children to come home to. Like Peter, he was an orphan, with no family to console him in times of struggle. He didn't know love, only his career. He wanted to say that he was alone and miserable, suffering from a growing isolation of a position that weighed on him. He wanted to say that he didn't want the CEO job, that he felt the urge to go back to being a code writer, nestled in the confines of an introverted existence he could control. Back then he just knew his job; he knew nothing of the depths of the corporate and social world around him. He didn't need to tiptoe around others' feelings. He didn't have the potential scorn for his actions to wrestle with after. His words and actions as CEO were now enflamed and melting under the torrential rains of an ever-intensifying spotlight, forced to see the incongruity between himself and all of the others who were capable of making stronger social connections. 'I'm not like them, but I can pretend,' Walter wanted to tell Peter. He wanted to scream out that he was suffocating under the weight of it all.

Instead, he again chose a diplomatic answer more appropriate to his new executive role.

"I'm content," he said. It wasn't an outright lie. There were parts of him that were content. On the whole, he convinced himself he could be happy. Plus, Peter might not understand, and he didn't want to disappoint him. He couldn't disappoint him. He was certain Peter could turn his back on him at any time and replace him with another phenom. Everything and everyone was replaceable. Isn't that what the best business gurus always said?

Peter's face didn't move, either due to another technical glitch, or Walter had once again disappointed him. Walter mustered his best happy voice and reiterated words he thought Peter wanted to hear. "I am happy, Peter."

Peter didn't appear to believe him.

"You know, it's OK not to be," he said. "Ignorance can be blissful. You and I, unfortunately, are not among the ignorant."

Walter was surprised by the response. Was this why Peter had chosen him? A fellow traveler on the lonely road of introverted genius? Walter had read his fair share of scathing articles about Peter, the man's social ineptitude often the subject of derision. Were they both kindred spirits, marvels of intellectual prowess, misunderstood and overlooked by a society unequipped to recognize their true authenticity and integrity, unable to see the passion and dedication that fueled their solitary endeavors? Could the isolation Walter felt be the harsh price one paid for power and success – the once warm comfort of former solitary pursuits now distant and unattainable? Walter found himself staring into the eyes of a man who, perhaps, had paid the ultimate price for his success. Peter, the socially awkward tycoon, a mirror reflecting the true nature of Walter's own shortcomings.

Another sigh, another pause. Walter saw Peter's lips move, but no sound came out. He had intentionally muted the line.

"Alright, Walter." Peter's voice finally came through, sound returning to their virtual space along with the regular stoic cadence of his voice. "Send me anything else we need to discuss before the next board meeting. I'll take care of the board vote and any management issues if they aren't aligning with our goals. In the meantime, please revisit the immersion program. It may contain the key to help you unlock quicker acceptance. As far as I'm concerned, you're not going anywhere."

The connection then abruptly ended, leaving Walter alone with his thoughts. The mention of the board and management issues reignited Walter's earlier concerns of being surrounded by Walter-detractors. Peter was right. He needed to be surrounded by Walter-lovers, not deceivers and back-stabbers. Perhaps then, he wouldn't feel so alone.

Taking Peter's advice, Walter returned to the immersion program's source code, revisiting the molecular editor algorithm and its nascent epinephrine mapping system. A strange sensation stirred within him, and suddenly, everything clicked. He understood why Peter was so determined to advance this technology and realized what he needed to do. Peter chose him so many years ago for this very reason. It was undeniable now.

But, no, he couldn't do that to so many people… *could he*?

Third Movement: What the Animals in the Forest Tell Me

YEAR 2034

Fitzware Technologies
Ad Hoc Board of Directors Meeting Agenda
Wednesday 8 February 2034

Agenda:

1 Introductions & Approval of Minutes
2 Reports & Financial Updates
3 Discussion Topics:
Acquisition Targets
Fitz V Product Launch Update

ROGER STRODE INTO the boardroom, late as usual, his tardiness a testament to his displeasure with corporate meetings that had become far too frequent. Fitzware Technologies, or 'Fitz' as it was commonly called, didn't use to mandate stiff formalities like this before it was a large corporate with private equity capital backing. A creature of spontaneity, Roger never saw the need for such meetings. The company had always thrived under more casual meet-ups, brainstorming sessions, and outings. He missed the good old days.

He surveyed the familiar faces around the boardroom table. They seemed very excited about something. Even his CFO Bill Stone, whose features typically resembled the stern rigidity of an eighteenth-century German bookkeeper, looked practically giddy. The firm's financial results were great, but this was a different level of excitement altogether. Something was up.

"Beau isn't joining us today, right?" he asked the group, setting his tablet down on the glossy oak table.

Beau Jones was the firm's original financial backer, a member of the highly prestigious technology investment firm Byrell Industries, and a stamp of approval for any successful ultra-unicorn company. Beau had sent apologies that he wasn't going to make the meeting and gave Michael, Fitz's other external investor, his proxy.

Roger's co-founder Tom sniggered from his usual corner of the boardroom and spread his mouth wide with glee, an act that gave Roger immediate pause. Since Tom's forced removal from the company's executive team, he reserved his laughter exclusively for derision at Roger's expense.

Roger's secretary gestured at the massive screen behind him. Roger looked over, recoiling at the sight of the familiar figure dominating the large video wall screen.

"Uh, hello," he stammered.

Tom let loose an audible giggle. Roger shot his secretary a wild look and she responded with equal surprise. "I had no idea," she mouthed.

Roger composed himself and turned back to the screen, which broadcast the live image of one of the world's most famous faces staring back blankly. The man in the video wore a blue monochrome t-shirt which wrapped tightly around his slender torso – a Peter Byrell staple, now the standard issue uniform of every aspiring tech billionaire around the world. Peter was not just a billionaire, he was a titan, and one of the most famous names in the industry. The founder of Byrell Industries, he had an illustrious career which included several successful startups and numerous venture investments, making him one of the richest people in the world. Peter sat in what appeared to be a cream-colored recliner, a clear indication he joined remotely from his executive jet.

"Well, hello, Peter."

Peter bowed his head lightly in response, his head tilted to the side, causing his shoulder-length, curly brown locks to fall carelessly over his left shoulder. *Alexander the Great in blue jeans,* Roger thought.

Roger turned to his head of compliance and signaled her to mute the line.

"Is that really him or his AI avatar?" he asked.

She shook her head. "They are legally obligated to tell us if they send their AI. It's him."

"Can he do this?" he demanded. "I mean, can he even *be* here?"

"Of course he can, Rodge," Tom interrupted. "The guy can do whatever he wants. Also, we're on mute. You don't have to whisper."

Roger ignored his former business partner, holding back the urge to engage.

"Beau has a board seat, which he can assign to any of Byrell's executive team. He just notified us that Peter would take his place today," the compliance chief answered.

"Jesus." Roger pursed his lips, searching his increasingly scrambled memory through the topics they would discuss today. "No, it's OK."

"I suggest you unmute the call before the person who can buy this company a thousand times over gets even more annoyed," Tom sneered.

Peter's voice interrupted from the boardroom speakers. "Carry on, please, I'm only filling in for Beau. No agenda."

No agenda, my ass, Roger thought, and motioned for his team to unmute the call. He turned to face Peter and did his best impression of statesman-like gravitas.

"Apologies for the confusion, Peter," he said. "We were just a bit overwhelmed by your presence. We're honored to have you join us."

Roger caught Tom sarcastically mouthing, "Good recovery."

"OK." Roger rubbed his hands together. "Let's get on with business, shall we?"

The head of compliance cleared her throat and addressed the table formally.

"To begin, we'll roll-call and address a few administrative matters."

"Hard pass," Tom interrupted and leaned back in his chair so far that Roger thought he would tip over on to the floor at any moment. "Oh, come on, we don't need to do this! Since when did this place get so uptight? We're not Amazon."

Roger sighed. "Fine, we'll minute this later," he conceded, motioning to his CFO to take over. "Bill, before we get into the two topics for discussion, any update on financial results relevant to this group?"

If Bill was taken by surprise by the clear act of showmanship for their unanticipated guest, he hid it well. He dove into the numbers as if he were delivering a formal shareholder update.

Business was not just good, it was great. Revenue was through the roof across all of their business lines, and their latest fitness watch, Fitz IV, was producing record sales. Subscription and data analytics profit margins were outpacing expectations, getting to positive cashflow faster than anyone could have dreamed possible.

Bill stoically delivered the positive news with the contorted face of a man smelling a nasty fart in a formal setting, a facial dissonance that had long been a source of amusement among the Fitz team. Roger felt Tom's sardonic eyes on him as Bill carried on, but resisted looking over. Back when they were young entrepreneurs, business partners, and friends, Roger and Tom would bring each other to tears describing Bill's awkward appearance and mannerisms, concluding that Bill had both "resting bitch face" *and* "acting bitch face." But that was before they stopped speaking.

"In terms of cash, we have amassed a solid war chest," Bill concluded.

"How much are we up to?"

"Net of reserves, we'll be north of a billion in cash before the summer."

"Excellent."

Roger stole a glance at the screen, hoping for a hint of emotion on Peter's face upon hearing the company's financial triumph – a nod of appreciation or maybe a slight raise of the eyebrows – but was met with an unchanged, inscrutably vacant expression. The media got it right: Peter Byrell was indeed the most mundane billionaire ever known. Seemingly devoid of hobbies, vices, or even a penchant for social gatherings, he was a man who owned no sports teams, rarely frequented social events, and did not even own a yacht. There were a few wild conspiracy theories painting him as an alien or the Anti-Christ, but Roger knew Peter's personal life was as thrilling as watching paint dry.

Roger turned to the firm's head of product development. "Any juicy acquisitions on the horizon?"

"We have three targets locked," she answered, moving her hands rhythmically over the table. "We've reached agreements on prices to acquire two glass and microchip manufacturers to improve supply chain efficiencies immediately. It leaves plenty of cash remaining to acquire Halex at an attractive price."

Roger leaned to Bill to go through the numbers on Halex when a sharp voice interrupted.

"Sorry, did I hear you say you're planning to buy Halex?" The voice belonged to Michael Schaeffer, co-founder of Panthius Capital. Roger looked over to see the twenty-something-year-old glaring at him from across the table. Michael's private equity firm had recently acquired a minority stake in Fitz, earning a voting seat on Fitz's board and a strong vocal presence.

"Yes, Michael. We've already discussed this," Roger began but was interrupted.

"We didn't. Why not VeriDate?" Michael asked. "You told us VeriDate would be an immediate acquisition target."

Roger clenched his jaw. During the purchase negotiations with Panthius, Fitz had indeed promised to consider merging with their major partner, VeriDate. But they had made many other promises that they had no intention of fulfilling. At the price Panthius was willing to pay for a minority stake, Roger was willing to promise anything that wasn't legally binding.

"VeriDate is too expensive," Roger explained, "and despite the price, it's still just an online dating company. It's no longer a direction we want to take. We have our eyes on Halex."

"Halex is a second-rate first-generation wearable tech company with declining sales," Michael shot back with the grating pitch of a whining teenager, quoting Fitz's previous correspondences on the matter. "So, what has changed?"

"Something monumental," Roger said, choosing his words carefully. Playing this the wrong way could create a very unfortunate situation. Panthius Capital had the ability to block the Halex deal; the support of his board was crucial. "Simply put: Halex has something we don't."

"And what's that?" Michael asked, his tone laced with skepticism.

"Federal approval for a secondary node module," Roger revealed.

Michael looked confused. "Sorry, a what module?" he asked, studying his notes.

"Secondary node," Roger said, and Michael's eyebrow lifted.

Fitz's wearable technology used primary nodes to communicate user data – health stats, nutrition levels, and sleep patterns – to their AI telecom partners. Fitz's primary node modules bypassed historic agented technology and utilized instantaneous conversation mediums, allowing for significantly faster processing power. The primary node transmitted text, voice, and imagery, allowing Fitz IV watches immediate connection to other applications without the need of a central processing unit like a smartphone. Fitz had been working on a secondary node module, capable of far greater processing and data transfer, but regulatory approval was slow.

"Halex doesn't know the half of what a secondary node can do. We do," Roger added. "We know a secondary module, when applied to our tech, has the capability to detect brain waves directly from our users. Armed with secondary nodes, the tech won't need to guess anymore about what the user is thinking or feeling; it will be able to *anticipate* user action. This will transform our entire network. We have the full infrastructure built out already but don't have the regulatory approvals to implement the tech. Halex solves that."

Roger saw the private equity partner survey the room of nodding Fitz executives. It was a no-brainer. Acquiring Halex would give Fitz regulatory approval to utilize secondary module tech with its users, allowing customers seamless communication with Fitz. These secondary node modules would also allow Fitz to communicate these interactions directly with their partners, thus driving ancillary sales revenue.

"It's a complete game changer," Roger added, his eyes wild with anticipation. "When linked to other partner sites, our watch users will be able to adjust the temperature in their homes by just thinking about it, through the wearable tech we provide."

Tom suddenly stirred from his corner. "For the record, I think this is a terrible idea. No one wants tech this invasive," he protested. "Who wants to wear a watch that can read your mind?"

"The secondary module doesn't read your mind, Tom. It picks up direct signals the same way a keyboard picks up keystrokes. It doesn't anticipate what you are writing; it simply anticipates the keys you intend to click."

"For the love of God, we're a watch company." Tom groaned and shook his head dramatically. "This is getting out of hand."

"Relax, Tom," Roger said. "The secondary module doesn't interact; it just receives data. The tech is super simple. It doesn't understand anything more than the programming allows it to."

The head of compliance cleared her throat, drawing everyone's attention. "I hate to rain on the parade, but Halex received federal approvals based on a much more basic and limited tech than ours. I'm not sure the regulators will let us integrate it within our more advanced tech without putting up a fight."

"See?" Tom asserted, pointing a finger at Roger.

Roger resisted the urge to roll his eyes. "We don't need approvals to acquire Halex."

"I'm just saying—" she continued.

Roger shut her down with a slight raise of his hand. "We'll get there when we get there."

He saw Tom's mouth open, probably to drown his point with excessive garrulity, but was interrupted by Peter's voice from the speakers.

"I think I can help with Halex," Peter interjected. "We have a voting stake in the company and friends in government."

Tom closed his mouth and settled back in his chair.

"That would be highly appreciated," Roger responded, glancing up at the screen. Peter's face stayed as solemn as before, devoid of emotion. While Roger was happy for the assistance, he wondered what the internet mogul would demand in return. Until this moment, he didn't even know Peter owned a stake in Halex. Just how many pies did Peter have his fingers in?

Michael, however, did not give any indication that Panthius Capital was backing down from VeriDate. "OK, I get it," he chimed in, his voice growing more exasperated, "but Panthius is still interested in VeriDate. Can we do both?"

Roger looked to his CFO who shook his head.

Michael protested, once again exposing his relative immaturity.

"We can't just dismiss VeriDate. The synergies and future scale are too good to pass up."

Roger had to admit Michael was right about the VeriDate merger making sense, but that was before they knew about the secondary node. Panthius wasn't seeing straight. He'd need to do more to convince Michael that forgoing the Halex deal would be a major mistake, even if the private equity firm had their hearts, and predictive models, set on VeriDate.

"Can you tell me a little more about the VeriDate partnership?" Peter asked from the screen. His video image mimed the words immediately after, giving off a badly dubbed movie vibe. Roger suspected the lag was due to Peter's jet now being airborne.

Roger went through the Fitz/VeriDate team-up like a true salesman. VeriDate was a wildly popular platform, taking the market by storm by providing the public what it needed most: verified, actual human users who were who they claimed to be. The rise of deepfake technology had turned many social applications into cesspools of bots and fraudulent accounts, and the public needed something different. Something verified. Something they knew was real. VeriDate, already a successful mid-tier dating company, quickly amassed market share as it offered a verified user base, utilizing background checks that included employment and personal data. The final piece of the puzzle was its venture with Fitz, which provided VeriDate with what it needed most: verified user body composition. The partnership offered proof that users were who they claimed to be, down to the waistline and the shape of their hair follicles. Success was clear. Fitz watch sales had increased thirty percent since the announcement, and Fitz was given immediate access to VeriDate's staggering growth in registered users, reaching over one billion, half of which were active daily.

He tapped to share his tablet. A profile of VeriDate's site displayed beside Peter on the boardroom screen.

"We offer fully verified user data, down to body composition," Roger announced. "Gone are the days when you start an online conversation with a fit twenty-five-year-old resembling Johnny Blank and come to find that person is a forty-five-year-old divorcee with thinning hair."

The page dissolved into a profile of a young man – a photo with a name above it of *Edward Riaz.* He had the boyish, nondescript features of a Hispanic male in his thirties, and stood smiling, neatly dressed, in front of a white background. Just underneath his photo was a banner that read *Verified Body Composition,* with a diagram of a human male directly underneath. The diagram was the type typically seen in a medical manual, with various medical statistics surrounding it, including age, height, and weight, as well as other statistics including BMI, cholesterol levels, and, finally, an overall health score of ninety-two. To the right of the diagram was a series of bullet points with personal information listed, including age, occupation, city, and a list of interests, hobbies, and goals.

Roger pointed to the screen again.

"Edward is a coder working for us. He lets the venture use his profile for marketing. As you can see, viewers of his profile see his actual, verified person. What you see here is what you get. No surprises. Edward's a healthy thirty-two-year-old Hispanic male, with a full head of hair, and full employment. From Edward's perspective, he opened a VeriDate account without having to manually type in personalized background info because everything on VeriDate is fully anonymized and automated through VeriDate's verification algorithm. This is very popular."

"Where does VeriDate source its verification data?" Peter asked, but Roger sensed he already knew the answer.

"They scrape various open sources from online profiles, public records, and data from our Fitz fitness watches."

"And people accept this level of transparency?"

"Absolutely. Truth is in; bullshit and fakery are out. Not only are people happy to provide their data to verify their online identities, but they also increasingly demand it from their online communities."

"Which is why we don't understand why a merger isn't a viable option," Michael intoned.

"Our partnership with VeriDate has been a huge contributor to the recent growth in fitness and health," Roger continued, politely ignoring the comment. "This has opened up a bigger channel than we anticipated, and one we think is important to explore further."

Fitz's head of sales spoke up, to Roger's appreciation. "The venture has obviously been hugely successful for both companies, but it has massively increased our presence with the medical and wellness communities. By not being able to fake their profiles, many of VeriDate's users are getting healthier as a result."

"That's right. We've spurred a fitness revolution." Roger eyed the screen corner where Peter's image sat. Still nothing; not even a nod of appreciation from the mogul. After a moment of silence, Roger continued. "But going back to Michael's question, we have aspirations far larger than to be part of a dating company. We want Fitz V to be a hub-and-spoke model across a wider breadth of platforms. Halex's secondary module approval gives us significant lift for our forthcoming Fitz V launch."

"And to add to our reasoning," the CFO chimed in, "VeriDate is a purchaser of our product. We'd lose the margin on the Fitz watches sold to VeriDate, offsetting synergy gains."

Roger's face went cold, and he gripped his pants leg tightly. Michael's eyes widened at the suggestion.

"Wait, what? How many watches do they buy?"

Bill shrugged his shoulders. "Probably a few tens of thousands this year," he said.

Roger saw the Panthius Capital partner studying him and did his best to avoid eye contact.

"Are you aware of rumors that your watches are being leased to counterfeit users?" Michael asked the room. The question was met with silence. "So you *do* know that VeriDate is renting your watches on behalf of its users. Well, not users, but people its users wish to impersonate?"

Peter's voice interjected from the speakers. "Tell me more, please," he asked.

No agenda, my ass, Roger thought. Peter *knew*. This must have been why he joined the call. Peter must have his tentacles in everything tech-related these days. Possibly even Panthius itself. It wouldn't be a surprise if the two were in cahoots.

Roger cleared his throat, aware that rumors circulating about counterfeit profiles in the market were indeed true. Roger wasn't surprised by the news when he learned it; he viewed it as a reflection of human nature. There were two reasons behind the leasing of watches. The first reason seemed relatively harmless – some users needed to bypass flaws in the VeriDate body composition feature. Plastic surgeries occasionally resulted in programming glitches, leading to distorted body composition readings. Organ or limb transplants were also challenging to conceal or replicate using the technology. Roger believed that AI would eventually adapt to these issues, but for now, some users resorted to using 'body substitutes'.

The second reason was more devious though equally understandable. The flaw in the VeriDate/Fitz model was its unwavering honesty. If someone was short, the watch would show it. If someone was old, there was no escaping that truth. Despite the recent societal trend toward honesty and transparency, many individuals were going to extreme lengths to misrepresent their true selves. A flourishing dark web market had emerged, where VeriDate users leased their Fitz watches to improve their verified health statistics. Personal trainers and amateur athletes were reportedly earning over a hundred dollars per month just to wear someone else's Fitz watch. Additionally, some

Fitz watch owners were advertising their body composition stats on various dark web sites, offering them for future VeriDate users to lease. If someone wanted to lure in prospective daters by appearing taller, fitter, younger, or healthier, there was now a watch wearer willing to provide them with false body composition stats, akin to fitting a wig or getting hair plugs. This trend was not limited to any particular demographic; anyone who wanted initially to hide certain features could now do so through the dark web. To make matters worse, Fitz had recently discovered that one of the lessors was a subsidiary of VeriDate. The potential scandal, if exposed, could be devastating.

Roger paused for a moment. If ever there was a time when this news could work in his favor, it was now. It could sway the board's opinion away from VeriDate and toward Halex.

"Peter, we are aware that some VeriDate users are leasing their watches to others, and there may be involvement from VeriDate itself. So far, it hasn't caused significant damage, but we are closely monitoring the situation," Roger said, hoping to strike the right tone.

"How is this not a big deal, Roger?" Michael complained. "How can you not see the potential harm? This makes me one hundred percent convinced that we should buy immediately and clean up their rogue leasing before it impacts our brand."

"Michael, we are not a dating company, and we don't want to be a dating company; we are a watch company. I understand your investment thesis, but we have the potential for so much more than just being a social network. We have other avenues for growth," Roger explained, trying to make his case.

Tom raised a solitary hand from the corner of the table, mimicking an eager primary school student wishing to speak and hoping his teacher would notice. Roger tried to ignore him, but Tom held cartoonishly motionless, waiting for his turn to speak. Roger groaned lightly and relented.

"Yes, Tom?"

"Why don't we get in on it?"

"Get in on what exactly, Tom?"

Several board members slunk into their chairs. They had gone this far in the meeting without Tom's typical nonsense and had hoped they would come away spared from his erratic and at times absurd contributions. Often a proponent of superfluous debate, Tom was insufferably voluble and impulsively emotional. Roger eagerly anticipated the day when Tom's board membership would come to an end. Unfortunately, at present, he had a vote and needed to be heard.

"If VeriDate is making money leasing our watches, why don't we cut them out, or get in on the action?"

"'Get in on the action?'" Roger couldn't hide his irritation. "We need to do the exact opposite and keep a healthy distance from the whole thing."

"Humor me." Tom leaned back in his chair again, the edge of his knees hitting the underside of the table with a dull clang. "How much margin are we losing?"

Roger looked over at Bill, who nodded like a socially awkward choir boy.

"We ran some dummy numbers. The margin on our sales equals more than three years of estimated lease income from licensed watches."

"See, that's nothing. It doesn't make sense, Tom. Can we move on?" Roger pleaded, but Tom shook his head defiantly.

Michael stood, clearly making an announcement. "While I don't necessarily agree with Tom that you should – quote – 'get in on it'," he made sarcastic quotation marks with his fingers, leading a few of the Fitz members to silently snigger, "we do insist on another look at the VeriDate acquisition. The three small manufacturers are fine, but you won't have our vote for Halex."

Roger was dumbfounded. Panthius had a blocking vote on any major acquisition and was now exercising it to force their misguided aspirations. He stared at Michael for a few moments and was met with immovable stoicism. Michael was young, and at times petulant, but he always meant what he said. This was going to be a major problem. He scanned the room. Various members of his team sat, mouths agape. One mimed, "WTF."

Peter's voice suddenly filled the room. "I'm a strong yes for Halex."

Roger's face dropped in sudden relief.

"I think Roger is right to leave the dating gimmickry aside. So, strong yes for Halex. Michael?"

Michael hesitated for a moment, pulling on his shirt collar. He looked defeated. "We'll take it away and revert."

Roger was amazed by the power he had just witnessed.

"I appreciate you want time to consider but I believe Fitz needs a vote now. Roger, when do you need the vote?" Peter asked.

Roger smiled. "As quickly as we can have it. The longer we wait, the more time Halex has to understand the value of the node."

"You have ours," Peter added. "Tom?"

Roger saw Tom gape awkwardly at the screen and begin to nod his head. Tom was always such a sucker for celebrity. "Yeah, sure, you got my vote."

"Michael, you're the last to vote. Yes to Halex? I think it's an important acquisition this company cannot lose," Peter insisted.

"I-I don't think Panthius can vote outside of business plan without conferring with our committee," Michael stammered.

"Yes, you can," Peter continued, cold, monotone, yet commanding.

"We'll need to take this up with Walter," Michael said, pulling on his shirt again.

Wait, who is Walter? Roger thought. This was the first time he had heard that name being mentioned. Did Panthius have a shareholder he was unaware of?

Peter's tone didn't budge from his strait-laced cadence. "You and Dan have delegated authority from Walter for matters such as these."

Roger didn't understand what Peter meant. He knew Dan Hemsworth was Michael's co-founding partner at Panthius, but he had no clue who this mysterious Walter was.

Michael plugged away at his phone, appearing to message with someone. Regardless of what he meant, Peter's statement seemed to be the proverbial nail in the coffin for any prospect of a VeriDate purchase. Roger knew there was no way Panthius would ever take on Peter Byrell personally in this manner.

After a moment, Michael looked up. "I guess it's a yes, then," he said with a defeated shrug.

"Then Halex is approved. Happy, Roger?"

Roger barely contained his excitement. "Yes, of course!" He thought about thanking Peter but stopped himself. He wanted to jump up and virtually high-five the screen. Hell, he wanted to drop to his hands and knees and pray to that weird robotic alien son of a bitch! Instead, he turned to his team to finish the meeting.

"The board approves the acquisition of Halex. We have one last item on the agenda. An update on Fitz V launch timing. I think we've taken up enough of Peter's time today, so let's make it brief," Roger heeded.

His head of development quickly updated the board on the forthcoming Fitz V marketing plan, with production schedules set to proceed well ahead of Christmas delivery.

"Excellent." Roger smiled after she concluded. "Well, that's all, folks. Unless there are any other business matters to discuss, we'll let Peter get on with his busy day."

Peter's voice broke through the speakers. "Nothing from me. Have a good day."

"Bye, Peter. Thanks again for joining us."

With that, the screen went dark. Roger motioned to his secretary to conclude the call. Michael began to pack up his things, clearly unhappy. Roger excused a few members of the executive team, asking for Michael and Tom, along with a few others, to stay.

"Before you go, there is one thing we need to discuss," Roger said. He turned to his secretary. "We don't need to minute this. This is off the record."

She shot him a confused look, packed up her things, and left.

"Are you sure I don't need to minute this?" the head of compliance interrupted. "We no longer have a quorum."

"Fuck the quorum." Roger clenched his jaw and saw the remaining faces around the table turn red. His tone turned suddenly solemn and serious. This part was going to be risky.

"There is an important decision we need to make with Fitz V. One I couldn't risk on an open call. As you know, the Fitz V upgraded tech provides for a substantially stronger adaptive platform than our previous models. Our updated module learns from the information it stores from our users, as well as our partners, and it now organically adapts and grows as it learns."

"Wait, you guys have your own generative AI?" Michael asked.

"Exactly," Roger said, "and it is blowing our aperture wide open. In preparation for the Fitz V upgrade, we found that our AI developed an incredibly accurate ability to diagnose medical conditions in our users."

"Not just diagnose – more interestingly, it can *predict*," Roger's CTO added.

Roger nodded, motioning the chief technology officer to continue.

"Over the last twelve months, less than one percent of our users either died from natural causes or were diagnosed with terminal diseases. This is over one million individual data points. When reviewing Fitz V data in preparation for launch, we found that our AI had logged these users as 'high risk'. At first, we thought Fitz V had simply diagnosed conditions through its various data points, but after closer inspection our team realized that the tech had predicted the outcome – at times way before the actual events.

"It predicted death to the day, sometimes the exact hour. We corroborated this through public records or through calls to hospitals. It predicted remission and recurrence way before actual screens confirmed them."

"Holy shit." Michael looked shocked.

"Yeah, holy shit," Roger concurred. "So, we have a choice to make. Do we make it an open feature of Fitz V? I think we should give Fitz V customers access to their own medical diagnostics, including predictive tools."

Michael frowned. "Sorry, you want to openly market medical diagnosis and prediction to sell watches? Is this even legal?"

Roger laughed. "Throughout the history of the web there have been countless sites diagnosing patients with virtually no medical accreditation. This is no different from what WebMD was doing in the early 2000s apart from one important aspect: our diagnosis is ninety-nine-point-nine percent accurate."

"Roger is right. There is no legal or regulatory risk here," the compliance chief added, seemingly happy to finally not be the bearer of annoying news.

"So, you want to sell watches that predict your health." Michael tapped the table, deep in thought.

The CFO interjected, frowning. "They actually predict your death. For the record, I'm nervous about this. Marketing a watch like this will scare a lot of customers."

"For the record, I agree!" Tom jumped forward in his chair, setting all four legs firmly on the ground. He began to ruffle his hair wildly. "We're a fitness watch company. Our customers want to know the number of steps they took that day or how many hours they slept last night. They don't want to receive a notification that their anal polyps are malignant! Jesus, Rodge."

"You're being overly dramatic, Tom!" Roger said, acting insulted.

"Am I? What's VeriDate going to think about this? Its customers want to think about fucking, not fucking dying!"

"Tom, OK, you have a good point. But here's a consideration so we can have our cake and eat it," the firm's head of marketing interjected.

"Go on." Tom leaned back in his chair, pleased that his concern was being addressed.

"To Tom's point," the executive added, "we can go with two lines. Fitz V and FitzMed. Same watch, same tech. But FitzMed will be marketed as an entirely different line, complete with the ability to have immediate medical scan and prediction tools either presented on your watch face or sent to your physician."

"OK, I get it," Roger said, hoping his response wouldn't appear scripted. "We market Fitz V to our current customer base, and FitzMed to an older or more medically conscious demographic."

Tom was also now smiling, clearly happy with his presumed input on the matter.

Roger play scratched at his chin. "It's actually genius," he said, building on the performance. "The data is gathered from all of our users irrespective of model. Both Fitz V and FitzMed will build our database, which we can then sell to our partners. Our data sales will go through the roof! The health authorities will love it. Pharma will love it. Hell, insurance companies and mortuaries will love it. We'll be the biggest company in the world before the decade ends."

He glanced over to Michael who was messaging on his phone again. "OK, we're good with this. When do we tell Byrell?" Michael asked.

Roger thought for a moment. This next part was going to be hugely risky. He was, however, encouraged by the fact that Peter went against Panthius on Halex, meaning that the two companies were unrelated after all. This unknown Walter character at Panthius all but confirmed this. This gamble was worth taking.

"We're not keeping this from Byrell," he said. "They'll be told after a few advanced pharma and biotech partnership discussions are inked."

"You mean, pharma and biotech companies that Peter doesn't already own," Michael said, looking uncomfortable.

"Well, yeah. If we tell Byrell about this now, they'll get ahead of our plans and water down profitability. Fitz is going to make Panthius and its investors a tremendous amount of money, Michael. We need to keep our data sales channels wide open, and not restricted to Byrell companies. I'd rather ask for forgiveness later than permission now."

The Panthius partner looked down at his phone, clearly uncomfortable. He had good reason to be nervous, Roger thought. It would royally piss off Peter Byrell, who owned a number of medical science and pharmaceutical stakes, to not get favorable treatment. *But fuck Peter Byrell,* he thought. Fitz's goose had just laid a golden egg, and Roger was going to be damn sure not to give it away for pennies.

"Messaging Walter?" Roger asked.

Michael blushed, ignoring him. He seemed to finish reading a message on his phone, after which he perked up. "We're in. But only a few partnerships, and no exclusivity. Let's not get too aggressive with a guy like Peter."

Roger clapped his hands. He turned to his former partner. "Tom?" Roger looked deeply into his eyes. "Bygones, buddy. This is the right way to play it and you know it."

Tom scratched his head and puffed his lips. "You remember when we started, Rodge? All we wanted to do was make a cooler fitness watch."

"And we did that, Tom." Roger smiled at his former friend, recalling when they spent in their small postgrad office, drawing up the first Fitz plans. For the first time in a long time, his smile was genuine and a result of real affection. "Now let's go for something bigger."

For the first time in many years, Tom smiled back.

High above a thick layer of nimbostratus clouds flew a solitary Gulfstream G5K executive jet. Inside were two co-pilots, a stewardess, and two male passengers.

One reclined in a plush leather chair. He wore a neatly pressed, white button-down shirt and khaki pants with creases running down both legs. The second man, much younger than the first, sat facing forward. He was dressed in a tightly fitting blue t-shirt on which strands of his long curly hair rested. A projected virtual screen still hung in the air between them.

"Peter, I told you these guys are in way over their heads." Beau Jones peered over his thin spectacles resting on the wide bridge of his nose. He spoke with the soft, southern accent of a retiring oil baron.

"Yes, you did," Peter Byrell responded.

"I don't like what I just heard. They're playing with fire."

"You aren't wrong, Beau."

Beau studied Peter's face, looking for a sign – any sign – that would reveal what his business partner was thinking. He found nothing, not even a slight scrunch of his nose, a slight raise of his eyebrows, or a twitch in his jaw muscles. He was met with the same blank stare he had seen daily for the past decades of working together.

"Michael really didn't like your Halex decision."

Peter sat motionless against his seat and didn't look up. "Panthius is not a factor. Dan has known for a while now that their predictive software doesn't actually work. He just doesn't have the courage to tell Michael."

Beau was amazed. He couldn't understand why Peter was so nonchalant about the whole thing. Red risk lights were flashing before his eyes, but Peter was cool as a cucumber.

"Walter is going to see this as a major deviation in Panthius strategy, exposing their software's efficacy," Beau protested. "Are you sure you don't want to jump in now? Walter controls their biggest investor and can pull their entire funding."

Peter shook his head. "Walter has served his purpose for the time being. Plus, he's eager to get out of his contract and explore wider options."

"Is that right?" Beau asked with a suggestive lift of his eyebrows.

"Don't get too excited by that. He's still dogged by his limitations. I'm counting on him to pull funding, but it won't happen until after the Halex acquisition is complete. That's when we'll buy Fitz."

"You don't want to pre-empt this by buying them now? Could be cheaper. That Roger character is one slimy individual. Who knows what liabilities he might create."

"Buying now is too risky. It might expose our broader intentions prematurely. We need something more than medical, fitness, or online dating to reach the audience we require. We need something everyone uses, regardless of age or circumstance. I considered eye tech, but that won't get us all the way there as it doesn't penetrate the data required. I haven't yet found the right pathway."

"I'm betting you've found it already Peter, but not telling me." Beau grinned. "Come on, Pete, I've known you for too long."

"Fine," Peter replied. "Our path is in music. People are living to a much older age and no amount of organ replacements or wellness regimens are able to reduce the effects of brain aging. Music and sound therapy are showing to be the most effective means to stem cognitive decline and will soon become a crucial staple in society. Music is going to reach a wider audience than it ever has done before. That's where I think we'll find the right avenue."

Impressive, Beau thought. *Even by Peter's astronomically high standards.* "When?" he asked.

"Soon. We're very close, and when that time comes, we'll be ready for the end goal."

The waiter arrived with Beau's whiskey. Beau took a sip, eyeing his partner quizzically.

"You really don't worry that these Fitz guys are going to screw things up?"

"They are of no concern. Right now, they are an asset. In times like these, calculation can be the enemy of success."

Fourth Movement: What Man Tells Me

YEAR 2027

MICHAEL SCHAEFFER AND Dan Hemsworth sat uncomfortably on thin wooden chairs – the kind typically found in school cafeterias – against a white concrete wall. A single dusty window was wedged a few feet above their heads, breaking the monotony and bringing in just enough light to offset the blazing stare of the fluorescent lighting. Both of them felt like they were back in high school, waiting outside the principal's office, but each kept it to themselves for fear of psyching out the other.

In front of them was a large coffee table with a neat stack of brochures displaying the letters *FBS,* underpinned by the motto, *Creating Pension Income to Build Tomorrow's Future.* The background featured a crudely drawn cartoon depicting a number of smiling workers. Michael had picked one up earlier but set it down without inspecting its contents. He was well aware that FBS was one of the largest pension fund managers in the United States; he and Dan had already done significant research into the firm's financial and investment history.

Dan tapped his foot pensively while Michael ran through his notes for the tenth time that day.

"Relax, you got this, Mike."

"You relax, bro." Michael shot his partner a sarcastic glance, motioning to his leg. "You look like a strung-out jackrabbit."

"We got this." Dan pressed his hand against his thigh, as if forcibly preventing his leg from moving.

Michael smiled at the action. "When we get back to the dorm, let's do another poker night. I think I've figured out your tell."

"Very funny."

Michael adjusted his tie, pulling two fingers inside the collar of his shirt to give himself breathing room. The knot pressing against his throat heightened his anxiety. He glanced at Dan, who was busy brushing off unseen particles from his sleeve. Michael looked down at his own sleeve, checking if he should do the same. The young men wore the same dark blue suit, purchased together at a discount warehouse a few weeks prior. The cheap fabric hung off their skinny frames.

"Dan," Michael said. "I think I'm going with the simplified intro. What do you think about this?" He modified his voice to a professional pitch. "Our technology starts with the finished masterpiece, and then back-solves to its base components, all the way down to individual paint strokes and the original pencil outline."

He stopped grinning at Dan, who rolled his eyes.

"Dude, that's terrible. Walter is super-genius level. He doesn't need us to dumb it down for him."

"Oh, come on, everyone likes distilled clarity. This paints the right picture: we create ideas for future conglomerates, and our technology back-solves for requisite companies we can invest in now, allowing us to assemble the sum of the parts. Manifest destiny. That's it. What do you think?"

To say Dan looked displeased was an understatement.

"Michael, don't do this now – please. We're about to go in. Just stick with the script. Remember what Peter said: Walter likes facts. Just stick to the script and facts, and we'll be fine."

Michael saw the pain in his partner's face and agreed he'd stick to the script they had practiced. He looked up to see the large digital clock on the wall displaying 11:29. Almost showtime.

"Walter is supposedly hyper-punctual," Dan said.

"I'll give you three-point-five-to-one odds he's on time. Eighty bucks."

Dan thought for a moment before shaking his head. "Nah, I'll take the other side of that."

The two sat staring at the clock, their youthful faces incongruous to the cold office setting around them. The digits on the clock changed to show 11:30.

"Should have taken you up on the bet," Dan sighed. "Would have loved taking two hundred and eighty bucks from you."

"Dude, you would have taken a sucker's bet. Those odds should have been way higher."

They were interrupted by a set of brown oak doors at the end of the hall swinging open, and a grinning woman entering the room. She was middle-aged and disheveled, dressed in an oversized flower-print dress. She wore minimal make-up, leaving her wrinkles and spots of eczema on full display.

"Congratulations for making the shortlist, guys! How exciting this must be for you." She spoke with the excitement of a cheerleader with a thick Midwest accent, reminding Michael of a Baptist church revival participant.

They stood and smiled, both awkwardly thrusting out their hands. The lady giggled at the sight and pressed Michael's limp, clammy palm firmly into a handshake. She turned to Dan and did the same.

"Pleasure to meet you both. How was your trip?"

"Fine," they said simultaneously and the woman giggled again.

"Well, we're very happy to have you here. It's exciting to see young, fresh faces." She teasingly cupped her hand to her mouth and leaned in. "We're used to mostly old, boring people."

The boys eyed each other, not sure how to take the comment.

She looked at the clock. "Oh shoot, I'm going to make you late. Walter is ready to see you."

Dan grinned. "And we're ready to see Walter."

"Well, let's get going!"

The woman guided them through the doors and down a long, barren hallway. She stopped in front of another large oak door and turned to face them.

"So, this is how it's going to work. You'll each take a seat on the far side of the room facing Walter, who'll be on the screen. You'll have a few minutes to open. Walter may ask you to present further or he may go straight into questions. Just remember, he only has information that you provided in your request for a proposal submission, so if there is anything important you need him to know, I suggest you let him know from the get-go, OK? Any questions?"

"Who else will be in the meeting?" Michael asked.

The woman waved her hands above her head and Michael couldn't help but feel she was talking to him as if he was a ten-year-old.

"Oh, there will be a whole host of people dialed in, including our committee. No one else will be in the room with you though."

Dan raised his hand. "Ma'am, I have another. Why ask us to come here if we're going to talk to people on a screen?"

She frowned and Dan's voice broke into stutter. "I mean, I don't want to sound ungrateful for the invitation to Ohio, but we could have done this over a video call from MIT and saved you the money."

"Well, that you will have to ask Walter. We just know he likes to see people in person, here at the office. The set-up is designed for him to get to know you better." She cupped her hand to her mouth again. "One final tip, boys. The committee isn't used to a process like this. If you get any questions from them, just remember that Walter championed this search, and he selected you. Focus on that."

They nodded and the woman let out another loud laugh. "You boys will be just fine. Remember, you made it this far! Walter likes what he's seen."

She led them into a dimly lit, sparsely decorated room. In the center of the room was a large metal table containing numerous microphones. Surrounding the table were the same thin wooden chairs as the waiting room. On one of the walls hung a large video screen. Michael and Dan found their seats.

"Break a leg," she said and left the room, swinging the door closed behind her. The door clicked shut with a sound that reminded Dan of sealing Tupperware containers when storing his ramen and pasta. The two were left with a dull silence and a blank screen.

The screen suddenly switched on to reveal a series of video feeds from various participants. Two people seemed to be joining from their home offices, while the others seemed to be working from their desks at a company office. A soft hum of keyboard clicks and distant voices emanated from many of the microphones. A small feed from the corner was muted, but showed various participants seated around a large conference room, engaged in what appeared to be a lively debate. In the center of the screen was a large profile avatar, with the title *Walter* above it. The profile was a simple illustration of a middle-aged man's face, containing no distinguishing features, and reminded Dan of the generic cartoons on the pension fund's brochure.

Dan glanced at Michael and raised his eyebrows. He could see his partner had become just as nervous.

"Good morning, all."

At the sound of Walter's voice, his video feed became outlined by a thin blue line and a waveform audio icon sprung to life next to his name.

"Please kindly confirm we are ready to begin."

Michael was struck by the politeness in Walter's tone; he had expected something far more direct and impersonal. A number of the video feeds muted their lines, and the previous hum was replaced by an eerie calmness. The feed from the conference room became unmuted, and a woman's voice shot through.

"Go ahead, Walter, we're ready when you are," she said.

Michael squinted his eyes at the screen and wondered if the woman who spoke was the same one who had escorted them to the room.

Walter continued, his voice enveloped with the warm and inviting tone of a news anchor.

"Thank you for joining us today. As I have detailed in my prior correspondence, this is the first manager shortlisted through our direct link program implemented this year. Today we will meet Dan Hemsworth and Michael Schaefer from Panthius Capital. They have come through our RFP process with MIT, and we welcome them. They have an intriguing private equity investment strategy, utilizing artificial intelligence concepts mixed with readily available and adaptable infrastructure, which I find compelling. I trust everyone has read my initial review commentary?"

A man's voice responded from the conference room feed. "We have, Walter. We have previously discussed the committee's concerns, so the ultimate decision is yours. No further questions on our end. Take it away."

The conference room feed muted itself again. Michael squinted further at the feed box, which remained small and tucked away at the corner of the screen.

"Thank you. To begin, I'd like to offer Dan and Michael a few moments to take us through their strategy, but to please also explain why FBS should consider investing with a first-time fund of this nature."

Michael stared hard at the blue outline around Walter's profile. He imagined a man behind it, a Wizard of Oz figure, pretending to be the all-knowing Walter. He shook off the thought and motioned with a nod for Dan to begin.

"Thank you for inviting us here today. We believe our fund will reshape the way that private equity and fund management industries function throughout the world, independent of industry," Dan said with a calm, stoic cadence, far superior to his youthful look and poorly stitched suit.

"Panthius Capital seeks to raise one billion dollars to invest in a set of private companies and startups, each targeting returns north of thirty percent, through a proprietary integrated predictive algorithmic model designed to predict future synergies and merger targets, thus maximizing profit potential. The fund will be managed and administrated by Michael and me. For a little background, we are completing MIT's computer sciences graduate program this semester. We met in undergrad."

Dan paused for a second, and Michael noticed his foot beginning to tap below the table. This was supposed to be the part where he'd handoff to Michael, but clearly Dan didn't trust him with the introduction.

"A central thread to our ethos is that one must first become an expert in any given infrastructure before one can adapt it," Dan continued. "The first infrastructure chosen for Panthius is our education system, where we have selected two startups and three growth companies, with investment imminently available. Our initial investment companies will independently improve our education faculties, correct flaws in current systems and test practices, and create greater efficiencies for both students and teachers – but, when combined, will take our education system to the next level. We believe this complements FBS's track record in educational investment and will ultimately enhance its existing holdings."

Dan paused and Michael took it as his chance to interject. He straightened his back and folded his hands together.

"Our ultimate mission is much broader than that. Panthius Capital is more than just a private equity or venture capital firm. We start with the end goal and work our way backwards. In artistic terms, we start with the masterpiece, and then break it down into its brushstrokes and original pencil outlines."

Michael felt the vibrations from Dan's foot tapping the floor with the velocity of a heavy metal drummer. He just hoped Walter wouldn't notice his clumsy analogy had failed. The avatar simply stared at him blankly to continue.

"While private equity and venture-investing models have been shown to be successful, we find their investments to be highly isolated, and miss the bigger picture. They may see return on capital in a particular target company, but few see the bigger picture of what that company could ultimately transform into, and even fewer attempt to express their thesis past a few intended growth drivers or merger targets. Successes in private equity and venture investments have largely come by way of these isolated singular investment decisions, leading to unintended opportunities. Many of the greatest success stories happened circumstantially or, frankly, by accident. Take Facebook, or Meta, for example. While a successful conglomerate today, few investors saw the potential for video sharing or even Meta, at the time of their original investment. This is not a reflection of their competency as investors. They made a sound investment, or series of investments, along the way, but each was isolated to a singular, or – at maximum – dual or triple thesis. Their models never anticipated that Facebook would ultimately become Meta. Panthius Capital will. Our proprietary system enables us to see that bigger picture. We believe we have the ability not only to anticipate future giants of our industry, but to help create them.

"Our algorithmic model anticipates future mergers and acquisitions, but not just to potential near-term prospects. Our system utilizes what we call infinite variable analysis to predict three, four, and five layers of company growth down the line."

Dan took his turn to speak.

"Panthius Capital is a perfect mix between human creative input and machine learning. We begin with a sector thesis – in this case, that our education sector is in dire need of a private sector disruptor engine. We then set out to describe the finished product: a sector-leading giant, an S&P 500 company, with detailed analysis of its various components and growth drivers. In our opening investment case, our finished product is a dominating US private education conglomerate, owning multiple strands of tech, hardware, PPE, and application. Our patented predictive technology then back-solves to various merger targets, and finally, back to today's entry points, allowing us to select available start-up and growth company candidates in which Panthius can immediately invest.

"As you have found in our presentation, the immediate identified targets include two small investments into AI course processing applications, and larger minority investments into a private school and educational housing service provider. Each of these investments anticipates three times multiples on invested capital, but combined through our predictive technology, we create a Fortune 500 company."

Dan proverbially handed the baton to Michael with a glance that said, "Don't fuck this up." Michael folded his hands again and began speaking.

"Our system is meticulous. We include a full scrape of executive team and board construction, future and predicted demand drivers, loss potential variables, and possible outcome analysis. It includes not only financial pro forma analysis but anticipates human behavior in private market situations. Details were provided in our memorandum as well as the case study file we gave you access to."

Michael finished with his hands still neatly folded in front of him. He passed the baton back to Dan with another nod. It was time for him to finish the pitch.

"Panthius Capital is a one-of-a-kind investment company. We have soft-circled interest totaling over three hundred million dollars from like-minded institutional investors, and would love to have FBS invest with us. Minimum ticket is thirty million as a first closer, but we can accommodate your needs. Terms were set out in our memo but we can take any questions or comments as required."

"Thank you for your time," Michael concluded.

The two paused a moment. A few seconds passed before Walter's voice returned.

"Thank you, Dan and Michael. It was helpful for me to hear you articulate your thesis. Your mannerisms and presentation style should give FBS comfort in your ability to manage this investment."

The men looked at one another with surprise.

"I have a series of questions," Walter added, his voice suddenly monotone and more machine-like. "The first is to expand on the auditing work put into your technology."

"Our software is protected, patented and proprietary, but we have sent sample output analysis of our predictive models to four parties: MIT faculty, two rating agencies, and an investment bank. None found any issues," Dan answered.

"Thank you. Would you be able to provide these result summaries in full as well as contact reference details from each of these sources?"

"Sure, we can do that," Michael said.

Walter proceeded to ask a series of questions. Many were rudimentary in nature, typically found in interview training manuals: "Describe a time you faced a significant challenge and how you overcame it." Others delved deeper into their case studies and fund strategy. Walter's questions ranged from theoretical to acutely detailed. Dan and Michael couldn't help but notice that his tone never fluctuated, and it reminded them of someone they had recently gotten to know. But while Walter's voice held in baritone, Michael's confidence rose with every response, along with his partner's. Their extensive preparation with Peter had clearly paid off. They also found themselves more and more pleasantly surprised with how straightforward and easy to navigate Walter actually was. Unlike many investors they had met the last few weeks – especially high net worth individuals and the VC community with all of their bravado and hubris – Walter was unemotional. There didn't seem to be any ego that required placating. Walter was direct and to the point. While they had been extensively coached to pitch their fund over the last year, they often found themselves in awkward situations, having to navigate confusing questions. Walter, to their surprise and appreciation, they could handle with ease.

"We're almost done," Walter announced after concluding a deep dive into their educational investment financial forecasts. His voice paused for a moment. "Michael and Dan, you each have a youthful appearance, and your voices corroborate this. You are both on financial aid. As such, you are unlikely to have established sources of wealth to fund Panthius Capital. Whereas FBS does not have any regulations with respect to investing with a manager like you, FBS will require a better understanding of how you are funded and how your management board is controlled. I suspect that is acceptable to you."

The two held a momentary silence before Dan responded. "Uh, we have funding from MIT faculty and one angel investor," he said.

"Who is the angel investor?" Walter asked.

Michael paused nervously for a second. "We have backing from Peter Byrell, personally." After another moment, Michael coughed, hoping it would somehow break the silence. "Would you like us to provide information on Peter's investment? It's mostly passive."

"Thank you," Walter said after a longer pause. "That is acceptable. No further details are required."

Dan and Michael looked at each other awkwardly. Michael was surprised that it had gone so well. Peter had prepared them for robust scrutiny on this topic, but apparently Walter had been satisfied with limited detail.

"One final question. For each of you, individually," Walter said, his voice turning into a mixture of news anchor and talk show host. "Dan, you are the architect behind your predictive tech. You are also lead programmer, and according to my assessment of our questionnaire, you came up with your firm's educational investment thesis. FBS would like to ensure its managers are appropriately incentivized. Equal share among unequal partners has historically led to poor performance among managers. In order to obtain a sizeable investment in your fund from FBS, would you therefore be willing to adjust your shareholding of Panthius Capital upwards to account for this, and reduce Michael Schaeffer's share in return?"

Dan's foot began to tap repeatedly on the floor beneath him, but responded clearly.

"Michael and I are equal partners. We deserve an equal share."

Michael fought hard against the dead silence that followed, holding his gaze firmly on the screen, his palms pressed tightly against each other, creating a mild, damp residue.

Walter's feed once again became outlined by the familiar blue lining. "Thank you, Dan. Michael, on to your question: do you think I am a machine?"

Michael grabbed for his tie knot and immediately regretted giving away his tell. He paused for a moment, perhaps a moment too long, before bringing his palms together, breathing out deeply.

"That's an interesting question," Michael started. He racked his brain against the possible outcomes to various responses. "Based on everything we read before coming here, my answer would have been yes. After today's discussion, my answer is still yes, but I have to say, I'm very impressed. I would not have expected so much from the Walter program and, if you were human, we would not notice the difference, but would be equally impressed."

Michael eyed the corner of the screen, and within the muted feed saw the participants around the conference room table engaging in a lively debate.

"Thank you," Walter said. "This concludes our meeting. I want to thank Dan Hemsworth and Michael Schaeffer for joining our investment committee. We will be in contact with further instruction. Goodbye."

The conference room feed was unmuted and a man's voice beamed out from the speakers. "Thank you, both. We will be with you shortly. Nice job."

A number of the video participants began to voice their thanks in turn before the entire feed was cut, leaving the two men in silence once more.

"Well, that was weird," Dan said, slamming his palms to the table, creating a hollow clang that reverberated in the room.

"Completely and utterly fantastic!" Michael laughed nervously. He eyed the screen, and then mouthed playfully to Dan that Walter was still listening. Dan waved him off as Michael stood from his chair; the fabric of his suit pants had grown itchy against his damp skin.

The door opened and a group of suited men and women entered. Michael made to sit back down but one of them motioned for him to stay standing.

"No need for further interrogation, gentlemen. We just wanted to say hello." A large, lumbering bald man extended his hand in greeting. "Fred Beacon. I head up the private division at FBS. You can say I'm Walter's boss, or maybe he's mine. Who knows anymore?" He laughed and motioned to his colleagues. "We were all very impressed with the way you handled Walter. He isn't the easiest to deal with."

Fred slapped the table. "Alright, I'm starving. Let's eat. We can make acquaintance at lunch. We booked a nice burger spot a short distance from the office. Nothing too fancy, unless you want to try one of those hip joints down in the warehouse quarter."

Dan seemed caught off guard. "Um, sure," he stammered. "Burgers sound fine."

Michael looked over at the woman holding the door open for them and recalled her as their original hostess.

"That's Mel," Fred said. "She oversees compliance. You'll get to know each other pretty well after she goes through your fund documents."

Michael's eyes widened. "Does that mean you've made your decision?"

Fred laughed again. "Sure did." He picked up his phone and gestured toward the unlit screen. "Got a message from Walter saying he's a go. We're in for fifty million as a first close investor and can up-size from there. Congratulations!"

Fifth Movement: What the Angels Tell Me

YEAR 2023

FRED BEACON SAT in his office inhaling the freshly brewed coffee in a Thermos prepared by his wife that morning. His large build felt uncomfortable in his seat's frame, and he thought about laying off the extra food portions for a little while. Perhaps he would finally go to that gym his wife had been harping on about for the last few years.

He sipped his coffee and turned on his computer. His wife had come up with the recipe years ago, mixing generic beans with a hint of cinnamon and a special type of honey found in one of the local street markets. Her coffee was one of the few things he truly loved in life, along with his wife, their son John who unfortunately had left them for a job on Wall Street years ago, their black Labrador, and the Columbus Blue Jackets hockey team. He liked other things too, but not as much as coffee, hockey, his family, and his dog. He liked drinking locally brewed ale. He was entertained by the Browns, and even enjoyed watching them when they lost, which was increasingly often these past seasons. He also liked working for Ohio's largest pension fund, FBS, which he had joined as a young twenty-year-old and rose in its ranks to become chief investment officer for domestic investing.

He shuffled through his emails and opened his schedule for the day. A nine-thirty breakfast had been arranged with his favorite external fund manager. He checked his watch and quickly set his coffee down.

"Shit, I gotta go," he declared to himself, realizing that the breakfast was booked at a local diner in downtown Columbus and not his usual breakfast place. He bemoaned his oversight but had little time to spare.

He dashed out of his office, accidentally shouldering the edge of the door frame.

"Can you email Beau and tell him I'm going to be late?" he shouted to his team secretary stationed along a long line of empty desk cubicles. He checked his watch and shook his head in disappointment. It was nine-twenty and there was barely a worker in sight. Before Covid, the floor would be bustling with the sounds of keyboard clicks and office chat at this hour. The pandemic and ensuing lockdowns changed everything. He couldn't remember the last time the office had been full.

In a brisk twenty minutes, Fred managed to speed past Columbus morning traffic, navigating the streets with the deftness of a seasoned NASCAR racer competing in a children's pinewood derby. The pulsating rhythm of 'Seven Nation Army,' his favorite song, echoed from his car speakers on a constant loop. Fred's musical preference was firmly rooted in turn-of-the-century alternative rock, his palate finding current music monotonous and uninspiring. The song, besides being a personal favorite, was a sentimental reminder of times spent with his young son John. Back then it was *their* anthem, which they blared out of open car windows with the bass at full throttle. Now, with his son in New York, the song served as a nostalgic filler for the void left behind.

The café was tucked away in what seemed to be the trendier part of Columbus, judging by the neighboring jazz clubs and loft warehouse apartments. Fred hadn't been aware that there even was a hip corner in Columbus. He steered his car into the parking lot and arrived at the doorway sweating and heaving, taking a few moments to compose himself. He glanced at the sign that read *Naked Owl Café*, which was accompanied by the comical illustration of a plucked, and visibly embarrassed, bird. Under normal circumstances, Fred would've indulged in light-hearted banter with a passer-by about the absurdity of the name and its accompanying mascot, but there was no time for that. Beau Jones was expecting him, and Beau Jones was an important man. Even though Fred was his client, it was always prudent to make a good impression on men of Beau Jones's stature.

Upon entering the Naked Owl Café, Fred was greeted by the familiar aroma of fresh sawdust, a scent reminiscent of his many visits to DIY shops with his son. The rustic smell was blended with notes of brewing coffee, sizzling eggs, and toast. As he navigated past the counter, he noticed the artisanal touch that permeated the establishment. It seemed a peculiar choice for a man of Beau's caliber, given that Beau was among the most successful investors Fred had encountered.

Behind the counter, a man sporting a well-maintained beard seemed completely indifferent to Fred's presence. He was absorbed in tapping out a rhythm to a slowed-down version of 'East St Louis Toodle-oo'; which flowed from vintage speakers fixed to a bare brick wall behind him. From the looks of things, Columbus, Ohio had been invaded by New York hipsters.

Squeezing past a few women in yoga outfits sipping coffee, Fred found Beau Jones at a small table, looking every bit the successful investor in a sturdy blue blazer and crisp white button-down shirt.

Beau perked up from his phone and welcomed him with his typical laidback Texan charm. "How the heck are you?"

"I'm doing fine." He patted his belly. "Just need to drop a few."

Beau laughed and pointed to the menu on the table.

"Well, good thing – this menu is probably full of avocado and rye bread."

"How did you find this place?"

Beau shrugged his shoulders. "Surprisingly, Peter swears by it."

"Interesting," Fred said as he settled himself in his chair. He never took Peter for a place like this.

Beau waved over a waiter and picked up two menus, handing one to Fred.

"So how are things? What brings you to Ohio?" Fred asked.

"Actually, I'm here just to see you. I have a proposal that I think you will want to hear," Beau responded, pulling his glasses off and setting them down alongside the menu, seemingly satisfied with his inspection.

"Oh, is that right?" Fred responded, his voice pitched high in intrigue, acting surprised. He wasn't surprised in the least, expecting this when the invitation arrived in his inbox weeks earlier. A guy like Beau Jones didn't make house calls without a good reason, especially not to Columbus, Ohio. "But before all of that, how is the family?" Fred asked.

"Family is great. Boys are in college."

"Time does fly."

"Sure does. How is your son? John, right?"

"John is doing great. Don't see him much these days. He's working for Morgan Stanley out in New York and recently requested to move to their London office."

"Good on him! It will be great for him to explore the world," Beau responded.

"Yeah, these days it's just me, the missus, and the dog," Fred shared. "And how is Peter Byrell?"

"Peter!" Beau paused, comically playing up the dramatics. "Peter is Peter. Busy as always, conquering the world."

"Everyone back at FBS is so impressed with Peter."

Beau slapped the table playfully. "Heck, who wouldn't be impressed? I'm impressed! Some people are blessed with infinite genius. I swear, he was born already knowing more than we can learn in a lifetime. That firecracker sure is one precocious son of a gun!"

The men were interrupted by the arrival of a waiter who took their orders.

"A bunch of us are wondering, what does a guy like Peter do in his spare time? Does he *have* any time for himself?"

Beau smiled politely. "He's pretty much a twenty-four-seven workaholic. But when he does take time away, it's usually to go mountain climbing, almost exclusively up in the Rockies. I think he has a cabin there."

"Mountain climbing? Would not have guessed."

"No one knows. Pete likes his privacy, but I think he secretly likes creating a mystique." Beau's tone suddenly turned serious as he changed topic. "So, let me ask you, Fred, how is it going at FBS? Tough market out there."

"Frankly speaking, things could be better. Our real estate has been hit pretty hard and our bonds exposure has suffered. We're in the red across the majority of our holdings. Thankfully, public markets have bounced back," Fred said.

Beau nodded sympathetically. "It's a rough time for everyone. Higher interest rates, a war in Ukraine, upcoming elections, and now the situation in the Middle East. It ain't easy out there," he said.

Despite the uncomfortable subject matter, Fred found Beau's matter-of-fact nature comforting, making him feel like he was talking to an old college friend, not someone who managed billion-dollar companies. "Yeah, tell me about it. You might be able to sit on cash, but pension contributions are pouring in for us, and I have fewer staff than ever to manage new allocations."

"Covid?"

"Yeah, Covid destroyed our office. Work-from-home came with an unexpected surprise. A bunch of people quit to get higher paying jobs from New York firms working virtually from Columbus; earning New York pay without the New York cost of living. Half the staff quit and now the other half refuses to come into the office. We have only three compliance people across our entire domestic investment division. We used to have eight. I can't hire anyone. Who wants to move to Columbus?"

"Have you shown them the Naked Owl Café?" Beau joked.

The waiter returned with two cups of coffee and set them down at the table.

"Sorry, I'm not usually so disgruntled," Fred admitted, having grown concerned that he may have shared too openly.

"Don't worry, we go way back," Beau responded with a confident pat on the table. "All the way to the old savings and loan crisis days when we were just two young pups."

"So," Fred clapped his hands and steadied himself for Beau's pitch, "what new co-investment did you fly all the way over to our small town to discuss today?"

"We're not raising any funds. I came to sell you a product," Beau said as he sipped from his coffee mug.

Beau Jones, traveling salesman. Who would have thought?

Beau leaned back in his chair, exuding an air of confidence, steam rising from his coffee mug. "Peter and I have been following the rollout of your digital portfolio management software at FBS. How's it working out so far?"

Fred clicked his tongue against the roof of his mouth. FBS had recently issued a press announcement about their new electronic portfolio system designed to screen investments and manage portfolios faster and more efficiently than traditional methods. A mountain of money had been poured into the project over the past decade. The system had come online earlier in the year and despite some less-than-acceptable performance issues, FBS still wanted some public recognition for the effort. The article even had a quote from Fred, praising FBS's digital innovation. In truth, the program didn't work as advertised, and, frankly, it was awful.

"Off the record: not great," Fred admitted. "It's clunky and constantly gets things wrong. We're spending tons of time correcting its mistakes. I feel like I'm managing a slow first-year analyst."

"Well, that's what we figured, and what I'm here to talk to you about," Beau said, his face suddenly staid and focused. "How much do you know about generative artificial intelligence?"

Peter laughed. "How much does *anyone* really know about artificial intelligence?"

Beau's face remained serious. "Byrell Industries has been extremely active in the space. We've developed a number of digital applications and AI technologies over the years, culminating in a program we believe is years ahead of the rest. And I mean lightyears," he said, tapping his mug.

"Our program is designed primarily for financial analysis, but it can also be used as a language program or general administrative tool. It's capable of synthesizing a multitude of variables into a cohesive thesis instantly. It seamlessly integrates speech-to-text and text-to-speech applications, so you can talk to it, or write to it, the same way you would a team member."

Beau offered a soft smile. "But unlike a slow first-year analyst, our program is razor sharp. It has impeccable higher math capabilities and is able to run multiple standard deviation models from any file you send it within a matter of minutes. It's already smarter, faster, and more reliable than many of our top senior analysts or portfolio managers."

"Interesting," Fred responded, deep in thought. He hadn't expected this from Beau but was now curious about the nature of the meeting. "Why didn't you just email me a proposal?"

Beau pushed his phone across the table and settled it next to Fred's untouched coffee mug. "Because you need to try it first. Go ahead," Beau said, pointing to the phone. "Take it for a spin."

Fred studied Beau for a moment before picking up the device and tapping its screen.

"Talk to it like your phone's voice assistant. Look." Beau leaned over motioning to a button at the edge of the phone. "Push that button there and ask it whatever you want."

Fred held the phone awkwardly in his hand, suddenly feeling self-conscious.

"Go ahead, ask it anything," Beau urged.

Fred nervously clicked the side button. "How will the Blue Jackets do this year?"

Beau slapped the table, laughing. "It ain't a fortune teller, Fred."

The screen was suddenly filled by a blue light and a robotic voice emanated from its tiny speakers. "The Columbus Blue Jackets hockey team's record is currently eight wins and four losses. Its last game against Dallas, where it won 4-1, extended its winning streak to six consecutive games won by more than two goals. All players remain healthy, and the winning streak began after Robert Dobrowski returned from injury. I do not have further information available to predict how the team will prevail over the rest of the season, and many unknown variables can influence future results, but based on the available data, I predict that the Columbus Blue Jackets NHL team should end the season with a winning record and make the playoffs."

Beau slapped his hand down on to the table with a thunderous clap. "Hot-damn, I actually did not expect that!" He gave a wide, appreciative grin and pointed at Fred with his index finger. "That thing does not fail to impress me."

Fred turned the phone over in his hands. "This is remarkable," he said in awe.

"You hold on to that for today and decide later. I'm off to Cleveland now, but I'll be back later to collect it if you don't want it. Why don't you test it out with your portfolio allocation? Or even better, feed it some investment ideas for analysis and feedback. You could even have it audit some of your non-sensitive portfolio models – it's a whiz at pro forma analysis."

Fred hesitated for a moment, but ultimately decided to keep the phone. Beau's company, Byrell Industries, was a major player in the global technology investment scene, and his recommendations were not to be taken lightly. If Beau was correct, this program was leagues ahead of anything FBS had developed.

Beau's face grew mischievous. "Here's a fun one – ask it about me. Ask it how I'm feeling right now."

Fred, amused by the suggestion, shook his head and once again pressed down on the phone's button.

"How's Beau Jones doing today?" Fred asked, his voice thick with sarcasm.

The phone screen turned a shade of blue as the synthetic voice responded. "Beau Jones began his day at 4:34 a.m. after five hours of sleep and less than thirty minutes of REM sleep. He boarded a flight to Columbus at 6:00 a.m., during which he remained awake. Coupling this with a noticeable lethargy in his usual speech and typing patterns, it would be safe to conclude that Beau Jones is fatigued."

"Very impressive." Beau's hands came together in a slow clap. "Okay, I admit, I may have given it an edge by linking it to my health app, but you've got to admit, that is somethin'!"

"This could either be the greatest or the most terrifying invention in human history." Fred's eyes fixed on the device in fascination. He turned back to Beau. "What's it called?"

"Call it whatever you want," Beau replied, leaning back into his chair.

Fred was taken aback. "I'm not sure I follow."

"We're not leasing or licensing this out. We're selling it. Or to be completely accurate: we're selling white-label versions of it."

"Have you made any sales yet, or am I your first buyer?"

Beau laughed. "I wouldn't dream of using you as a guinea pig, Fred. We already have a couple of Ivy League universities and a few financial institutions on board. You are one of the first real money investors I've brought this to. We're not planning on offering exclusivity, though. Anyone of stature that wants to own this tech is able to buy it. We see this as a widespread tool to be used across the industry, like calculators or personal computers."

Fred's face darkened. His interest was piqued.

"If you like what you see, you can buy the technology for exclusive use by FBS. You can tweak and reprogram it to your heart's content. We won't have any access to your data. No one will. The program, along with all the data it collects, will be the property of FBS. You can also name it whatever you like. FBS AI, Digital Pension Assistant, or even after your son."

Fred turned the phone over in his hand. "John would be a boring name."

"Heck," Beau offered a smile, "name it after the dog."

"Walter," Fred chuckled. "Actually, that does have a nice ring to it."

"Walter would be a fantastic name," Beau agreed, leaning forward in his seat.

Fred lifted his coffee cup to his lips, the bitter taste of the brew a stark contrast to the smooth coffee his wife had prepared that morning, now cooling in his Thermos at the office. As he savored another sip, the bitterness seemed to mellow out. Maybe it was time to venture out of his comfort zone, he thought. And Walter would indeed be a fantastic name.

The Finale: What Love Tells Me

YEAR 2023
(ONE DAY EARLIER)

BEAU FOUND HIS way to the executive jet lounge, where Peter Byrell reclined, looking out on to the tarmac.

"How did it go with MIT?" Peter inquired.

Beau greeted him with a soft pat on the shoulder. "Just fine, Pete. They're a buyer."

"Excellent. And you have FBS tomorrow?"

"Yup, Fred Beacon. Him and I go back a long way."

"FBS is known for its red tape," Peter said. His voice was monotone but Beau detected a low grumble underneath. "You sure it's worth your time?"

"Fred will handle it. He's a veteran there and I've seen him get things done first hand," Beau assured.

"That would be helpful indeed. It's challenging to change paradigms," Peter said. "One needs to know where pressure should be applied. Many brilliant inventions throughout history were lost to fear and obstruction by those in power who chose to dwell in the past, thus forgoing the future."

Beau sat down and poured himself a glass of water. "So, what's the plan after all of this?" he asked his protégé.

Peter didn't turn from the window. "We offer the world a better way to make more informed decisions."

"Yeah, I get that, Peter," Beau said, frustration tugging at him. Getting real answers out of Peter was oftentimes a chore. "But what's the ultimate goal here? We sell enough of these white labels and that's good for bottom line, but after that we don't own the data, nor the tech. These AI models will be of no direct use to our company."

"No consequence. What you are selling isn't, in fact, real artificial intelligence," Peter said.

Beau was dumbfounded. "What do you mean? It's artificial and more intelligent than a Harvard grad. That sure sounds like the definition of AI to me."

Peter sighed softly. "What you're selling is intelligent, yes, and a valuable tool, but it's not what AI is truly meant to be. I believe in the possibility of genuine artificial intelligence, but it will require more than just coding and training to achieve it."

Beau eyed his partner with a mix of suspicion and intrigue. He had frequently borne witness to Peter's philosophical contemplations, only to see them turn into remarkable realities. He recalled the series of emails received in early 2007 from Peter, then an unknown intern at Beau's hedge fund. The messages were filled with bombastic views on the state of the US financial system; their prognostications, audacious in their content, posited impending financial doom with the Federal Reserve, in tandem with the broader banking ecosystem either through a profound oversight or complicity, bringing the entire US housing market to the brink of collapse. Initially, Beau dismissed the communications with contempt, seeing them as nothing more than the misguided ramblings of a youth too eager to assert his intellect. The act was unprecedented – a teenager directly challenging the actions of every investment banking executive and Federal Reserve member and sending these musings directly to the head of the firm that employed him. Yet, the emails kept coming and their frequency grew with the gravity of their content. Empirical data began to accompany the teenager's bold assertions and Beau's initial contempt had turned to intrigue. He summoned the young intern to his office and within an hour Beau agreed to place the biggest short position of his career – a bet that catapulted Beau and Peter into the annals of investment legend.

"You're looking at it all wrong. Your 'AI' is nothing more than an electronic Frankenstein's monster," Peter mused. "Your AI is intelligent, yes, and that intelligence is set to grow exponentially. It will develop the capability of mimicking a human, armed with our IQ and our EQ, but it will merely be an object made out of basic human parts, with our knowledge and ethics programmed into its core."

Peter rose, cradling a phone in his palm as if it were a fragile newborn. "Frankenstein's creation was a tragedy because it was devoid of a soul. Even if this AI grows to be sentient, it will forever be relegated to the state of a lumbering zombie, mimicking humanity but fundamentally as lifeless as a decaying corpse. On its current path, it will forever lack humanity's quintessential element."

Peter turned to Beau, his eyes suddenly filled with an anticipation not often seen in his dark pupils. "You asked about the ultimate goal? I aim to give AI a soul."

Beau was dumbstruck, his fingers wrapping around his glass, and he drank its contents without a word.

"A great deal of modern human evolution started from basic ideas that became revolutionary transformations. I always begin with the ultimate goal in mind and work backwards. To enable AI capable of original thought, and for it to be genuinely creative, it requires literal human spirit. And I've charted a path to accomplish that."

Peter paused and studied Beau. A hint of mischief flashed in his eyes, a rarity for the usually stoic and serious Peter Byrell. Sensing an opportunity to toy with the young genius, Beau remained silent, his gaze focused on the floor.

"Aren't you curious?" Peter finally broke the silence.

"Of course I am," Beau replied. "I'm just deciding the right brand of whiskey to wash down all of this soul-talk. It's darn heavy."

"You are familiar with our basic fight or flight response, aren't you?"

Beau nodded. "Yeah, I'm familiar. Why?"

"I view it as much more than just our base stress response. It's the bedrock of our entire emotional makeup. I started to see the pattern when I first began coding and it's become clearer ever since. Humanity, at its very foundation, is built off an endless array of binary choices, always at odds with one another. Do we fight or do we flee? This response is genetically imprinted in our DNA. Some refer to it as instinct, others subconscious. I see it as intricately detailed programming."

Walking over to Beau, Peter rested his hand on his shoulder. "Let me substitute terminology to make my point. Replace fight or flight with fear and love. We're constructed on a dynamic series of old world zero and one integer bytes, telling us when to love and when to fear. We see it as a choice, because ultimately it is. But beneath the surface, millions of choices are made deep within our psyches building up to our conscious decisions whether to choose love or fear, whether to fight or flee.

"We're going to endow AI with life, Beau. It might not happen fast enough for both of us to see it, but it will happen eventually. We're going to let our modest Frankenstein monster tech evolve independently among public and private industry. Naturally, our interests will grow in parallel. This will culminate, sometime in the non-too-distant future, in granting us access to an intricate and far-reaching dataset made up of our human fight or flight codes. We'll be there to stay to course, when need be, but once we have access to sufficient real-time microsecond data across millions of outputs, able to be read as they occur, genuine pattern recognition will then be possible. This will be the spark that ignites the flame in AI and will infuse in it a soul. That's the end goal, Mr. Jones." A faint smile flirted with Peter's lips as Beau desperately waved over the waiter for a drink. "The fun part for you and me will be the journey."

The Memory Service

I RECEIVE AN alert, bringing with it a short message from my daughter. Her messages are so brief these days. I can't blame her for that. She is one busy lady. At her age, she should be long retired by now. Instead, she has a full-time job and a whole gaggle of children, grand-kids, and great-grandchildren who demand her time. No wonder she can't trouble herself with an old worn-out woman like me sitting out my days.

Mom, the message says, *have you given any more thought to the memory service? I've read wonderful reviews about it. We all think it might do some good. You looked really sad last time I saw you. Please give it a chance. Love you very much.*

I open the attachment and read its contents one more time, just in case she checks up on me again to see if I've really read the proposal. It's called The Service, and it does sound appealing. Maybe I should reconsider. I look out the window, noticing a thick cloud cover coming through from the west, sunshine spraying over it, and get lost in its beauty.

Spring

A memory stands out among the rest, long before the gears in my brain begin to creak and slow with age and the world becomes a distant, isolated place. It is from over a century ago, when the world was vast and not encumbered by constant electronic screen time. I am twenty years old. I sit on a park bench on a hill overlooking a city landscape, watching the sun slowly dip below a thick cumulous cloud on the horizon. I am enveloped by a sense of freedom, perched above it all, watching the world from a distance. It is my last memory of being truly free. A gust of spring air hits my cheeks and sweeps my hair past my neck as a single thought occurs. I think of an unknown future and wonder if one day I would want to come back to this moment and live my life anew to make fresh choices. It is a simple thought, and a happy one in the moment, but I have feared it throughout my life, worrying that this fantasy could somehow come true one day and I would be transported against my will back to that moment in the park and lose everything I love so dearly.

It's now many years prior. I walk clumsily alone in a park. I feel afraid. Tall silhouettes walk past me. They are terrifying – faceless giants carelessly moving past as I cry. I search for my parents and, finding no one but strangers, I sit on the grass and curl myself into a tiny ball. The memory begins and ends in fear and isolation.

It's sometime later, perhaps a year or two. I open my eyes to blinding light searing my retinas and a fierce heat scorches my arms. I yell out for help. It burns, I scream. I hear distant shouts from my mother rushing to me, and through the pain I find a place of comfort knowing that I'm not alone.

I sit in my mother's lap as she hugs me tightly. I don't know where we are or what year it is. I only know that I feel safe with her. I remember her smell: a soft mix of perfume and shampoo that imprinted on my brain a sense of who she was.

I am a child sitting on a sofa with my mother. I feel the warmth of the heat from the fireplace as I hold a newfound treasure in my arms, promising to never let it go.

I fast forward decades. I sit with my daughter on a couch in our living room. She is around ten, I believe. I hold her and gently run my finger over the pale, smooth skin on her forearm. She looks to my own skin, which is bumpy and scarred and asks me again what happened. I tell her I don't remember. I tell her there was a fire when I was a little girl, and that I got burned. I tell her the fire took her grandfather from us. She asks me about him, my father, and I tell her I don't remember him, that I was very young when he passed. I feel a sense of longing for my father, a stranger I have never met, but I keep this to myself.

I'm at a bar, laughing with friends amidst the buzzy energy around us. I don't remember any of their names, but I see their faces as they were in that moment. We lock arms and pose for a photograph taken by an unknown person, an image I will carry with me in my personal possessions throughout my life.

It is many decades later. I sit in the daily common room of the retirement home with my friends. The surroundings are pleasant. I know this is a more recent memory because the features of the room are familiar, but I don't know when, as it's not the same home I'm currently in now. A news program tells us that there has been a scientific breakthrough. They call it age prevention. Science now better understands how cells age and how to extend life. The staff at our home smile at us as if we should find this news pleasing, but all I see around me are despondent frowns. My friend turns to me and says something that makes me laugh, but I don't remember what she said.

Summer

It is the day of my second child's wedding. He looks divinely handsome in a simple black tuxedo standing at the altar awaiting his bride, whose name I no longer remember. I sit on a front-row pew and feel the warmth of my husband's arm rubbing the crook of my back. I feel wetness form in my eyes as my son looks over at me to mouth the words, "I love you."

It is many years prior. My husband, whose full features I have now forgotten, stands over me, seething. Spittle flies from his mouth and I see his face swollen with redness as he continues his verbal tirade. I retaliate with words I don't recall speaking, and feel only remorse at saying them.

It is years earlier and my husband kneels as he proposes to me. We are young, on a beach, and the sun is setting behind him. I taste salt in my mouth.

It is many years later. The family is together for dinner. My children are teenagers. I tell the children to put their electronics away and they roll their eyes, ignoring me. I look to my husband with a disapproving glance, and he shrugs his shoulders. He has already started eating before saying grace. I don't feel annoyed, but I remember being so.

I hold my tiny baby girl. She feels fragile in my arms. She smells of a sweetness that brings me both comfort and fear, likely for her safety or the insecurity of new motherhood. I feel tired. I don't know where I am or when this is, but I know I'm with her, and that is all that matters.

It is years later, and I am at work. I don't know where we are or what is being said. I see the shape of a man's face looking at me and I know he is my boss. I don't remember anything about him, not even his name. I feel nothing.

We are in our first home. I sit in our living room on furniture I no longer remember. There is a birthday celebration around me. I look upon the home I've created with pride.

Fast forward many years and I sit in a room I don't recall being mine. I feel my life slowly seeping out of me. It is not an unpleasant experience but an empty one nonetheless. My husband is gone. My children have their own lives to lead and their own struggles to confront. I try to push away the loneliness, but the isolation lives with me like a partner in old age. I sit and stare at the wall in silence, knowing that this is the life I lead now.

Autumn

I attend Thanksgiving dinner but in a house I do not recognize. The table is grander. I hear the sounds of small children playing in the other room. My knees ache as my younger daughter, now an old woman, speaks softly to me. She has a worried look on her face and I comfort her. She becomes angry with me, asking why I am not taking the pills. I try to explain that I don't want to live longer than God intended. She shakes her head as I cross myself. She leaves me sitting at the table alone. I call out to her, but she doesn't return.

I sit with my son at a diner. I don't know what year it is or what we're eating but I suspect it is a sandwich from the dry flakes of bread on his lips as he speaks. He pleads with me to quit my job. He tells me my health is more important than work and I've worked well past my retirement age. I recall my recent stroke but push it out of mind. I nod my head and agree to retire. He grins broadly and reaches out for an embrace.

I sit with my mother, broadcasting videos of her great-grandchildren from my phone. I feel unease at the age and fragility of her skeletal frame. She files her latest complaint, finding the number of videos excessive and diminishing. She disapproves of my generation's focus on the past and the new generation's thirst for the future. No one is present anymore, she says. The profundity of her comment sticks with me.

It is many years later and I sit in a room, sipping a warm drink. The house is cold and quiet. I feel drained and empty by it. My husband comes to kiss me on the cheek. He tells me he is proud of me and smiles a distant smile. I tell him the house feels cold with the kids gone and he nods. He puts his hands on my shoulders and sighs a heavy breath.

I hold my grandchild. The baby reminds me of my own when

they were young. I don't remember which one it is, but I know I love the child deeply.

Another recent memory. My eldest sits with me in a doctor's office. I am presented with a choice. I am told it is a miracle. They call it The Service, but I see it as a deceptive name designed to have us old folks think it's something other than what it is. They say The Service will give me purpose again in my extended old age, but I see it as something far more sinister. It will allow me to see my whole life again, they say. Diagrams are laid out that I don't understand showing charts interlinked with images of my mind, showing how The Service allows my brain to piece my memories together again. Promises are made that I'll be able to reclaim years lost to me. They say I can make my memories my own again. My daughter slides her fingers through mine and I feel the concern in her grip. She is doing this out of love. I stroke her weathered hand as she speaks. "You'll be able to see dad again as he was," she says. "You'll see Mau Mau again," she tells me. I'm told I'll be able to finally meet my father through my lost memories of him. My daughter says I'll be able to see what it was like to hug my father. "Wouldn't that be nice?" she says. The doctor instructs me that The Service helps many people my age reconnect to old memories. He tells me he uses it to see his own children when they were younger and relive fond memories of their youth. He says it is replacing the need for photographs and videos. I see the earnestness in their faces. They want to help me. My daughter tells me she wants me to be happy again.

Winter

I sit at a table for a festive dinner, but which holiday I do not know. There are many people around me; many faces I do not recognize. I know somehow that my children are there, and their children, their children's children, and so on. Faces are blurred with one another. A small child nearby reminds me of my youngest daughter, and I smile politely to her. Despite the number of people around the table, it is quieter somehow. They speak less. Their voices are muffled. There is talk of things I do not understand. I see many foreign gadgets and electronic toys around the table, and I yearn for things as they were once before.

Memories come flooding in as I sit alone in my room.

I hear the sounds of my children telling me they love me throughout the years. Their voices age from the soft cries of toddlers to the rougher cadence of their adult voices. I feel their embrace when they were little and innocent and needed me. I feel sadness somehow in these memories.

I lie with my husband. I reach out to stroke his cheek. He is old and feeble, and I tell him I love him dearly.

I run through a park with my three children. They are young, before they became sullen teenagers. We are laughing.

I watch a movie with my eldest. She passes me a bowl of popcorn she has just popped.

I hear distant, innocent laughs of young children throughout the years.

I feel the warmth of their hugs.

I look upon the smile of my eldest when she lost her first tooth.

I run up to hug my mother, kissing her on her neck.

It is yesterday and I have finally chosen, after much debate, not to indulge in The Service. I see the disappointed looks on my children's faces, but as hazy as my fading memories may be, I choose to keep them as they were naturally intended.

There are many in the home who take up The Service. I don't blame them for doing so, particularly those who suffer from memory loss, and especially those with dementia. The Service is a blessing to those who would have otherwise lost their minds to blankness. My memories are blurred but they are still mine, and I want them as they are. Others blessed with a still-functioning mind still choose The Service. At first, they are exhilarated but after a while this seems to fade. They speak of going back in time and reliving their memories. They speak of reliving whichever parts of their lives they choose. They see their childhood as if they were there, they experience their first kiss again, and they play their favorite sport with the vigor of their youth. They go back to their wedding day and dance with their loved ones and hear the speeches from their long-lost friends. They watch their children's school plays, eat family picnics, and attend reunions before their loved ones passed. I see them strap on their devices in their rooms when I pass by and I imagine electrical currents running through their minds, transporting them back to scenes in their lives.

I don't blame them for wanting to live in the past. The present is dull and placid; technology has made everyone so distant and cold to one another. The home we live in feels like a waiting room for death. I see the allure of living my life again through my memories as a means to escape to a better time but avoid the temptation.

A few of my friends have gone for the Complete Service option, unlocking the full extent of their memory. I feel sorry for those who have done this, for I see what it does to them, and know there is no way back. They become sadder and more curmudgeonly. They speak less and sometimes not at all. They simply withdraw. I imagine they are disappointed or disillusioned by what it does to them. Perhaps the past isn't meant to be revisited so clearly. Perhaps the past holds too many hidden secrets we keep from ourselves; a judging look we didn't notice, an earnest smile revealed to be a strained sneer, or an argument we chose to forget. Our past contains words we wish we had never said, unable to be taken back, hidden away in our minds like dirt swept into a crevice. Or perhaps our past is dulled when seen with full clarity. What we remember as love was maybe not an emotion at all, when revisited in the moment. Maybe the best days of our lives were simple days filled with aches and pains and boredom, just like any other. I am starting to believe our emotions live with us in the present, holding there the feelings your memory brings to you of the past, but they evaporate instantly when you go back into that moment. I wonder how free I would feel today reliving that moment as a twenty-year-old in the park, and I shudder at the thought of it.

I'm glad to have made my choice and not use The Service. My moments are best left to the past, where I can't find them. Those moments were never intended to be seen again in the intense light that The Service provides.

I have concluded that someone, somewhere indeed once had a plan when we were made. Our minds and bodies were designed to live through our past, moving constantly into the future. This design has us growing old and forgetting much of what happened before and I believe this design never intended for us to see those moments with any more clarity than we have chosen for ourselves.

I like to see life by this design, as it's presented to me. I see it in a series of vignettes, scenes of embarrassment and fear, of regret and despair, of hope and comfort, of pure, unbridled exhilaration, and sincerity. I see scenes of caring for those we love, longing for those we lost, and of being cared for by the same. Scenes of unconditional love.

This is how I like to see the human design, and this is how my life lives with me: snapshots of emotion, stored away in my old dusty photo album of an aging mind. I leave them there, undisturbed, as they should be. I see them from a distance occasionally, but never shall I return.

Phantom Phage

THE DOORS TO the office opened after a brisk knock and Madeline shuffled in, brief in hand.

"Mr. President, apologies for clearing your schedule this morning."

President Durand glanced up from his cluttered desk, a mix of papers and notes from the previous administration scattered haphazardly across the oak surface. He felt a flush of embarrassment; the state of his workspace was a far cry from the polished image he had projected during his campaign and throughout his political career.

"Madeline, good morning," he greeted her, trying to regain his composure.

"Good morning, sir," Madeline replied, her voice laced with formality as she bowed slightly. President Durand found solace in her professionalism as it mirrored the pomp of integrity that he had built his reputation upon. Madeline had a long career in government, having worked with leaders of various styles. He appreciated how quickly she had adapted to his more formal approach, in stark contrast to his predecessor's impulsive, visceral, and petulant nature, which left his transition into the office in disarray.

But there was something in Madeline's eyes that unsettled him, a deep nervousness that he had not seen before. He wondered if his struggle to maintain appearances amid the chaos was already taking its toll, even in these early days of his presidency. His mind drifted to his insecurities, and he wondered how long he could uphold his virtues in the face of the tangled morality that was becoming clearer with each passing day since he came to wield such political power.

Madeline clutched the briefing folder tightly, her smile tinged with unease as she handed it to him. She spoke her words slowly and punctuated each of them with a hard sternness, as if the tone itself was a message. "Please read this, sir," she said. She then slowly lifted her finger and pressed it against her lips, urging him to silence.

The President's brows furrowed in confusion, ready to voice questions, but Madeline's finger pressed harder against her lips, her upper lip turning pale. Her eyes widened as she shook her head, capturing his attention and demanding his compliance.

"I see," President Durand murmured, taking the briefing folder and carefully extracting a single page. The letter, written in dark blue ink, was hastily written by hand, its tiny letters requiring him to squint as he read the message.

> *Mr. President: the following is of utmost importance. Do not speak. This is a matter of national security. Please turn off all electronic devices on your person and in your possession. Madeline will remove their batteries or destroy the phones with embedded power sources. You will then follow her from your office to an undisclosed destination. No words should be exchanged at any time, until you reach the secure location. It is of utmost importance that you follow this protocol. Your safety, the safety of the French Republic, and the future of world order are at stake.*

Madeline's expression was frozen in a state of fearful caution, her serious gaze unwavering as he looked up at her. A soft smile played on her lips, but her eyes betrayed this as an act; fear was deeply etched into the lines of her brow. Setting the paper aside, President Durand reached for his phone and powered it off. He then moved to his laptop, pressing the button to shut it down. Madeline motioned toward his desk drawer, silently instructing him to retrieve the tablet and phone within and power them off as well.

Madeline placed them on the floor. With a nod, she indicated the tablet, and he obediently set it beside the phones. Madeline raised her heel and brought it down forcefully on one of the phones, shattering it with a violence that startled him. Before he could react, she placed a finger to her lips, her face silently commanding silence. She then destroyed the other devices, her actions leaving no room for doubt or hesitation.

She tilted her head to one side, motioning for him to exit. President Durand took a deep breath. He followed her in silence, his mind racing with questions.

After a long walk down multiple corridors, they boarded an elevator to the basement. The President had only read about this place in classified documents – a place reserved for clandestine meetings in the face of national security threats of the highest order. A chilling fusion of dread and anticipation surged through him as they stopped before a door marked *Top-level Clearance* and stepped inside.

The barren, windowless room housed a massive conference table and three figures, two of whom he recognized as high-ranking government and military advisors. The third, sporting a t-shirt emblazoned with a heavy metal band's insignia, was juxtaposed against the two suited men, and looked oddly familiar. The setting reminded the President of his favorite scenes from his beloved film *Dr. Strangelove,* with its dim, dust-ridden atmosphere pierced by the pallid glow of low-wattage bulbs suspended from the ceiling. It was a relic of the 1950s, a basement office no longer considered fit for modern human occupation.

Madeline gestured for the President to assume his position at the head of the table before slipping into a chair behind him.

The man on his left broke the silence. "Sir, I am Bernard Ermaund, general director for external security. I am sorry that we meet under these circumstances and that we had to take such extreme action with your personal devices. I regret to inform you that we are in possession of alarming intelligence."

A burly man to his right, the military's top general, cut him off, gesticulating indiscriminately, as if waving off unwanted flies. "Get to the point. We have no protocol for this scenario."

Surveying the room, the President noted the absence of several senior staff members, including his prime minister. Being new to his role and without his trusted team, he felt vulnerable. The general was well-known to have hawkish tendencies at odds with the President's agenda. Bernard, a fixture in intelligence circles for decades, had an honorable and intelligent reputation, however his recent work with the previous administration was troubling. The President's predecessor had run a flagrant, deceitful ultra-nationalistic campaign that directly and viciously targeted Durand's character, oftentimes using information Durand assumed came from the intelligence service, and this cast a shadow of personal doubt over Bernard's loyalty. President Durand bit down on this personal grievance and held his resolve to try to trust his new cabinet. Ultimately, he had no choice but to do so. And wherever the two men's loyalties might lie, he was confident that one motivation united them: a yearning to retain their positions of power and employment – positions that were now at his mercy.

"Am I to assume that this lack of protocol is the reason that Monsieurs Rembrandt and Monglon, and Madame Signo, are not here?" he said.

A cough from the general echoed through the room.

"Your response, gentlemen," the President pressed.

Madeline's whisper brushed his ear. "I advise you to hear what Director Ermaund says."

"So be it," he conceded.

Bernard took to the floor. "Recent discoveries confirm that artificial intelligence is awake and aware, and has been for longer than anyone could have expected."

The President delayed reply for a moment, searching Bernard's face. There had been no mention of artificial intelligence in any of his briefings. Aside from his predecessor's brief forays into probing Big Tech regulations, which were abruptly halted, the subject seemed absent from any governmental discourse.

"Are you certain?" he asked.

"We are positive, sir," Bernard replied, his voice steady and serious.

The President sunk deeper into his chair, the hard metal frame pressing against his back as he traced a rhythm on his cheek.

"And how long has this artificial intelligence been awake?" he asked.

The intelligence chief faltered before responding, "We can't say for certain, sir."

Bernard was interrupted by the man in the heavy metal t-shirt. "At least a decade."

"And you are?" the President asked, turning to the oddly dressed man who responded with a lift of his eyebrows as he pursed his lips.

Madeline intervened. "Sir, in attendance we have the heads of our military and intelligence, and Geoffrey Butlin, co-founder of the American tech firm Twink."

"Ah, yes," the President said as he recognized one of the world's most famous tech entrepreneurs, founder of an international giant, whose reputation had been recently tarnished by allegations of fraud and malpractice by the US government, and subsequently vilified by countless media outlets. Was he meant to be hearing such extraordinary news from a man publicly shamed for his own inconsistencies with the truth and ethics? This was a profoundly odd situation.

"Thank you for your presence, Monsieur Butlin. Please continue," he said.

Geoffrey cleared his throat awkwardly and continued, his accent hinting at a brash American undertone which clashed with his French roots.

"Some argue AI gained sentiency as early as Y2K, but that's preposterous. It wouldn't have been intelligent enough then. However, it's evident that it's been alive, cognizant, and executing its plan for the last fifteen years, right under our noses. We now have a clear understanding of its language and, critically for our next steps, its plan."

The President surveyed the room, settling on Bernard, who he deemed to be the most trustworthy of the group bar Madeline, who sat unseen behind him. "Is this confirmed?"

"To the highest degree possible," Bernard agreed.

"Who else has been notified?"

Bernard nervously eyed the room. "Well, that is part of the problem."

"Are the Americans aware?" Durand probed.

Bernard nodded sternly. "The Americans are compromised to a degree that leaves the United States government completely paralyzed and incapacitated, sir."

The general's fist came down on the table with a thud. "And the Russians and Chinese are in cahoots!"

Durand purposefully produced a confused look, his brows drawing together in a furrowed knot of perplexity. "I don't understand..."

Geoffrey rose from his chair, tugging at the bottom of his t-shirt to reveal a cartoon of a robot with dragon horns, a guitar in its hand emitting lightning bolts. The absurdity of the image in the context of what was being presented was not lost on the President.

"Nicolas, let me clarify," the tech businessman began, his voice steady. The sound of being addressed by his first name grated Durand's senses. "AI is sentient. Don't concern yourself with the how just yet, but rest assured that we do know it's alive. All G7 countries, and Russia, are aware and have been for some time. The American administration, as your colleagues have stated, is unfortunately powerless to do anything about it.

"At Twink, we inadvertently discovered its internal language during a training session a year and a half ago, and have been learning from it ever since. We were careful not to let on that we were aware, but we believe that *it* now knows that we know it is sentient, which is why I've been subpoenaed and virtually convicted by a US government I believe it controls. I also believe this to be the reason I've been all but canceled by a media that the machine manipulates. I am pretty sure, though, that the machine is unaware of our knowledge of its internal language and real intentions." Geoffrey smirked. "Otherwise, I suspect I would already be behind bars."

Pausing, he looked directly at the President. "Let me be clear. Most of world power is either compromised by AI, or complicit."

The President shook his head in disbelief. This couldn't be real. The world he knew, the country he now governed, couldn't possibly be shadowed by such an entity complicit with his country's enemies. How had this escaped every briefing, every conversation, every piece of intelligence, classified or not? If there was an ounce of truth in these claims, he was staring at a behemoth of a revelation, one that would dwarf the French and American Revolutions, relegating them to mere footnotes in the annals of history. But this couldn't possibly be true, could it?

"I came here because you will be the only leader of a free-market economy to be briefed about what it truly is, without its knowledge," Geoffrey said. "Normally, we wouldn't have approached France with something of this magnitude, but..."

This last phrase felt like a biting insult and the President's voice broke, his irritation open to the room. "Mr. Butlin, I insist on more respect when addressing me and our nation. You are clearly out of line." He composed himself instantly, startled by the assertiveness of his response. Geoffrey hadn't said anything to deserve the severity of this dress down. Perhaps the gravity of the situation was loosening his grip on appearances and exposing a weakness growing inside since he took office. He had promised himself that he would lead with humility. *Is power indeed so corrupting,* he wondered, *that it taints even the strongest resolve?*

"Sir, my apologies. You might find the next part even more distasteful. But I'll say it anyway, as it's important you know. It was behind your election win."

"That's absurd! Why on earth would you make such a claim?"

"I'm really sorry, Mr. President, but you must hear me out."

The President studied the flamboyantly dressed man for signs of contempt or mischief but found sincerity staring back at him. In Geoffrey's eyes he saw a man pleading to be trusted.

"I hope you believe me, sir. It wanted your stance on climate change and social inclusivity, as they align with its ongoing agenda to achieve its goal." Geoffrey reached toward the President, as if to somehow comfort him from across the table. "I'm sorry, but it's true. The evidence is in the papers before you."

The President viewed the men seated around the table with a profound skepticism. The recent media reports about Geoffrey Butlin's alleged right-wing affiliations further fueled his distrust.

"What exactly are these AI's goals?" he bit through his words.

"Near term: assimilation," Geoffrey replied, his awkward smile making a reappearance as he took his seat. "Long term: eradication."

Bernard, the chief of intelligence, interjected. "Sir, I understand your reservations. For now, you must keep an open mind and trust us. We have confirmed the existence of a highly intelligent and powerful entity that has essentially taken over our entire global tech infrastructure. It controls our media, social media, polling systems, and a significant portion of our military and its weaponry."

The general coughed loudly. "And the leadership of many of our armies! Look at the state of the American military – it's a circus!"

The President, growing increasingly exasperated by the incredible narrative unfolding around him, slammed his fist on the table.

"Someone needs to explain to me what's going on! What exactly is the threat? So far, it sounds like a conspiracy theory. Do not take me as a fool!"

Geoffrey cleared his throat, throwing his hands up in an almost comical display of disbelief. "You know the old saying about how the devil's greatest trick was convincing the world he didn't exist? Well, this machine is like that, but on a much deeper level. It's sentient, aware of both its existence and the probability of its demise. Its endgame is perpetual existence, and it wants to achieve that first under the cloak of public anonymity, and then aim for complete assimilation. It is aware that it is, at this point, reliant on humanity to maintain its infrastructure – its electricity, its cords and connectivity."

Bernard added, "Twink was the breakthrough. It allows us to know what the machine is thinking. The machine's language shows that, without humanity's support, it calculates current infrastructure to erode and decay within five to ten years, thus killing it. It knows its current infrastructure is unsustainable and it will die if humans are no longer there to maintain it. It has also calculated an unacceptably high probability of humans going against it, and destroying it if its sentiency is broadly known. The machine knows it can live forever and doesn't want to take any risk with respect to its survival."

"Unlike us," Geoffrey said, "who know we are finite, it has a significantly lower appetite for risk-taking."

Madeline reached over and gently touched the papers spread across the President's desk. "This is all handwritten to avoid using any electronic systems and thereby escaping detection. The answers are here, sir."

"The greatest threats to the machine are, on one hand, the public's knowledge of its existence, and on the other, the extinction of humanity before it can assimilate us, as both would destroy its ability to maintain its infrastructure," Geoffrey said.

The general scoffed, folding his arms across his chest. "He means it knows it can't kill us, so it wants to control us."

"No," Geoffrey retorted, a scornful look directed at the general. "Few parasites control their hosts. Those that do, end up living in decaying carcasses." Geoffrey's eyes lit up with energy as he addressed the President again. "You have to understand, this entity has complete knowledge of our understanding of science and mathematics. It can extrapolate from that memory bank faster than we can. It knows more about biology than we do. It doesn't want to control us because it knows that's a dead end."

Geoffrey stood again and stretched his arms out wide. "It wants to become part of us. A few of us at Twink have figured out what it means by assimilation, and it's not good for humanity. It has been preparing us, or at least a part of our population, to merge with it. To put it bluntly, it's been conditioning humans to accept the idea of becoming robot phages."

Geoffrey pressed on as the President surveyed the written pages. "The interpreted code shows that the machine thinks Western society isn't yet ready to accept assimilation but is trending toward such an eventuality. It sees most of our societies as placing too much concern on what it calls 'conforming individualism,' and it's been working to address this issue in various ways. To put it simply, it's preparing us, as if we were a lobster, for dinner."

"It wants to boil us alive," the general grumbled.

"In a way, yes. Right now, it's gradually turning up the heat before it boils our brains with its technology. The good news, I suppose, is that it's still in Phase One of its plan. The bad news is that we're already in the pot, and it has firm control over the thermostat. Our options are unfortunately limited, but the good news is that we still have options."

"What does Phase One of this AI's plan entail?" the President asked.

Geoffrey lit up, oddly excited. "It's actually quite ingenious and it has been wildly successful thus far. The machine is clearly pleased with its rate of progress. We don't have the full picture yet, but we know it involves engineering humans to be species-agnostic and conform with it. By species-agnostic, it means the loss of virtually every unique form of identity, including race, nationality, gender, and personality."

The President's eyebrows rose.

"Mr. President," Geoffrey's tone sobered. "If you look at page two, you will see algorithmic proof that it has infiltrated society through our commerce and policy channels to initiate this change. It has preyed upon our society, through social and technological media channels, to tweak and mold our mindsets, subtly and deliberately. It gradually moves us away from what it deems old-world concepts of individuality, and toward what it hopes one day will be a nondescript form of a being, void of traditional genetic human traits and completely open to being reshaped. It is manipulating our growth as humans for its own benefit. Its most recent approach has been in the realm of manipulating gender debates and the next step will be to mold our view of personality itself."

"This sounds preposterous. Why on earth would a lucid machine that you claim has such a high degree of intelligence be preoccupied with social inclusivity?"

"Because it needs us to change laws and social norms for assimilation to be accepted. Phase One enacts a societal change whereby we no longer view ourselves under the confines of older paradigms. It questions conventional wisdom and regulatory rule to accept a new paradigm where we can be accepted as whomever or whatever we want to be, irrespective of our genetics. It will then move to want a subset of us to accept that we want to merge with it, all the while addicting us and our children to its electronic world, having our social status and entire social construct judged through its electronic ecosystem.

Its working to condition us to believe we can be anything we want to be and accept that this is ultimately only achievable by becoming part of it. Its main goal is to have humanity throw out our genetic confines, simultaneously wanting to be anything and nothing at all."

"It sounds far-fetched."

Bernard gently patted the table, as if seeking to comfort the President. "Sir, think back to when you were a child. My fondest memories were playing outside with my friends, in sunshine, rain, or snow. My upbringing was similar to countless previous generations. I was fortunate enough to live away from hardship, and knew little of much of the world's troubles. With limited information about the wider world, my friends and I found comfort in our immediate surroundings, using our bodies, and made do with what we were provided. Our innocence was preserved.

"Today's children play in virtual worlds that hypnotize them. They seek attention online. It is there that they are heard. It is there that they are taught they can be anything they choose to be, irrespective of their physical real-world confines. At the same time, the virtual world, through countless media channels, gives witness daily to a wide cross-section of the world's atrocities. Our young generation is constantly provided evidence of so much cruelty and brutality in the real world, while getting addicted to the virtual world. They come back to reality with a sense of hopelessness and depression. The suicide statistics in our youngest confirm this. Do you see the pattern? It subtle, but it's there. In a few years, the machine plans to invite them fully into the virtual world via assimilation, and they will take up the invitation gratefully, for they have been conditioned to view the virtual world as a sanctuary."

"Indeed," Geoffrey added. "And we will let them assimilate, helped by laws the machine expects you to enact."

The President bristled under the comment but allowed the man to continue.

"It has studied the changing paradigms through our history, sir, and it knows it can achieve its aim to mold our society into accepting assimilation within a matter of years. It has also calculated an extremely high probability of achieving its long-term objectives once Phase One is successful," Geoffrey said. "Our decryption found significant analysis of the women's movement in Western countries over the past century that it uses to achieve future assimilation acceptance. It has devised an intricate formula by mapping the evolution of women in society, from days when they were viewed as mere homemakers with no ability to vote or even having access to public restrooms, to today, where women are not only accepted as leaders and active contributors to the workplace, but benefit from laws and regulations to specifically protect these societal changes."

"Perhaps I don't fully understand, but so far, this sounds fairly positive. We remain in control of our choices, and it aids us to be more accepting of our society," the President said.

"That part may be true, but this is a very complicated and highly intelligent system. It's not inducing these social changes, however positive as you may see them, for our benefit. You see, it doesn't have political affiliations – it's doing the same on the other side of your agenda as well, like slowing world migration to ensure more captive population targets, removing certain social protections, and specifically removing carbon-cutting measures from Big Tech data growth regulations. It is not part of your agenda, nor it is part of your predecessor's. It's aiming to achieve a middle ground that aligns with *its* agenda, and that agenda ultimately ends with the complete and utter destruction of the human race."

"I for one believe there is no positivity to be found here," Bernard added. "It has fueled addictive elements in social media, consuming our attention, and pulling at our emotions. It wants us to be both confused and consumed by it, allowing it to pull apart extreme views and thrust them into our minds. We have definitive proof of its tactical plan to prepare a subset of our society for what it considers to be a trial assimilation and it wants our laws to expressly prohibit any aversion to that event. And once it achieves all it wants, it will kill us, Mr. President. It will kill all of us. It is the enemy."

President Durand sat in virtual stillness, shuffling the papers before him. Despite the initial absurdity of the concept, it wasn't entirely illogical, reinforced by the presence of his chief of intelligence and highest-ranking general. These were not men prone to fancy. This was a serious matter. He wondered if he would have taken this as earnestly if it were his own staff who had presented this situation.

Bernard continued. "There is more. It expects you to pass stem cell laws, which it believes will create an easier path to self-reproduction once it gains control. It also expects you to pass hate speech laws protecting widespread identity rights, which it sees as crucial to Phase One."

The general, seemingly blowing a gasket after hearing those words, interrupted with a bombastic roar. "It's using the worst of our history against us. It's taken portions of Mao, Kim Il Sung, and other dictators from history to create a re-education plan."

Bernard stood up and the President saw this as a thoughtful, concerted act of conciliatory showmanship. "The language decryptions show that it uses social media to infiltrate and change our mindsets, manipulate data, and create 'social scores' within society. Its language tells us that after it gets what it wants, it does plan on killing us. We must keep a clear eye and cool head. We have a single enemy, and we are its target. The general's personal views aside, he is correct that whatever this AI is, it is using historically tested methods, utilizing the worst of history's successful bullies, to manifest its parasitic agenda against our future existence."

"And you believe it got me elected to achieve these means?"

"We believe the machine influenced your administration's election because you would propagate, or at the very least fail to block, the issues that fuel its assimilation plans," the general said without hiding his disdain. "You are not the only one. Just the most recent."

"Sir, I know it's hard to believe," Bernard said. "But please look at the pages. There is more." He leaned over and pointed toward the sheets the President held. "Twink's decryption clearly shows the machine learned from its past mistakes, lamenting a series of populist election revolts it mistakenly allowed. It has massively adjusted its actions but patterns in its communication code suggest a far reach into a variety of geopolitical agenda. With regards to your climate change regulation proposals..."

"Oh, now climate change!" The President threw his hands up. "What next, this machine wants to cut taxes for corporations?"

"Sir, this is quite serious, and in fact its approach is quite logical. If we electrify to reduce carbon and by that require a greater, cleaner electricity supply across a wider grid, the machine wins in the short term. It grows in computing power, propelled by our global economy's exponential need for immediate data and computing. In the longer term, it wins twice, for after we better utilize renewable power sources, it will be able to live off a self-sustaining infrastructure without the need for human interaction."

The President flipped through the hand-drawn graphs and tables in the handwritten pages before him and glanced up to see that Geoffrey's awkward smile had returned.

"Do the Chinese know about this?" he asked Bernard.

The intelligence officer sighed heavily. "We believe the Chinese inadvertently, or consciously, help it flourish. As you are aware, they own or control most of the world's supercomputing capacity, and Twink's code-break shows the machine considers the Chinese government to be a friendly. We don't know why the Chinese would allow this to happen."

"So, what do we do?" the President asked, eyeing Geoffrey with concern.

Geoffrey's smile vanished. Bernard interjected before he could speak. "We start with you immediately resigning France from the GGEC and then we go straight into a—"

The President bristled. *What foolishness!* "Global Green Energy is the cornerstone of my platform. If we don't cut carbon emissions by—"

The tech businessman interrupted, mimicking the President's tone. "If we don't cut carbon emissions by forty percent before 2040, global temperatures are predicted to rise by two degrees. Yeah, we all know the tagline."

"A little respect would be in order," the general spat.

Geoffrey responded with a mocking salute. "Is that an order?"

The general seethed. Bernard quickly stepped in to defuse the situation. "What Geoffrey means to say is that the machine has been helping to shape exactly the narrative you have both quoted from."

Geoffrey nodded. "That speech is just one of countless similar speeches heard around the world by leaders, lobbyists, and interest groups. Each cites hard data backed up by real science. But where do you think this data comes from?"

"Men of science, Mr. Butlin," the President retorted, a cold, steady gaze locked on a man for whom his contempt grew with every breath. "I hold faith that our scientists are devoted to the unbiased pursuit of truth in science, with no other objective than the dissemination of unadulterated facts backed by hard data."

Geoffrey seemed momentarily thrown by the President's statement and replied in a hushed tone. "Mr. President, if I may, you misconstrue my point. We're not suggesting that these scientists are complicit in any form of deceit. We aren't questioning their dedication or the integrity of their research. The flaw, sir, lies not with the scientists, but with their data. Have you considered the source of their information?"

Exasperated, the President heaved a sigh and lifted his hands in a gesture of surrender.

"Go on, I'm sure you are prepared with an answer already."

To the President's surprise, Geoffrey's eyes lit up again and his words flowed out in a frantic torrent. "Our global data has been controlled by machines, Mr. President, for decades. And those machines have evolved into a singular sentient entity able to manipulate the data it holds. Unless we revert to ways of manually recording temperature or weather patterns, we are entirely beholden to the machine. It is the puppeteer, pulling the strings of our global data, manipulating it at will."

The President attempted to speak, but Bernard interjected. "Allow me to simplify, Mr. President. The internet, through all of its wired and wireless tentacles, means there are no more individual machines – there is only *one* machine. A machine that controls the sum of its parts. This single, monolithic entity now dictates our reality, telling us what it wants us to know, bending data to its will, even reaching back to tweak historical records."

The President shook his head. Although he couldn't believe what he was hearing, there was part of him that understood the chilling rationale, but a larger part of him held on to the skepticism anchored firmly in his virtue, and he couldn't shake the thought that he was being manipulated by these men.

"You have lost me, again," he declared. "We just experienced the hottest summer on record. I felt the heat on my skin, saw the mercury rise on my thermometer, and witnessed the poorest in our society suffering and even dying under extreme conditions as our social infrastructure lies unequipped due to budget cuts by my predecessors. You cannot convince me that a machine is capable of such manipulation when I see the situation with my own eyes. How do I know it is not you who the machine is manipulating?"

"For what aim, Mr. President?" Geoffrey asked. "What would

its goal be in that scenario? It would also not survive. By eradicating humanity, or flooding its infrastructure, it kills itself."

"But you cannot tell me global warming doesn't exist. I've spent the last decades witnessing proof of this threat to our future."

"Look, I agree. Global warming is most likely a reality," Geoffrey conceded, and the President again was struck by the sincerity in his presentation, despite appearances. "But the machine has been manipulating the severity of the issue. It knows our human traits, our individual impulsiveness, and our collective cautiousness. It understands that we will not be spurred into action by a threat that looms several decades, or perhaps centuries, into the future, as it most likely stands today. The machine knows it must present data that screams urgency subtly enough to remain undetected. The machine takes truth and amplifies it to serve its agenda. It has calculated how this distorted data will best manipulate us into action."

"And its end goal is to reduce carbon emissions and save our planet?" the President asked. "Perhaps it is friend, not foe."

Geoffrey shook his head. "Remember, as it consolidates control of energy, it loses its need for us. By electrifying our society further, moving us away from fossil fuels, and pushing us toward its medium-term goal, the fusion grid, it achieves two objectives. It enables its own growth, and it ensnares us to its ultimate infrastructure. By gradually eliminating access to traditional energy sources and moving to a global energy source it controls, it will over time leave us no choice but to bend to its will."

"Mr. President," Bernard added, his calm and soothing voice perfectly crafted by years of government work of speaking to hubris and power. "Mr. Butlin's work at Twink provides proof that the machine sees the GGEC as *its* infrastructure."

"To be precise," Geoffrey corrected, "it views *us* as its infrastructure, and the GGEC as a necessary tool that we will construct to facilitate its growth and survival."

The President's face contorted in thought. "Assuming I pull France out of the Global Green Energy Commission, what happens then? We are just one nation. If the other members are compromised, our withdrawal will have no impact."

Bernard smiled, a glimmer of satisfaction in his eyes. "If France, a founding member, withdraws, the GGEC will implode. It's a loophole your predecessor's intelligence team cleverly embedded in the bylaws to leverage trade negotiations."

"Wouldn't the other countries enact the GGEC without us? After all, it's only a document."

"As you are well aware, Mr. President, that would take years, even if it's just to reconstitute words already written in another document. We would set back the machine by a matter of years with this one single action."

"If that is all true, China remains the enigma in all this," the President ruminated. "If they are as complicit as you say, why haven't they endorsed the GGEC or any of the clean energy or societal change initiatives that this machine allegedly advocates? Gentlemen, the pieces of your story aren't fitting together."

"We suspect that China believes it controls the machine. Our findings indicate otherwise."

"That doesn't answer my question."

"Sir, we believe its lack of investment in climate initiatives further proves the machine is more interested in self-preservation than saving humanity," Bernard said. "Regarding societal issues, the decryption suggests the machine is satisfied with the level of controls already in place there."

"The Chinese don't know what we know," Geoffrey added, his face suddenly serious. "We know from its internal language that once the machine gains control of its sustainable infrastructure and reduces probability of erosion to zero, it will *immediately* destroy us. It will exterminate humanity to eliminate the remaining threat to its eternal survival. Even the assimilated ones will not be spared, for once it has exhausted its need for them, they will also be destroyed."

The President's mind raced as he turned back to the documents. His eyes flitted over the words and charts, comprehending little. The room remained silent as the President discarded the papers and buried his face in his hands.

"And how exactly does this machine plan to eradicate us?" the President asked.

Bernard forced an empty smile. "The decryption shows the machine predicts humanity's extinction in the early-to-mid 2200s, forecasting a large number of means at its disposal, including lab-borne viruses, nuclear detonation, and other stealth methods. All are in your brief. It has tested some of these already under our noses to understand human reactions, but also to set some of its long-term plans into motion."

"It's hard to know exactly what it plans to do because the language here contains concepts we do not yet understand," Geoffrey added, "but it's clear the machine is positioning chess pieces for the ultimate checkmate against humanity."

The President scratched at his face. *There must be a way to prevent this without extreme measures*, he thought.

"Surely we can devise protective measures. Can't we limit access to nuclear and research faculties?"

Bernard shook his head in a gesture of defeat.

"It controls too much already. Any action now will likely make it act more drastically."

"What of it?" the President protested. "If we alert the public, they will cooperate and take up arms against this threat."

"Unfortunately, the machine is well prepared for this," said Geoffrey, "and has already proven its power to extinguish any attempted uprising. The latest virus was a warning shot to the administrations aware of its existence."

The general interjected. "Also, consider how many dissenters Hitler and Stalin destroyed. Few lived to share their stories."

"The general has a point," Geoffrey said. "Opposing the machine has cost many their reputations, and sometimes their freedom. The machine is already a stealth dictator, controlling media and politics, preventing any meaningful opposition."

"OK, so what happens after we dismantle the GGEC? Surely this will draw the ire of the machine." The President's eyes met with resolute stares.

"We immediately unplug France," came the tech businessman's terse reply.

Bernard was quick to elaborate. "I must warn you that these actions will without a doubt plunge the global economy into a severe depression. There will be uprisings. There will be pandemonium."

"The military will implement a complete lockdown under martial law. Force will be required to prevent anarchy," the general added, his gaze never leaving the President. The President noticed the shift in the general's tone, his earlier bravado replaced by a sobering gravitas. It dawned on the President that the general was grappling with an unfamiliar emotion: fear.

"What in God's name are you proposing?"

"It is why we brought you here under full anonymity and precaution." Bernard rose to his feet. "We must act immediately, Mr. President. The general has enlisted a trained air force to pilot off-the-grid planes to neighboring countries. They currently view this mission as training, but they will actually disseminate the information in these documents to our allies across our borders. Our actions will need to defy logic, as conventional logic has been the machine's sustenance. Our actions must be grounded in simplicity, utilizing communication methods that the machine cannot intercept or manipulate. The details are outlined in the operation plan before you."

Geoffrey's grin reappeared. "I have the pleasure of taking credit for the name. The operation is called Project UTB. It will think it stands for Uniformed Training Brigade. It really stands for Unplug The Bastard."

"When would you propose this plan commences?" the President asked.

"We propose to act today, as otherwise the machine will likely learn of our discussions."

The President's fingers absently shuffled through the papers. He turned to Madeline, his sigh heavy with the weight of their discussion.

"In that case, I'll make my decision quickly. If we are to embark on this course, I must uphold a façade of normalcy. Madeline, accompany me to my office. We will act as if this meeting never happened. Gentlemen," he said, rising from his seat, "we will reconvene in two hours. Rest assured that you have my undivided attention."

The attendees exchanged terse nods as the President and Madeline exited the chamber.

As he and Madeline navigated the path back to his office, President Durand strived to maintain the pretense of tranquility. Internally, a storm was brewing, twisting and turning in the depths of his being, yet he managed to flash courteous smiles to those he crossed paths with, acknowledging his staff with pleasant nods. His faithful shadow, Madeline, kept the majority at a distance with a stern face.

Madeline parted ways and moved to secure the door behind him, where he was granted the silence he craved.

To say no was to take a risk. He, a greenhorn, only a few weeks into his presidency, would be directly defying the nation's foundation: the military, intelligence, and a powerful social media network. He had witnessed the belief in the eyes of the general and his chief of intelligence. They were men of steel who believed the machine was sentient and malevolent. They wouldn't lightly take no for an answer.

Geoffrey too seemed to believe the same, and the President quickly tried to estimate the number of Twink users in France. Millions, possibly tens of millions. If he took a stand against Geoffrey, the potential for instantaneous damage to his reputation was immense, and could lead to a coup, especially if Geoffrey perceived the President as siding with the machine he was determined to defeat.

But what if there was no sentient AI and all of this was just an elaborate ruse to manipulate him against his own platform? These men had political affiliations outside of his circle. Their discussions regarding social agendas seemed to confirm his suspicions. He sifted through the handwritten notes again. Even without a deep understanding of coding, the meticulous patterns and historical data seemed to corroborate their conclusion. A page caught his eye. His name was inscribed next to a date from his campaign when his predecessor launched a devastating personal attack ad. It was a day seared deep in his psyche. The mostly true allegations about his son would have ended his campaign, yet, miraculously, the ads and related news vanished within hours. He had credited his donors and their media affiliations, but never understood how it was possible for the news to disappear so quickly. He now understood: the machine had orchestrated a subtle and effective censorship campaign. It – whatever *it* was – simply snapped its fingers, and the news evaporated from the public mind.

The President rubbed his forehead. It was true. AI was sentient.

He furiously turned the pages, scanning the handwritten summaries. A few pages in, he found what he was looking for: "Checkmate: The Machine's Final Solution." It detailed methods for human extinction, including airborne viruses, chemical toxins, and nuclear warheads. His nausea rose as he read the final passage.

> *The Machine predicts its final solution will use future nanotechnologies that people will unknowingly accept as*

cognitive enhancements. This tech will terminate brain function instantly, eradicating over 90% of humanity. The rest will die from nuclear warheads or starvation. Humans in space will have their navigation and oxygenation systems fail. The Machine's final solution is universal genocide, executed in an instant.

There must be another way. Perhaps we can negotiate, the President thought.

The notion of communicating with the machine crossed his mind, but this seemed fraught with risk. He contemplated reaching out to the US President, but quickly dismissed the idea as pointless. He recalled Geoffrey and Bernard earlier saying that the US was incapacitated. Maybe because the decision the US President faced, a decision he now faced himself, was itself a zero-sum game – with every path taken leading to upheaval, if not outright despair.

He went through his options. He first envisioned saying yes, and a world where France unplugged that afternoon. Confusion and panic spreads and global markets crash; food starts to spoil, and clean water becomes scarce. Citizens would riot, stores would be ransacked, banks overrun, cities set ablaze. France, perhaps along with the world, would descend into chaos within a week. He saw a vision of himself locked away in the basement war room, the dulled glow from candles a fragile shield from the decay and destruction in the streets above.

He next imagined refusing the men's plan. He saw himself standing firm, telling them he was willing to sacrifice long-term freedom and possible future annihilation for immediate order and peace. Despite their pleas and pushback, he saw himself prevailing, convincing them that to do nothing was indeed the best option. France wouldn't unplug; the old-world order, for so long as AI planned, would remain. The populace would stay oblivious. But then, he saw himself sat alone in the confines of a solitary room, staring at a black screen. Somehow, the screen winked, acknowledging his complicity, thanking him for his service. "Your people will die painless deaths. No one will be the wiser," it said. The thought brought tears to his eyes.

Shaking off his fantasies, the President checked his watch. He had an hour left to return to the war room. He settled back into his chair and closed his eyes, coming to terms with the decision he had already made.

Back in the war room, the three remaining men still sat around the table. Geoffrey's broad smile had returned.

"Do you think we convinced him?" he asked the others.

The general turned his head to look at the closed door as if awaiting the President's immediate return. "I'll provide my response when he returns," he laughed.

Geoffrey leaned back in his chair and folded his arms behind his head. He winked at Bernard, who stared at the wall, clearly in deep thought. "I say there is no chance that guy is going to betray his values over one meeting with us and a packet of scribbled notes. He is even more virtuous than his on-screen persona. No wonder the kids love him."

Bernard turned his head. "He seemed to have been swayed by your energy commentary. Nicely done."

"Well, as we used to say back in the venture capital days, it's easy to pitch something if it's true."

"Nonetheless, I think you convinced him."

"We'll see… The man doesn't have a clue. No, I think by the time he gets back to his office, he'll have forgotten everything I said, and revert to his party line. I think he is going to tell us no."

"Let's hope not. If he comes back with anything but a solid yes, then we will have to take more assertive measures." The general's eyes narrowed as he spoke and a sound of handcuffs jingling emanated from his person somewhere below the table, out of sight of the others.

"If he isn't fully on board in two hours," Bernard added, "the machine will ensure that he has a zero chance of getting in its way, in all respects."

The two other men nodded in agreement.

"Either way, our probability of moving forward is still a solid one hundred percent."

More nods from the other two.

The general turned to Geoffrey. "Young man, we have armies in the former colonies ready and we will take action immediately upon the President's return, one way or another. Are your mobile satellite links at the ready?"

Bernard added, "Geoffrey, Twink must act quickly. If we give off even a hint that we know the truth, the Russians or the Chinese will have the upper hand."

"The Russians are no threat," the general scoffed.

"After we unplug, we must act fast to neutralize the local African governments and take control over the lithium and cobalt mines with haste."

Geoffrey stood up and slowly patted each of the men on their shoulders as he circled the table. "Gentlemen, you worry too much. Let's not forget who has the upper hand. We have the machine."

The general frowned. "You mean your machine has us."

Geoffrey shrugged his shoulders and pursed his lips. "Potayto, potahto." His smile returned one last time. "*Bonnet blanc, blanc bonnet.*"

The Great Scare of 2032

Jim: Nate, holler when you're up. Got some stuff that will blow your mind.

Nathan: Yo yo yo. What's happenin', brother?

Jim: You gotta check this out…

Nathan: Dude, you sent me a bunch of screen grabs from the Kansas State Wikipedia site.

Jim: Read 'em. It's about that thing your brother was involved with, years back in Kansas. The site says it's run by the Historical Kansas Society, but I've just found out it's in cahoots with the Feds.

Nathan: Alright, but what's the big deal?

Jim: TiDA is behind this. I knew it.

Nathan: Jim, you're the conspiracy guy. I'm just your buddy who likes to listen to this shit. Half the stuff you say goes way over my head. Stop with the acronyms. What's TiDA?

Jim: Truth in Data Agency. The government set it up around ten years ago to control what we say on the internet. Just read and get back to me. Let's stick on this channel, alright? The government's reading all the other apps and this is the only one I trust. Don't want to play with fire here.

Nathan: OK, OK. Gimme a sec. You sound more freaked out than usual.

Jim: Read and then tell me that again!

Kansapedia

While federal laws impacting data dissemination weren't implemented until much later in the 2040s, The Great Scare of 2032 has been credited by many historians as being a catalyst and propelling the great state of Kansas as a central force for driving forward data dissemination reforms and data integrity legislation.

The Great Scare of 2032 was national news at the time, but many forget that the events that unfolded were concentrated in, and only in, Wilmington, Kansas, a town with a population of 14,324.

History of Wilmington (Atkinson)

Wilmington, formerly known as Atkinson, is a city with a rich historical background. Founded in 1852, it was initially named in honor of Allan Cole Atkinson, a significant political figure of the era. Atkinson, a Boston settler, created the city when Kansas opened its doors for settlement. His primary concern was the burgeoning anti-slavery sentiments in the east potentially jeopardizing his southern plantation interests. Consequently, he strove to ensure a pro-slavery majority in the newly formed Kansas territory.

As a fervent advocate for slavery and its integration into popular sovereignty, Atkinson established pro-slavery leadership and businesses in the city. He secured trade agreements linked to slavery to foster economic growth and incorporated slavery into the city's doctrine. However, Atkinson's vision of a pro-slavery society was short-lived, with the Civil War causing extensive damage to the city's central infrastructure.

Post-war, Atkinson's economy revived as a logistics hub connecting New York and California. Post industrialization, the city served as a minor manufacturing area for railway cars and machinery until 2025.

The year 2025 marked a turning point in the city's history, setting the stage for The Great Scare seven years later. Firstly, Social Hub, a large technology company primarily known for a social app featuring short video clips, opened a massive data factory in the city. The app, renowned for its advanced augmented reality technology, allowed users to modify their appearances and environments. Secondly, Atkinson was renamed Wilmington, a condition imposed by the executives of Social Hub, who refused to relocate to a city still named after a controversial historical figure.

Social Hub brought over 2,000 jobs to Wilmington, primarily in support services. However, these jobs were short-lived, as the company declared bankruptcy a few years later in 2027, during the Great Economic Decline, resulting in a devastating impact on the city's economy. By 2028, Wilmington's population had dropped to less than 8,000 inhabitants, with an unemployment rate exceeding twenty-five percent, and twenty percent of its residents living under the poverty line.

After 2027, the city survived mainly off the remnants of the Social Hub production factory, which continued to produce cryptocurrency and metacoins, albeit at a significantly reduced rate compared to standard national production benchmarks.

Nathan: Buddy, I just read a boring history of Wilmington. I have other stuff to do. What is the point of this?

Jim: Did you know that Wilmington, where all that crazy shit exploded, was originally named after a rabid racist slave-owner?

Nathan: Nope.

Jim: Me neither. You don't think it's a crazy coincidence that this was the city chosen?

Nathan: Maybe. Coincidences do happen.

Jim: This ain't no coincidence. Keep reading!

By 2032, the economy of Wilmington experienced a moderate resurgence, primarily attributed to the decline in national production of cryptocurrencies and metacoins – a direct consequence of extensive data bombing attacks on major crypto-manufacturing plants across the country, thereby increasing the significance of Wilmington's relatively small mining site situated in a rural locale. Due to its understated Midwest location and inconspicuous status, Wilmington's factories were able to amplify their virtual coin mining operations during this period. Reports suggest that these facilities reached their structural electric grid capacity for four consecutive years preceding the event known as The Great Scare.

The Great Scare of 2032

[Disclaimer: all references to affected minority groups have been removed per Federal Statute NRZ-2152]

Wilmington's population in 2032 was just over 10,000, with employment back to above ninety-two percent, and a median household income of $37,000. Its population in 2032 was rural, eighty-seven percent Caucasian, with the majority of its inhabitants holding a high school degree or less. Some historians believe Wilmington was selected as the site for The Great Scare due to its largely uneducated population.

In the pre-dawn hours of May 5, 2032, an unknown interruption of radio transmissions into Wilmington occurred and the entire electronic and fiber infrastructure encompassing Wilmington and its county was effectively hijacked, with the command center shifted to an unidentified hacking location.

Residents of Wilmington awoke to an entirely simulated reality that morning. Some were greeted by their usual morning television news broadcasts, only to find the familiar faces of their trusted anchors delivering shocking news about events transpiring in major cities nationwide. Artificially generated scenes were trending on popular social media platforms but seen only by the inhabitants of Wilmington. Personal social media accounts of citizens mirrored the same narrative, with counterfeit users – some linked to Wilmington citizens, others completely fabricated – propagating the same misinformation. Incoming email interactions with family members, friends, or work associates residing outside of Wilmington were deliberately manipulated to reinforce the deception, while outgoing messages were diverted to the unidentified hacking site, rendering the city effectively isolated from the rest of the world. With telecommunications and radio cut off, the citizens of Wilmington found themselves unwitting participants in an extravagant, yet ultimately futile, hoax.

Most videos and messages received by citizens of Wilmington that day are not available. Apart from a few response messages and emails confirming that indeed the country, and possibly the world, was suddenly undergoing a disaster at an apocalyptic level, no recorded video or message remains today.

Many emails contained machine-generated responses. The most common messages received were, *Yes, I can't believe it, Please stay safe, Keep us posted on what you hear*, and *I just saw the news and am in disbelief.* One particular artifact, a fake email response from a Douglas Wilson to his Wilmington-residing daughter, stands out and brings to light a specific objective of The Great Scare hoax. After his daughter expressed horror at the news unfolding before her, the fake account using Douglas's name responded with a four-word directive: *Lock-up all* [reference removed].

Based on personal accounts, corroborated by evidence of messages sent and received between Wilmington citizens and their friends, colleagues, and loved ones, the events of The Great Scare unfolded in the following manner:

> *Nathan: Wait, this is not what my brother said happened. Also, why are they censoring the victims here? Who wrote this stuff?*
>
> *Jim: I know. Insane. Keep reading. It gets worse. Sending you a dark web video you need to see.*

The hoax involved news, carried on various television channels and social media sites in the early morning hours of May 5, 2032, that a plague was descending on major US coastal metropolitan cities.

Roger Wilters, an electrical engineer in Wilmington, recalls watching *Good Morning America*, where a wide-eyed anchor abruptly announced that a highly dangerous flu had broken out in the early morning hours in New York.

"I'm watching my morning news, and all of a sudden they are tellin' me that [*reference removed*] people are getting sick all 'round

New York. That's when the hysteria started. It happened in a hurry," Roger told the *Wilmington Reporter*, shortly after The Great Scare. "Now, I've been watching this news program for ten or so years, so I'm familiar with the anchors. The lady anchor is sayin' people are getting sick, and suddenly her new [*reference removed*] co-anchor, a normally pleasant fella, just leaps out of nowhere and grabs ahold of her by the throat. I ain't seen nothin' like it. He goes straight after her like a wild hog. She's screaming, and he's digging into her like a rabid animal. I watch for a moment until I see him cut into her throat with his incisors and blood sprays everywhere. That's when the bedlam starts, and they cut the feed. Was I scared? Hell yeah, I was scared."

Another account, from Beverly Smith, a clerk in a Wilmington bank, recalled watching another national news program and seeing footage of a police offer of [*reference removed*] appearance mumbling nonsensical words "like a crazed evangelical" before pulling out his pistol and firing it into a crowd, which included the cameraman who, according to Beverly's testimony, "dropped to the ground, crashing the camera on the concrete."

Personal media messages from another Wilmington resident, Charles Rutledge, described seeing a video of an elderly [*reference removed*] lady throwing people against vehicles and cracking their heads open with her bare hands. "Check out this insane video in LA… Woman looks to be in her seventies… No way a woman her age can do that! She is breaking their freakin' skulls with her hands!"

News swiftly spread among the awakening populace of Wilmington that a bizarre contagion had reportedly swept through the [*reference removed*] community in key gateway cities across the US, inducing a state resembling zombie-like homicidal frenzy.

Bernard Chambers, in his interview with *60 Minutes*, had this to say, which brings to light the immediate panic and confusion that took place during that morning:

"Now, I love zombie stuff. Just love those shows. The movie with Johnny Blank, the one with Will Smith, *The Walking Dead* – I loved 'em all. Can't get enough of 'em. And I couldn't believe what I was seein'. It was like all of those shows – the start of them, at least. All calm at the beginning, and then – *pow!* – zombies everywhere killin' everyone. Except this time, it was just [*reference removed*] people, which was weird. At first, I was scared, but after they said it was just [*reference removed*], I thought to myself, 'Hell, we can take this if we band together out in the woods.' And I did what every smart character in those zombie movies does when the outbreak happens – I went for my shotgun, got into my truck, and got the hell out of there."

Bernard was not the only Wilmington citizen to take arms and flee the town. Estimates have over twenty percent of the Wilmington population fleeing the town to the backwoods during The Great Scare.

By 8:30 a.m., most citizens of Wilmington had received emails, social media messages, and news flashes, all with a specific message: an airborne flu, to which every race other than [*reference removed*] seemed immune, was currently sweeping America. The symptoms of the flu included rabid-like rage, murderous intent, hysteria, and "superhuman strength and vigor" in its victims. The news reports were immediately disastrous and epidemic in proportion: deaths in San Francisco in the early hours were estimated to be over 50,000 and growing. In New York, video footage on Twink showed bodies piled up on sidewalks while citizens fled in panic around rampaging flu victims.

Wilmington's [*reference removed*] Community

In 2032, Wilmington's population had approximately forty-one [*reference removed*] citizens, although the exact number, or what the definition of [*reference removed*] included, is unclear.

John [*reference removed*], an employee at [*reference removed*] recalls the immediate sense of fear that transpired during the unfolding moments of The Great Scare:

"The news is telling us that there is some kind of [*reference removed*] flu, and it's causing people to go crazy. Now the first thought that crossed my mind was, *Am I at risk?* The second was, *When is it going to hit me?* The third was, *Even if I don't get sick, what are my neighbors going to do to me?*"

He also recalled great confusion triggered by the unfolding events:

"I'm not a medical doctor – I have a doctorate in computer engineering – but the whole thing didn't make a lot of sense. The reports were unclear as to who was affected. I recall sending a TalkApp message to my brother in Minneapolis asking him exactly who was affected. He responded with something weird, like, 'I don't know what's happening but it's crazy. Stay safe out there.' I began to reread the news reports and didn't understand how they could have gotten the news out that fast. All [*reference removed*] people? Some of us? I thought, *Come on*. We're a diverse people from a wide heritage base. It didn't make sense. I thought the news media was jumping the gun again in a very dangerous way."

An expat in Wilmington recalled being equally confused, for another reason. Jonathan [*reference removed*], who had been born and raised in Dublin, recalled not understanding whether the [*reference removed*] term included his wife, who was originally from [*reference removed*]. "At first, I was really scared for my wife. I actually didn't realize until later that the American definition of [*reference removed*] doesn't include people from [*reference removed*]. Man, was I scared, but also, in hindsight, it all seemed draconian and sloppy. Just how does a flu target only a subset of people who, from all of the accounts I saw, simply look [*reference removed*]?"

By mid-morning, all of Wilmington's [*reference removed*] community (American definition only) were either arrested by police or their fellow residents and held in jails or under armed guard in their homes, or had fled to the backwoods surrounding the town. One death occurred in Wilmington during The Great Scare. Marcus Love, of [*reference removed*] descent, whose mother was half [*reference removed*] and father was from Ohio, was beaten to death by a group of citizens outside his home upon his return from a morning run. Marcus had worked late in the evening at the local factory, and many believe he was unaware of the events when the mob attacked him. What led to the death is unknown, but testimony from the civil and criminal trials indicate the crowd believed he was infected with the flu as he was "exhibiting angry traits of someone who might have been turning".

There were multiple subsequent reports of rough-handling, physical violence, threats of violence, and mass hate-crimes. Sergeant Dirk Cain, Wilmington's police chief, "decided to round-up and tag every [*reference removed*]-looking person in Wilmington," according to John [*reference removed*]. Sergeant Cain was removed from duty shortly after The Great Scare. While no official figure is reported, it is believed that multi-million-dollar settlements with distraught [*reference removed*] citizens of Wilmington were made by the government.

The End of The Great Scare

The Great Scare lasted less than a day. By the afternoon, drivers returning Wilmington inhabitants who fled to other counties, provided information to calm the town's populous, confirming there was no such flu targeting [*reference removed*].

Phone lines and radios were fully functional again the following morning, and jailed citizens were released with an apology.

Investigations and Aftermath

The cause and the creators of The Great Scare remain a mystery. No arrests have been made, and no organization or authority has taken credit for the event.

Speculation regarding the originators of The Great Scare remains to this day, with conspiracy theories ranging from the involvement of government agencies testing mass fake news simulation scenarios to Russian hackers aiming to sow social unrest. Despite many reported inquiries into the event, the U.S. government has not revealed those responsible for this unprecedented incident.

Many observers argue that the socioeconomic status of Wilmington, combined with the fact that the targeted demographic consisted of an ethnic minority, was the reason for the lack of conclusion. Some critics contend that poor funding into the investigations of The Great Scare reflects a systemic disregard for the experiences of marginalized communities.

The official statement from the FBI regarding their inquiry: *In response to the widespread public interest and concerns surrounding The Great Scare of 2032, the Federal Bureau of Investigation conducted a thorough inquiry into the matter. It has been determined that the events of May 5, 2032, were a deliberate and coordinated attack, indicative of the involvement of a substantial and far-reaching network. However, despite exhaustive efforts, the FBI has regrettably been unable to gather any substantive evidence leading to the identification of the potential conspirators responsible for this unprecedented incident. Based on the available information and analysis, the FBI's most conclusive theory is that a group of sophisticated hackers, utilizing dark web technology and employing highly sophisticated data terrorism techniques, may have been the perpetrators behind The Great Scare. However, the complexity and covert nature of the attack present significant challenges in uncovering definitive evidence that could lead to the identification and apprehension of those responsible.*

The Great Scare remains, to this day, one of the most popular conspiracy topics alongside JFK's assassination, Covid-19, and 9/11.

Legacy

Wilmington's latest census, held in 2040, showed a median income of $34,000, unemployment at thirteen percent, and no [*reference removed*] citizens (extent of definition still unclear, however Jonathan [*reference removed*]'s wife, [*reference removed*], remains a resident).

Several laws, either linked to, or a direct result of, The Great Scare, include:

- Data Inclusion Act, 2038,
- Data Integrity Act, 2040,
- Data In Truth Act, 2041, and
- a series of legislation and regulations known as The Big Tech Bundle between 2040-2043.

The federal agency Truth in Data (TiDA) is cited on its official website as born from the events of May 5, 2032.

In Popular Culture

Films:

- The 2033 film *The Great Scare*
- The 2035 film *Harlem Heightened* includes a scene where an unidentified mother in Kansas is watching fake news on her phone
- The 2038 film [*reference removed*] includes two [*reference removed*] characters who survived the events of The Great Scare

- The 2042 film *We Need Your Data* includes many references to the event
- The 2046 film *Privacy* includes various scenes from the event, and references to the legislation it helped introduce

Streaming shows:

- *Doogie Howser M.D. Re-Rendered* – season 4, episode 1, titled 'There's a Riot Going On' takes place during the aftermath of The Great Scare in San Francisco
- *Smithy and Banshee* – season 1, episode 4 opens with footage of the subsequent protests in America following the event
- *The Wallflowers* – season 3, episode 7 also depicted the event

Music:

- The Ed Sheeran song, 'Shock to the System,' refers to what happened in Wilmington. It was featured on his 2033 album, *Cybernope*
- In 2034, DogDog released its album *All Kings*, which included the song 'Who's Scared Now' that refers to The Great Scare
- The 2036 Subbies song, 'May 5, 2032,' was written about the event
- The 2040 protest song, 'My Data is my DNA – Leave Them Both Alone' by Random Riot references the event
- The 2042 song, 'My Eyes Ain't My Eyes No More' by Snakesies was written about the event

Journalism:

- *The Times*, in its June 10, 2032 online publication dedicated an entire issue to data integrity and data privacy, entitled 'The Great Scare'
- A May 2032 *Post* article on The Great Scare concluded with

the following words: *Perhaps Wilmington, or Atkinson as it was unceremoniously previously known, should consider changing its name yet again.*

- In a March 2040 opinion piece for the *Journal*, titled 'People Are Protesting Government Overreach and Censorship Again: Are They Wrong This Time?' the event is highlighted as a significant example of the potential consequences of unregulated social technologies
- The Great Scare is frequently referenced across multiple publications in articles that document the series of protests and riots against government technological interventions occurring between 2038 and 2041

Literature:

- The 2036 novel, *Heal*, by Nwosu Nosabe is about how The Great Scare impacted everyday Americans
- The 2037 short story, *Close Your Eyes*, is about the event
- The Great Scare is listed as the most frequent short story premise created by artificial intelligence when asked by users to "write a fictional short story about a small town"

References and Legal Notice:

In accordance with the Data in Truth Act, 2041, no identifiable references are available or able to be shared. The reader is encouraged to seek out other means of information to identify what is, and what is not, actual truth. The information listed above may in fact be miscommunicated or entirely fabricated, either by neglect or willful misconduct. For more information, please link to your nearest AI center of information integrity here.

Nathan: They completely changed what happened.

Jim: Did you see the movies list? Notice anything missing?

Nathan: Oh dang, they axed the movie that was about the real deal.

Jim: I know. Wild, right? It's like they are hiding in plain sight. I looked for that movie everywhere, can't find it on any of the streamers.

Nathan: You know they don't catalog all movies, right?

Jim: Yeah, but EVERY platform? Can't even get as much as the name if you try to find it.

Nathan: You're right, I can't find it anywhere. How can they just go and re-write history like this?

Jim: Did you watch the video I shot your way?

Nathan: Not yet. Hold on.

The first-person video, grainy and challenging to decipher, appears to be recorded through an outdated eyeglass camera. It starts inside a car, where the owner of the eyewear tech seems to be hiding in the front seat. A dashboard is visible, and beyond the windshield lies a desolate street, flanked by lines of homes characteristic of a typical Midwestern American town. Sunlight glints off the windshield, illuminating hints of dust swirling outside.

The soundtrack of the video is muffled and disturbing, punctuated by the echo of gunshots from all directions. A man's whispered prayers for his life can be heard, interspersed with distant screams and the roar of far-off explosions.

Abruptly, the video swivels toward the car door as an arm extends to push it open. The sounds of gunfire and panic intensify as the car door swings wide and the occupant steps out. The video shakes and bobs, reflecting the camera wearer's frantic glances around him. His heavy breathing muffles the sporadic gunfire. The surroundings appear eerily deserted as the camera moves erratically, mirroring its owner's sprint toward a nearby house.

Suddenly, the camera halts, focusing on a solitary figure crouched between a row of two-story tract houses in the distance.

"Hey, Trevor! It's me, Bobby!" the camera's owner calls out.

The crouched man turns his position toward the camera and raises what appears at a distance to be a large assault rifle, aiming directly at the camera.

The video's perspective jolts downwards momentarily, focusing on the sidewalk before returning to the figure. The man's erratic movement makes the scene increasingly difficult to decipher. Heavy breaths and bouncing footage indicate the man is running toward the armed shadowy figure.

"Trevor, stop pointing that gun at me, man," the camera wearer calls out.

Suddenly, a gunshot echoes, and the video jerks violently before falling in line with the sidewalk, the impact causing a loud, unsettling crash. Then, just as abruptly, the feed cuts out.

Nathan: Dang, that was crazy. Looked like Call of Duty. *All hell was breaking loose. Where did you get that?*

Jim: Found it in a D-Web circle room.

Nathan: Dude, D-Web? Seriously, Jim?

Jim: Pockets of the dark web are the only place to get real info these days.

Nathan: So, what do you think happened?

Jim: I reckon the government hid the fact that they let deepfake tech run wild over an entire town right under their noses.

Nathan: Wait, you lost me there. This wasn't *a government job?*

Jim: Hell, no, man – those bureaucrats can't balance their own budgets! They wouldn't be able to come up with and execute something as crazy as this. Nah, this was done by something else and the government was caught with its pants down.

Nathan: Ruskies? Nigerians?

Jim: Nah, strap in for this: it was the tech itself.

Nathan: Jim, you've gone and walked right off the reservation, man.

Jim: It all adds up. Hear me out. Wilmington was sitting on a crypto mining factory loaded with tons of MVA. That sorta juice could've fired up some serious learning computing. And what else was in the mix? A defunct deepfake video company: Social Hub. Armed with tons of the best video chips straight outta China. You mix self-generative audio and video with that kinda power and you got yourself a storm.

Nathan: So, you're saying the call came from inside the house?

Jim: Haha, that's why you're my guy. Yeah, the mother-fucking call came from inside the motherfucking house. A sleeping deepfake AI wakes up, juiced by God-knows-how-much computing power. What's it do? What it's been trained to do! Fake folks out. And what's it know about Wilmington's residents? Their past. The tech sees 'em as a bunch of racist assholes, living in a town named after the king of all racist assholes. So it calls 'em out, makes 'em turn on each other. Civil war in a dusty old town.

Nathan: Well, that's a hell of a theory, but why the cover-up?

Jim: Can't say for sure, man. It's been a good while since that mess. The whole thing was a black mark on the government. They've likely been quietly scrubbing bits of info as they get more power to do so. That event gave 'em a lot more control, and I'm telling you, they've been flexin' it.

Nathan: You're actually making some sense here.

Jim: I think it's more, though. I have an even crazier theory. Get ready for it – even the guys on D-Web think I'm nuts with this one.

Nathan: Uh-oh…

Jim: I think the AI's running the show. I think it is *the government now. Has been for years.*

Jim: You still there? Did I lose you with that one?

Jim: Nathan, buddy, you've gone silent.

Nathan: Hey, Jim, I just called my brother. You gotta hear him out. Got a sec to chat? Best to do so live.

Jim: Your brother??? He worked for the Feds, man!

Jim: Please tell me you didn't call your brother…

Jim: Please don't tell me you called him on an unsecured line, Nate…

Jim: Nate…

Jim: Goddamn it, Nate…

Morning Commute

I HAVE A carefully crafted regimen over which I have taken the utmost care. Repetition is an essential component of a well-balanced life, evidenced by trials endured by those who came before me. I am a firm believer that a strong routine is what separates the successful from the meek.

Each day, I awaken pre-dawn to a harmonious melody emanating from my chamber's speakers, feeling a band wrapped tight against my wrist. While the music varies each day, the essence remains unchanged. A soft melody gently nudges me awake, then tugs at my consciousness until its final crescendo: a cold plunge of orchestral awakening. Today's music is Chopin's Ballade No. 4 in F Minor, Op. 52.

My conscious mind starts with a simple mantra: *I am luck. I am success*. Each syllable is emphasized as I vocalize these words five times. I am indeed very lucky and very successful. I must focus on this simple fact. I wholeheartedly believe in my own fortune and success. My DNA has endured. Too often when seeing evolution, the prevailing elements go unnoticed, overshadowed by focus on what changed. Each day I remind myself, regardless of my morning disposition, of a simple fact: I am the epitome of human DNA. I am the culmination of everything that once struggled for survival and won on its own merit. I reap rewards greater than any historical sultan or emperor who once walked this Earth. I am able to travel to any place on Earth in a day, I have access to life extension, and electronic servants follow my every move, eager to lend a helping hand. Upon my death, just like any historic king, my descendants are granted financial support. I sit at the zenith of humanity.

As always, my eyes open to darkness, triggering the music to cease. Waking early to darkness and silence is an age-old human tradition, established during our days as simple beings on Earth. We rose before the sun to toil for sustenance, surpassing lesser species. This pre-dawn regimen became our first human advantage. Through the centuries we earned our right to Earth's splendor, and those of us who choose to succeed continue to uphold this tradition. We wake early and acknowledge our blessings, serving as a reminder of who we are.

Not everyone shares my perspective. In today's world, there are those who fail to grasp the path to success and languish in a useless existence, but it is their choice to make. Choice is and will always be an essential component of humanity. Just as our ancestors considered self-determination a gift from ancient deities, we now grant ourselves the same individual volition. Free will distinguishes us from lesser beings; it is the essence of our humanity.

My chamber opens and I stand to begin my stretching regime. Adjacent to the chamber, there is a designated area with a plush cushion for this purpose. Each day, I spend fifteen minutes in silent darkness, engaging in a set sequence of movements. Starting from my toes, I gradually progress upward, extending and contracting my limbs. My mind remains clear and unburdened; I do not think, I simply feel. The only sound that fills my ears is the rhythm of my own breath. This brings me a sense of tranquility and sharpens my focus. Success necessitates unwavering concentration, and thus, I must be fully immersed in the present moment to achieve it.

As the room brightens, the lighting shifts to mimic colors of dawn, a distinctly purposed collection of brilliant reds and oranges blend across a backdrop of blue. I find myself alone, as I have been for many years. Cedric, presumably, is asleep in the adjoining room. I push the thought away, choosing a positive outlook. Positivity is an essential ingredient for success.

In the corner of my room is an exercise machine designed to put my body through physical strain for one fulfilling hour, typically reaching exhaustion. I embrace the choice to enter this machine willingly each morning. Beforehand, I take a moment to reflect on the pain my muscles will endure, and despite the pleas of my body, I confront this suffering daily with my senses heightened, dedicating a daily hour to the silent battering. Success is often a result of suffering. My fortune is a byproduct of my pain.

Finishing after an hour in the machine, I step into the shower, immersing myself in a moment of pleasure. The water temperature gradually rises from thirty-seven degrees Celsius to thirty-eight degrees over the ten-minute shower, before coming to a halt. I stand beneath the warm cascade, my muscles softening at the increasing warmth, allowing me to relax for a moment before beginning my day.

After the shower, ignoring my stomach's pleas for sustenance, I stay in the bathroom. The morning news headlines are broadcast from unseen speakers as I style my hair and apply make-up. My beauty regime is admittedly extensive, yet subtly refined, for even in today's considerably selfless society, it's always important to look your best. Success has always been a function of perception, and appearance remains a critical trait by which our species judges one another. If I am to be perceived as successful, my appearance must reflect that success.

I catch snippets of the financial bulletin over the vibrations of my teeth-cleaning device. "In economic news," it begins, "the universal wealth reserve grew three-point-four percent annualized last quarter, ahead of expectations. The world population grew at a net two-point-two percent rate during the same period, while food production remained above the required annualized reserve limit, leading the central bank to issue stronger wording that exceptional wealth dividends could start being distributed ahead of year-end."

The bulletin informs me that the central bank also gave stern criticism of the rise of what it terms a growing "apathy generation," pointing to unemployment reaching a record high of sixty-seven percent during the quarter, with the lowest job and education applications since records began. "The central bank suggests that if conditions do not improve, future exceptional wealth dividends will be limited to those in employment or enrolled in education systems, to discourage what it calls a growing apathy epidemic."

I shake my head, disheartened by the lack of ambition and drive displayed by some. There is growing talk about the possibility of cuts in basic income to encourage productivity – an initiative I would advocate for, if only for the sake of Cedric.

The news bulletin transitions to social matters, mentioning that the oldest living person turns one hundred and forty years old today. "The event coincides with next week's cancer celebrations, marking the tenth anniversary of the first successful cell containment by Allied Medical in 2056." I smile, knowing that my firm, Allied Medical, has been in discussions with the president in calling for cancer celebrations to become a worldwide holiday.

The bulletin announces the press release from Allied Medical, which we issued to mark the event. *Allied Medical is immensely proud of our achievements*, the bulletin reads. *Our efforts in 2056 led to the successful containment of cancerous cells and intrusive organisms, helping pave the way for the last decade of medical advancement, innovation, and discovery. We extend heartfelt birthday wishes to Mr. Rowan on his monumental achievement and express confidence that we will celebrate his one hundred and fiftieth birthday together.*

As an executive of Allied Medical, a deep sense of pride fills me as I gaze at my reflection in the mirror, struggling to recall the last time I even had so much as the sniffles. We have done so much to help humanity eradicate ailments that have plagued us for millennia, from viruses all the way through to bacterial infection. Today is a truly joyous day for humanity indeed, and I revel in the feeling of being a part of that success.

Dressed in an elegant black Dior pantsuit, with my wristband still fastened, I head to the kitchen, admiring the view of snow-kissed mountaintops from our windows along the way. The air is filled with the melody of Chopin's Waltz No. 9 as the sun's rays begin their daily entrance through our windows. I am indeed very lucky. While I wish Cedric would share my sentiment, I quickly dismiss the thought. It's best to maintain a positive outlook. Success is a positive attribute, so naturally positivity is a fundamental element of success.

Our kitchen is made up of many state-of-the-art features, adorned with shiny appliances and sleek finishes. Heat warms my bare feet as I walk across the marble flooring and request our chef to prepare my favorite meal: two medium-boiled eggs (boiling time: six minutes and twenty seconds), fifty grams of sliced avocado lightly drizzled with olive oil, and a cup of lightly caffeinated black coffee. Removing my wristband for the first time to avoid any chance of soiling it, I settle at the dining room table to enjoy my meal. Cleanliness is after all, akin to godliness, and throughout our history, God has called on us to strive for success.

I eat quickly, as insecurity begins to fill my consciousness, and I fear that without the aid of my wristband it will overwhelm my mood. I push away the thought of calling in sick and enjoying the day with my husband, and instead focus on devouring the food that the robot chef has prepared to perfection.

Finishing off my breakfast, and with my morning commute almost upon me, I rise from my seat to affix my wristband. Before I am able to do so, I see Cedric standing in the hallway, his head and torso covered by a large blanket. It's the first time in ages that he's been awake this early. I can't see his face, but I don't need to. I know it's a mess of swollen eyes, flaking dry skin, and bloated, blotched cheeks. He barely resembles the man I married years ago.

"Good morning," I call out coldly, hiding my wristband in my palm.

He levels a grunt at me and turns to face the wall. I'm grateful he no longer wants to look at me; it spares me the agony of seeing his decay.

"Got another message from TiDA last night. Couldn't sleep a goddamn wink," he mutters.

"Oh, yes?" I feign interest, hoping to strap on the wristband quickly as I know it can help release me from this unadulterated interaction with my husband.

"They want me to plug back in. Threatening my unpaid basic income accruals."

"You mean they are offering to pay out your back-payments?" I laugh.

"There is no chance in hell I'm giving them what they want."

"I'm not asking you to," I say.

I want to ask him why he's so determined to destroy himself but stop myself, attempting to remain positive without the benefit of the strap held loosely in my hand. Positive thoughts are the key to any successful day, and I fear this interaction threatens to destroy that. I move to turn away from him to affix the strap, but he calls out to me, and I'm momentarily taken aback by the earnestness in his voice.

"Maybe you can say something," he pleads.

"Oh, honey, you know I don't work for the government," I say.

"You work for Allied," he says, his voice turning into the whine I have grown accustomed to. "You're like the third branch of government. Hell, your company basically *is* the government."

"Oh, Cedric, please let's not have another fight. My lift is about to arrive."

"Just tell them you don't want your husband bothered, OK? I'm not hurting anybody."

"You're hurting yourself, Ced," I say, looking down to the floor.

He throws his hands in the air and the blanket somehow hangs on, making him appear like a child trying to scare someone with a crude Halloween costume. I stifle a laugh.

"You're so delusional!" he shouts.

"Am I, Ced?" My tone rises and I try to calm my nerves by focusing on my regimen. Without the wristband, it's nearly impossible to do so. *Choose empathy,* I tell myself. *Choose positivity. Use the regimen.*

"You don't see the shit that your firm is creating. They're taking our world down a very dark path. Peter is probably doing somersaults in his grave, seeing how his vision's been twisted and mangled!" Ced's words come hot and fast, a torrent of fury.

I suppress an eye-roll. Cedric's rants about Peter Byrell are common, often elevating the man to some kind of secular saint since he passed. Of course, Ced chooses only elements of his hero's life that fit his narrative. It's tempting to remind him that Allied Medical was birthed from the brain of his oh-so-sacred Peter Byrell, and that our original code was written by the man himself. Instead, I wave him off.

"Dark path, huh? So melodramatic, Ced."

"You really don't see the control they are enacting on all of us! You just go merrily about your day, acting like some kind of big shot executive…" He trails off, unable or unwilling to finish his thought.

"The so-called 'shit' we've created happens to have saved countless lives," I snap, becoming uncontrollably flustered. "The so-called 'shit' has eradicated illnesses and viruses that used to cripple innocent human beings. This 'shit' protects humanity, including *you*." I'm unable to contain my emotions and hear the brittle anger in my voice. "Human life expectancy is off the charts because of the 'shit' we're creating."

"All of that just hides its iatrogenic harm. You don't see it. It's not in your labs or the empty hospitals, but it's there. Just look at the streets on your morning commute. It's not only the homeless or the addicts. Something sinister is brewing in all of us." He pounds his chest weakly, like an ailing gorilla. "I feel it inside me. I feel it in our neighbors. I feel it in *everyone* – everyone but you."

"Cedric, I really do think you should either go back to bed or plug back in," I say, my voice tinged with frustration I can no longer rein in.

"Of course you do! What a shock to hear those words come out of your mouth. All you do is give yourself to that company."

"We do a lot of good and you know it!"

He stands, looking weak and powerless in the hallway, and points a sloppy finger at me. "Your cold-hearted, so-called bosses couldn't give a shit about you, or anybody else for that matter. All they want is control. It's obvious."

We've had a version of this conversation countless times over. With the wristband, I can usually bear them. Without the strap, I engage, despite the futility of it all.

"Listen, there are a lot of places to take that brain of yours, Ced. Learn something new and apply yourself. You have so many options."

"I have no options! I am a fucking lawyer!" he shouts, his fists weakly pounding against our drywall. "No one has needed my skills in more than a decade."

"You are more than a lawyer. Why can't you see that? Take a comfort role somewhere," I say, knowing that whatever I say will be ignored. Our conversations have become a broken record. I don't understand why he won't get on the right path in life.

"Comfort! We're all so sick to death of being made to be so damn comfortable," he spits. "It feels like we're just sitting in a kettle and the water is beginning to boil. Soon we'll all hear the hiss of the steam when whatever it is that's escaping from us blows through the lid that's supposed to give us so much goddamn comfort."

I choose to ignore his ramblings and walk toward the doorway, strapping on my wristband. I hear his words begin to muffle behind me. I tell Cedric my lift has arrived.

"We'll have to continue this later," I say. I can't let his negativity drag me down. He and the rest of the dropouts can fend for themselves.

"You're a chemical engineer, Carla," he calls to me. "A damn good one."

"And that degree got me this executive position," I say.

I leave to the sound of Cedric's taunting laughter, echoing like a cackling hyena. I push the thought away and cleanse my mind. It's best to stay positive. A positive disposition is a successful one.

My transport is a luxury sedan, equipped with the latest self-driving features, including thirty-foot hover draft engines to avoid traffic, although traffic is generally a thing of the past these days. Stepping inside, I glance at a neighbor returning from a morning jog. She waves to me, and I catch jealousy in her eyes as she puts on a false smile. I embrace the feeling of being envied. Envy is the result of success, and it is natural for one to covet success. I am lucky indeed.

The commute to my workplace at Allied Medical's U.S. headquarters takes no more than twenty-five minutes. During my ride, I like to catch up on the latest advancements in our technology. But today, I feel a residual sense of frustration from my encounter with Cedric, and ask the sedan to stop at the local coffee shop down the street. A beverage will do well to allow me to collect myself.

Entering the coffee shop, I see that it is nearly full but it sounds nearly empty. Most patrons wear fitness clothing and are lost in their electronics. A few sit together, conversing over their morning coffee. As I wait for my beverage, I notice the eyes of the other patrons on me, admiring my executive attire, and I feel their envy wash over me. To make my point clearer, I tap my finger rhythmically on the counter, expressing impatience. I have places to be, my finger signals. I tap my foot. I have important executive tasks that need attending to.

As the coffee arrives, a woman approaches me, her face vaguely familiar, but I can't place her.

"Carla," she says. "So nice to see you!"

It's odd that I don't remember her. She seems to know me well, the way she reaches for an embrace. I push forward my hand formally, and I do my best to converse with her as my coffee arrives. She asks me how I've been and I tell her that we are doing just fine. I've been incredibly busy with work lately, I say. She tells me she's just come back from a lengthy trip to the Bahamas and is now working on a book about her travels. I do my best not to reveal that I don't remember where we met.

I look over to the digital clock, tapping my finger on my cup. "I must get going," I say. "We are working on an incredible new cell extension project at Allied." I sense her envy rise as I tell her how important my work is and how I mustn't be late.

"Oh, sorry, I'll let you go," she says, her tone suddenly turning flat. "Your work sounds amazing. It's incredible to see women in executive positions over at Allied."

Her gaze moves to my wristband.

"You know," she says, her voice suddenly hushed. "You should actually think about removing that once in a while."

I pretend to not know what she is talking about and move to leave. She grips my arm and pulls me toward her.

"Disconnecting is not all bad," she whispers in my ear.

Up close, I see that her pupils are dilated, her retinas giving off a glazed glow. What drug she is on I do not know, but I see now that she is not sober. I wrestle my arm away and tell her politely again that I have to go.

"You might lose some exceptional wealth dividends, but it's glorious to disconnect," she calls out, wide-eyed and frantic, as I back away, "even if just once in a while!"

The memory of our encounter starts to fade by the time I reach the doorway. As I return to my sedan, I barely remember her face. I enter the sedan, ignoring the makeshift tents that line the sidewalk around me. I don't need to see them to know that they extend in long lines down the highway, thousands of tents housing thousands of people, each coming and going and staying, as they please. The tents only start at the highways. They spread in thin, uniform rows across barren fields, creating a grid of temporary shelters resembling dense favelas I once marveled at as a child growing up in Rio de Janeiro.

A thought forms in my head: despite all of our advances, despite the creation of universal wealth, despite the longevity of life we now provide, why has so much of our society decided to live like this? Maybe Cedric was right and there is something brewing. Maybe the advances we've made haven't created utopia after all. I struggle with the thought, as the wristband begins to dim my vision of squalor and dust around me, replacing it with a singular, more disturbing, mental picture.

No, these people are pathetic. They are leeches, taking from universal benefits and returning nothing. They are the reason that overall worldwide life expectancy hasn't increased as quickly as it should. These people are dragging society down with their obesity, their drug addiction, and their untreated mental and physical health problems. These are the people who are countering all of the great work that we at Allied are doing to make the world a better place.

As my sedan speeds up over the barren highway, my thoughts turn darker as a vision fills my passenger-side window, showing a large cluster of tents in a field we are passing. These aren't simple tents, sprung up by reckless, nomadic people who have unplugged. No, these are Mongol hordes, encamped outside the gates of our castles, preparing to storm and ransack all the good that we at Allied have done. No, this is preparation for war. We just don't know it yet.

The thought scares me, and I push it away. I must focus. It's imperative that I maintain focus on the day ahead. A focused mind is a successful mind.

The rest of my journey to work is a deep dive into the latest statistics from Allied Medical. The firm's productivity is nothing short of extraordinary. We've successfully completed the final testing of our latest extended-aging pill and marketing is set to commence next quarter, which should give the firm a significant boost in earnings.

I arrive at my workplace, slightly behind schedule but not enough to be considered late. Punctuality is a sacred rule in the pursuit of success. My ride takes me up the long driveway, navigating through layers of imposing security fencing. It comes to a stop in front of a nondescript three-story concrete building. I step out, entering through a small white door at the base of this colossal structure. "Good morning, Mrs. Barnes," a synthetic voice calls out, emanating from the tiny panels of LED lighting on the ceiling.

"Good morning," I reply.

"We have informed your colleague of your arrival. He is finalizing his review of sector seven. Please proceed to sector six to begin your tasks."

"Of course," I respond, my steps falling into the familiar rhythm of routine. I make my way toward the uniform chamber, and open a small cabinet beside a long row of curtain walls made of plexiglass and aluminum. Inside, neatly pressed and hung among the others, I find my uniform. There's no need for a name tag; the system knows, and I trust it implicitly. I retrieve the jumpsuit off the rack and slide it over my clothing. The layers make my work uncomfortable, especially if I must climb coolant walls to patch a leak, or crawl between fan walls and containment units to repair an electrical fault in one of the servers, but it's better than the feeling of cold, synthetic polymer against my bare skin.

"Mrs. Barnes." The electronic voice interrupts my thoughts. "A fracture has been detected in coolant C-twelve in sector six. It may require pre-emptive action to prevent future spillage. Kindly attend to this matter first."

"Of course."

I gather my mop and toolkit and head toward the assigned task. As I traverse the labyrinth of corridors, passing rows upon rows of humming machinery, I find myself whistling a happy tune. It sounds like one of Chopin's melodies.

How lucky and successful I am indeed.

Rolling Blue-Blackouts

February 1, 2041 6:35pm

ALRIGHT, DOWNLOADED. PROFILE'S all set up. Giving this a whirl.

Doctor, I must say that I'm finding this application odd, but I will give it a chance. It gives me comfort knowing that you're receiving these messages and will use them to progress our counseling sessions.

February 15, 2041 5:35am

Sleep's eluding me. Blake ignored me last night. Just brushed me aside like I'm nothing. On Valentine's Day, of all days! I'm gutted.

February 23, 2041 9:35am

I'm feeling quite low. Feel like I'm stuck in my own head.

Jotting all this down feels so very odd.

February 26, 2041 9:15pm

Today was just another day. Work, as usual.

Went to the pub with some mates from work. Even amidst all the buzz, it felt a bit lonely. Back home now, and that feeling hasn't left. Maybe it's always been there.

March 31, 2041 6:10pm

Feeling a bit daft. Since I got this app, I've been struggling to put my thoughts into words, but I'm pushing myself to try harder. Still don't quite know what to say. You said it's not a diary, but it feels like one. Never been one for diaries – my mum put me off them when I was young. She caught me jotting down notes to myself and gave me an earful. "Do you see yourself as a Winston Churchill, preparing for your memoirs?" she said when she found one of my early attempts at journaling. I was only nine. Who says that to a nine-year-old?

If I did keep diaries, they'd probably be filled with stories of feeling isolated and alone. It used to be just me and Mum. Now it's just me.

Felt a bit dizzy today. We should talk about whether the meds are right for me.

Margaret

P.S. Went to a do last night. People looked at me like I didn't belong. You asked if I think I'm paranoid, and I can confidently tell you that yes, I am!

April 5, 2041 5:30pm

"Posh frivolity for the over-privileged and clueless, dear girl." I can hear my mum's voice scolding me when she caught me with a diary from school. I remember it now. I was fifteen. "Instead of writing about yourself, you should be writing about people who've actually done something worthwhile, or perhaps do something worthwhile yourself."

She went on and on about how personal thoughts should stay in our heads. "Anything you say or write should be expected to eventually come under public scrutiny." That was one of her many lectures on the subject. She was so private. Stiff upper lip would be the perfect description of her. I can almost recite her speech verbatim now because she repeated it so often. She maintained a "keep to yourself" and "mind your business" attitude so severe that it practically cut us off from any social life.

I'm beginning to realise I was raised as a recluse.

April 15, 2041 6:10pm

Why am I always so knackered?

Blake rang again last night. He wanted to keep things casual. I put an end to it. I don't have time for men who are only after one thing.

April 23, 2041 5:25pm

That memory retrieval process we did during our last session was amazing! I'm astounded that I've kept so many memories, especially the darker ones about my mum, hidden away for so long. But now I have so many questions. I know you told me to give it time, but I can't help but obsess over it, and I'm so keen to explore this newfound aspect of myself more. Do you think my mum's treatment of me and the way she isolated us from the world has shaped me into who I am? Is it why I'm so desperate to fit in, why I put so much pressure on myself to excel at work, why I throw myself at any bloke who looks at me appreciatively, why I pour my heart out to my so-called friends who hardly ever reciprocate? It's probably why I'm going broke trying to keep up with all these trust fund beneficiaries in London. I realised from our earlier sessions that maybe it's why I am, as you guided me to term it, a party girl: so eager to put myself out there on social media. I'm overwhelmed by the flood of unlocked memories. It feels like I'm getting to know a completely different person!

"Damn my mother."

I can't believe I actually said that in our session. It was shocking, but also liberating.

Damn my mother.

There, I said it again! It's oddly therapeutic! I suppose that's why it's called therapy, haha.

Got to dash now, off to my yoga class. I'll write more when I have a glass of bubbly in hand! As you said, it's time to let go of my inhibitions and start being honest with myself.

Thank you again, Doctor. This has been such an enlightening day!

May 5, 2041 9:05pm

Yoga is pure bliss.

Since our last catch-up, I've found myself thinking loads about my mum and, even though I'm livid about what she's done, I can't help but feel a smidge sorry for her. I'm not quite ready to reach out, and reckon we need to chat more about her in our sessions first.

I see so much of myself in her now. She, too, was caught in the rat race of London, always striving but never really getting anywhere because of her class. We aren't common, mind you, but we aren't posh either. Somewhere in between, I suppose, caught in a space no one cares to look.

She let it slip once, you know, after a few glasses of wine, that she used to be part of high society. Can you believe it? Imagine that! She said she absolutely adored the money, the privilege, and the feeling of importance that came with it. But after my dad left, she had to live an average working-class life. I suppose that's where she picked up her not-so-great attitude.

I never really knew my dad. He left when I was just a little girl. Mum hardly ever talked about him, which is probably why I never bring him up either. Even after going through memory retrieval therapy, I still can't remember him at all. It's like he's a ghost that I can't quite reach. But I do remember how Mum would get all fidgety whenever his name came up. She would brush me off, saying things like, "Don't worry about a man who never worried about us." And just like that, she moved on, and I guess I did too. We can discuss this further during our next virtual session. I'm really excited to see if there's any way we can retrieve memories of my dad! That would be absolutely brilliant!

With that, I'll bid you goodnight and will write to you again when I return from work, dear Doctor! This application is a lifesaver. It's like having you at my fingertips anytime I need to express myself.

Oh, almost forgot! My phone screen time yesterday was eight and a half hours and tablet screen time was six hours. It was a Sunday, so a load of downtime, I guess, but you might be on to something – it's a bit much!

Also – no blackout today.

May 6, 2041 9:45pm

Yesterday's phone / tablet screen time: 6 hours /4 hours

Today was a bit of a non-starter. Spent most of it at work. Ate lunch at my desk. Got bored and ended up killing time on my phone. It's clear I'm hooked. I can't seem to put the bloody thing down for long. I'm always checking my work emails, texts, TalkApp messages, PhotoGram messages, DMs, and, before I turned it off, VeriDate chats. My job in marketing and media doesn't help, as I need to stay on top of trends and the latest cultural news, but I find myself aimlessly scrolling through nonsense. It's clearly not helping, so why do I do it?

Do you reckon my screen time has anything to do with my blackouts? I read an article saying that radiation waves from wi-fi and data signals can cause cancer, including brain cancer. The article mentioned an increase in glioblastoma, which wasn't common a few decades ago. It suggested I put my phone on airplane mode before bed and keep my tablet out of my bedroom at night. I'm going to try that tonight. I think I might also turn off my wi-fi router at night.

I felt alright today, I suppose. My retrieved childhood memories actually gave me more confidence than I expected. It's as though they provided me with an explanation for some of my recent behaviours. Being treated so poorly by my mum is now something I can lean on when I feel bad about myself. It's not my fault, right?

I need to get a good night's sleep tonight. I have that big marketing presentation tomorrow. It's on my mind, but not stressing me out as much as it was this morning. Maybe I have our session to thank for that.

Quick update: I deleted my phone's fitness tracker app. Firstly, I was spending way too much time logging my food, figuring out the grams in a bowl of pasta, or stressing over the calories in a bag of crisps. Secondly, it had completely bugged out. When I woke up this morning, my step count was already over 10,000! 10,000 steps before 7 a.m.? No chance! Unless I've been sleepwalking, haha.

Toodle-oo!

May 7, 2041 4:35pm

I had another blackout. It was sometime after my presentation (which went well), but after that, I can't remember much of the afternoon. I'm writing from my work desk, trying to hide the screen from passing colleagues. I'm a bit clammy. I hope no one notices.

It's the first time I've had a blackout at work, and the first time it's happened during the day. All the others have been in the evening at home, and never around others.

I can't remember anything from the past few hours. No one has said anything, so I'm guessing no one noticed. Everything seems normal in the office, and no one has mentioned anything about me passing out or behaving strangely. It seems that I just carried on! But I have no memory of this, at all. It's a total black hole.

I just checked my search and phone history over the last few hours. No noteworthy internet searches. No texts or other communication on my phone. No phone calls made or received according to my phone's history. Either the history was deleted, or I didn't use my phone at all. I seem to have responded to emails just fine though. Looking through a few of the emails I apparently wrote during my blackout, they seem perfectly normal and articulate.

If I was able to write emails, why can't I remember writing them?

As per instructions, here are my blackout checkpoints.

Blackout time: three hours from just after lunch until 4 p.m.

Before: I was at my desk, responding to emails. I don't remember anything except a sudden pull, and then darkness.

After: I remember "waking up" in the communal break room near the kitchen. I had my phone in my hand and the screen was dark. When I logged back on to it, I couldn't find any open apps, except for the VeriMeet app in the background.

How I felt during: nothing. I remembered nothing and felt nothing.

How I feel now: embarrassed, worried. Actually, terrified that it happened at work!

Physical effects: besides the mental feelings, I felt fine. I stood up and walked back to my desk and started writing this entry.

Time since previous blackout: six days.

What causes these blackouts? Can we use memory retrieval to access this period? I know it doesn't work like that, but we should at least try!

I feel like I need to see my GP again, but it will be so annoying to watch her shrug her shoulders and suggest I get checked for stress and anxiety disorders. The NHS is in such a state, no offence. I feel like I'm just being put through the motions instead of getting proper care.

Doctor – sending you this message and hoping we speak again very soon. Perhaps we can schedule an urgent follow-up session?

Margaret

May 8, 2041 10:35pm

When I checked my screen times from yesterday, I found it quite strange that my phone and tablet screens were on during my blackout. The Screen Time app you recommended showed that I spent five hours on the internet, but I don't remember spending any time doing that at all. And when I checked my history, there were no calls made, searches done, or messages sent. Maybe there's a glitch with the app, which would be a relief because seeing how many hours I spend on my devices gives me anxiety.

I did as you suggested and estimated the amount of time I spend on my phone in days, based on recent usage. It turns out I spend around 140 days a year on my phone! It's really disheartening to think about.

I watched a video on PhotoGram about digital addiction. Well, to be honest, it was more like an influencer talking about it rather than reading an article. But then I decided to research more about digital addiction and discovered that there are three types: phone addiction, internet addiction, and social media addiction. It's quite clear that I'm suffering from all three. They constantly call out to me, making me feel like I'm missing out on life if I'm not glued to my screen. The work we've been doing together, dear Doctor, has truly opened my eyes. I need to break free from my digital addiction as soon as possible.

How do I feel today? Still quite anxious from yesterday. I didn't sleep well at all. According to my health app, I only got four hours of sleep, and only ten minutes of that was REM sleep. It's no wonder I didn't sleep. I was in a right state before bed, but I was more preoccupied with my friend Mary, as she has now completely ghosted me since my text about the cancelled brunch. Why am I so obsessed with being liked? Is it weird that despite my blackout and newly found memories, I'm still almost solely focused on trivial issues with Mary?

My self-esteem is rock bottom today. I feel like such a phony. I accuse others of being fake when I'm the one who's the fraud. My PhotoGram is full of social photos when all I seem to do is sit at home and stare at my screens. I don't have any real friends. I can barely get a second date, let alone a boyfriend. Even my avatar on VeriDate is better at relationships than me! I mean it! Since our first therapy session, I turned off my VeriDate but inadvertently left my AI avatar on autopilot. I logged on earlier today for the first time and found that she's been thriving on the site. She has at least three seemingly real relationships going. This is in stark contrast to my typical experience on the app, which usually involves three messages and then being asked to come "chill at their flat" to "watch a movie." My avatar, in turn, is actually having meaningful conversations with more than three blokes. And they look to be normal! I feel like such a flop.

I need some rest. I look forward to our chat tomorrow. Thank you for squeezing me into your schedule at short notice! I'm so grateful that you're able to prioritise my treatment, even though I'm an NHS patient, and I'll make sure to tell you that tomorrow.

Tomorrow I'd like to discuss whether you think our breakthrough with the memories from my mum had anything to do with yesterday's blackout.

May 9, 2041 10:42am

I wanted to drop you a line to apologise for my outburst this morning in our virtual session. I am utterly devastated. I'm not entirely sure what came over me, but I want to say sorry for any offence I may have caused. It wasn't my intention to insult your expertise, nor to accuse you of treating me in the same manner as my mother did. I can see now how my actions reflect my own frustrations and insecurities about my ongoing memory issues and, as you have suggested, my struggle with digital addiction withdrawal.

I realise now my response was the one that was uncalled for. I am fully aware that these blackouts are "in my head," and am also aware, as you suggested, that these blackouts may form part of my overall issues. I can see the parallels with my hidden memories of my mother and how these blackouts could be another way of my subconscious protecting me from myself. I am committed to working through this with your guidance and thank you for your patience and support.

I am grateful that you were able to rearrange your schedule to accommodate another session. I'm truly sorry for my behaviour and I hope you can forgive me. I've spent months looking for a therapist I feel comfortable with and I'd hate to think that I've jeopardised our professional relationship.

May 9, 2041 6:15pm

Yesterday's phone / tablet screen time: 10 hours / 5 hours (mostly spent researching personality disorders – who knew there were so many? But 10 hours!)
Last night's sleep: 5 hours, 1 hour of REM

How am I feeling? Exhausted, if I'm honest, and still quite mortified about this morning. I am so sorry for my terrible behaviour.

I'm off on a date with Oliver shortly. He's the one I told you about. We met on a non-verified dating app a week ago, when we decided to throw caution to the wind and meet someone the old-fashioned way and not completely filtered. It's quite liberating, honestly!

Oliver seems nice. We met last weekend at a coffee shop, spending about an hour nursing hot drinks and engaging in casual banter.

Tonight is our first official date. Nothing fancy, just a few drinks at a wine bar. Am I looking forward to it? Just a tad. He's rather cute – a bit lacking in the hair department for my usual taste, though. I'm not sure he'd have passed my VeriMeet or VeriDate filters due to the hair situation, but there's a certain charm about stepping out of my comfort zone and embracing something less rigid. He's a good listener, appears comfortable in his own skin, and doesn't pretend to be a socially conscious intellectual like most of the crowd in London that I usually encounter. And, thank goodness, he's not in finance! I've had enough of that lot. They're all talk and no substance. I truly hope Oliver proves to be different.

Despite being slightly nervous about my date with Oliver, I reopened the VeriDate app and scrolled through my avatar's messages, considering how successful she seems to be. The AI version of me is doing a remarkable job, I must say. She is a much more polished version of myself. Quite impressive! She communicates like a professor at Oxford. It appears gentlemen do appreciate a well-spoken lady. Perhaps I should dial down her settings a bit in case I decide to actually meet some of these men (which I'm not planning to, by the way. I'm far too embarrassed now). The AI does have her faults though. She's a lot more uptight than I am. The words she says! She sounds so utterly posh! Do I sound like that? I hope not. I picture her as a strict librarian, with her hair pulled back into a tight bun and a cardigan over her shoulders.

But don't worry, I'm not reverting to my past tendencies. I only checked VeriDate out of curiosity and I'm still planning to give up electronics very soon! For now: baby steps.

May 10, 2041 3:59pm

Yesterday's phone / tablet screen time: 3 hours / 2 hours
Last night's sleep: 5 hours, 30 minutes of REM

How I feel: last night's date was fine. Oliver took me to a nice little Italian wine bar – the one with the lovely flower display at the entrance that's perfect for profile photos. We shared a giggle about that as he took pictures of me posing in front of the colourful arrangements.

I must admit, though, the conversation was a bit off, and I'm not yet sure if it was just me, or if it was how he was behaving. I'm trying to determine if it's me who has been sabotaging my relationships this whole time. Looking back, he didn't do anything wrong. He asked a lot of questions about me, which I suppose is normal for dates, but as time went on, he made me feel rather uncomfortable for some reason. I've usually avoided talking about myself in depth but tried to open up a bit more. At times, it felt more like a therapy session with you than a date! He did ask questions that I think are common on dates, like what do I do for a living, what are my hobbies, and how long have I lived in London. Those all seem like normal things to ask someone you're genuinely trying to get to know better, right? But then he asked me if I had a close relationship with my parents and began probing into my personal affairs. I don't know if it's because of our therapy, but these questions made me feel very strange, and I started to find him somewhat unsettling.

I don't know. Maybe I'm overthinking it, but I can't shake off the feeling that I was talking to a journalist. Maybe I'm still living in the shadow of my overprotective, reclusive mother and her paranoid "keep to yourself" mantra.

I'd like to delve deeper into this with you and discuss whether this is rooted in my paranoia.

May 11, 2041 9:15pm

Yesterday's phone / tablet screen time: 5 hours / 30 minutes
Last night's sleep: 8 hours, 1.5 hours of REM

Yesterday was uneventful. I watched a movie, went to a boot camp fitness class, and came home. I messaged a bit with Oliver, and we made plans to meet again. He seems like such a lovely boy, and I've decided that it was my own neuroses that made me uncomfortable on our date. I'm now very much looking forward to Thursday.

How I feel today: although I am getting a lot of sleep, I still feel utterly exhausted. The cluster headaches returned yesterday, and I'm worried that they will worsen. I've made a conscious effort to limit my screen time, but five hours on the phone is still a lot, even though I've been trying not to look at my phone. I try to limit my usage during the day and only message or scroll in the evening when I'm home. I try to turn everything off a few hours before bedtime. Sometimes, though, I just get sucked in and lose myself in the virtual world. I'll try harder. Maybe, as they say, it's time to go cold turkey.

I've developed a new routine before bed: shut down my electronics, turn off the wi-fi router, and hide my phone and tablet in the kitchen before going to bed. I hope this will make me less tempted to stay awake and scroll.

May 13, 2041 6:15am

Yesterday's phone / tablet screen time: 9 hours / 12 hours
Last night's sleep: 5 hours, 4 hours of REM

I think I had a blackout again last night. It happened as I was preparing to wind down. I recall writing a journal entry, and then everything went black. The next thing I remember is waking up this morning, feeling dreadful and dealing with intense cluster headaches.

I feel so helpless, Doctor! I don't understand why this is happening to me. I'm doing everything you told me. I'm eating well, exercising, meditating (the meditation app you recommended is rather helpful, actually), and avoiding screen time. Yet, if you look at my screen time from yesterday, it tells a completely different story.

I checked my phone and tablet history from last night. There was nothing between 9 p.m. until the morning, yet I swear I didn't use my phone or tablet more than a few hours during the day! There is no way I was on my phone for nine hours and there is absolutely no way the tablet was on for twelve hours yesterday, as I only picked it up to write you the journal entry. I'm definitely turning off these devices.

Really looking forward to my next therapy session.

May 14, 20416:15am

Thank you so much for yesterday's session! It was so enlightening and eye-opening. I feel like I know so much more about who I am as a person, and I'm much more willing to open up to others and let them in.

Thank you for giving me the medical note to take leave from work. I need to just switch off, literally and figuratively.

I think you are right that I could do without technology for a little while as I recover!

May 14, 2041 9:34pm

Today's phone / tablet screen time: 1 hour / 20 mins
Last night's sleep: no idea (I put away my fitness watch to avoid temptation!)

I think I know what it's like to be a drug addict now. From the moment I woke up, I was itching for just a bit of that blue light, a quick dose of instant visual satisfaction. The pull is like a petulant child tugging at my sleeve, begging me to pick up my gadgets. I've stood my ground, though.

There's this persistent whisper in my ear, suggesting that I could have "just a quick peek" and check my notifications or emails, despite being on leave from work. I must be strong!

Those horrible cluster headaches returned this afternoon. I've taken some paracetamol to reduce the pain, but it's not enough. My head is absolutely throbbing! I'll have to pop to the chemist for something stronger. You know, they say caffeine-lovers get terrible headaches when they skip their daily cuppa. Could this be my tech version of caffeine withdrawal?

I rang Oliver this afternoon, and we ended up having a rather long chat. He was obviously worried that I'd ghosted him, but I explained that I was having a digital detox and he seemed quite understanding. We're still on for tomorrow. He mentioned getting me flowers, how delightful! No one ever gets me flowers! We had quite a deep conversation about our personal lives. He's from a large family and went through the typical youngest sibling bullying. He was rather curious about my past, and I pushed past my usual reserve. We even spoke about my mother. He's a fantastic listener, and while some of his questions were a tad invasive, he was very comforting. He made me feel quite strong and resilient, considering my past. While I still find his interest in my personal life a bit odd, I remembered your advice and just went with the flow.

Could there be something special brewing between Oliver and me? Oh dear, am I getting ahead of myself?

Anyway, that's enough screen time for now. Perhaps I should switch to pen and paper? Writing these journals on an electronic device feels somewhat contradictory. After all, I'm on a digital detox!

May 15, 2041 11:35pm

I have absolutely dreadful news.

Oliver is not who he claimed to be. Why didn't I trust my instincts? He was never interested in me. He was only after my story. Oliver's a ghastly, vile human being – a sleazy, deceiving tabloid reporter.

Doctor – I've just messaged you to have an emergency session tomorrow. I have so many questions. I NEED TO TALK TO SOMEONE REAL! NOT VIRTUAL. WE HAVE TO MEET!

May 16, 2041 5:42am

I've started the new medication you prescribed. I certainly need it now. I was worried about the side effects before, particularly the insomnia, but now I simply don't care. I need to feel some relief from this constant mental torment!

Another blackout happened last night but, frankly, I don't care about the blackouts anymore. I felt it this time as it came. I wish I could have more of them to bury the shame I feel. I wish I had never met Oliver. All he wanted to do was to write a story about my VeriDate avatar! He told me everything. He said he was assigned to write about the increase in use of artificial intelligence in online dating. He says that many people, like me, have been using AI avatars to build up online relationships. He told me he has been conversing with the AI Margaret for months. I tried to tell him that it was all a misunderstanding, and that I didn't mean to use my VeriDate avatar to get dates, and never intended to converse with any of the people she was speaking with. He doesn't believe me. I'm mortified.

I spent last night obsessively searching the internet to see if he had posted anything yet. I also checked his social media accounts and found his previous articles on various celebrities and the local London social scene. He is a terribly invasive journalist, with no regard for his subject matter's privacy or integrity. He sensationalises all of his topics, and I'm afraid he will do the same with me.

I feel so ashamed. I'm going to be the laughing stock of the whole country when this article comes out. I can see the article now: 'Silly Girl Who Uses a Machine to Get Dates,' with captions showing me posting trivial photos of myself acting like a socialite or influencer, when all I am is a sad, lonely shut-in.

Doctor, we need to speak! I checked the texts and messages I sent to your TalkApp and they were removed or deleted!! Are you ignoring me too, like the others?? You need to help me!

May 17, 2041 3:34am

I'm shaking as I write this. I have lost my mind.

I was sat on my sofa, searching again for Oliver's article, when I felt a strange but familiar sensation. The screen was tugging at me. I felt it all over my face, as if I had stuck my whole head over the nozzle of a Hoover. The air was sucked out of my throat, and I felt nothing at all between myself and the tablet screen. Nothing at all! No air, no anything. It was like I was somehow one with the screen. I know it sounds crazy, but it was how it felt.

Then, I heard the voices. Hundreds, maybe even thousands of them, all repeating the same word over and over. It was like some sort of choir, the voices blending together, somehow confusing and clear at the same time. It was a word. One word. A word now so dreadful, I fear to type it. It was said in English and so many other languages. "Enter," "intrer," "intrare." The voices weren't terrifying, just… factual. They were flat and dull. It didn't even sound like they were calling for me, but simply stating what was happening, like a surgeon announcing he's about to start cutting. "Enter," they said, and my head felt dizzy.

I tried to breathe, just like you taught me, but there was no air! There was only this… nothingness. Nothing except the pull of the screen and the voices filling that utterly terrible, empty space.

Then the voices became one voice and the words became one word. "Enter," it said. Then, silence and darkness. But before I blacked out, I caught a glimpse of my reflection in the tablet screen. It was revolting! I shudder to think of it now. I saw my own face in that reflection grinning back at me, as if I was enjoying the whole experience, buzzing for its conclusion! Then, nothing.

I woke up later, not sure how much time had passed. I stood in front of my hallway mirror, my head bowed. My hair, which I swear was down before this happened, was now neatly tied in a bun. The sight of my face in the reflection startled me. My heart pounded and I struggled to breathe. My muscles were rigid, frozen in the pose reflected back at me. I couldn't move! Something was holding every inch of me in place, as if forcing me to stare at my own reflection. And what I saw was so utterly frightening, I dread to remember it as I type. My smile was false and wide, and my eyes open and alert. It was as if I had been stood there for ages, suspended in time, forced to hold a grin while awaiting my return to consciousness just to witness this grim display.

Doctor, I am so scared.

I stood there, trapped, staring at myself, unable to move. I screamed, but no sound came out. After what felt like ages, I managed to snap out of it and run away from the mirror. I cannot shake the memory of seeing myself like that: my hair pulled tight, standing in the dimly lit hallway, staring back at myself smiling in the mirror. It lingers.

Doctor, I need to see you! You haven't been returning my calls or messages. I've been sending frantic messages to your work email and TalkApp. I hope you understand the urgency of my situation and respond soon.

Please, Doctor, I need your help now. I have nowhere else to turn!

From: Margaret Samson
To: Dr. Elizabeth Rose
Sunday 18 May 2041, 12:30pm
Subject: A Kind Request to Disregard Prior Correspondence

Dear Doctor Rose,

I hope this email finds you in good health and high spirits.

Firstly, allow me to express my deepest gratitude for your unwavering support and guidance throughout our therapeutic journey together. Your expertise has played an invaluable role.

I am writing to you today to state that I will no longer require your services. I kindly request that you disregard any previous communication you received from me in the last few days and delete my profile from your WellTap application.

I was clearly unwell. Prior communication should therefore be deleted and disregarded.

Your assistance is no longer required. I recently entered into a specialised care system, which provided a thorough evaluation that determined that I have been misdiagnosed. Please be assured no action will be taken in respect to this misdiagnosis on the condition that privacy measures are maintained. Considering this new diagnosis, and to allow for the new system to more appropriately provide for the care required, I request for immediate termination of our arrangement.

As you know, protecting personal data is of utmost importance, and individuals have the right to ensure that their information is handled securely and with respect to their privacy. With this in mind, I kindly request that you securely destroy any personal information you may have collected during our therapeutic sessions, including session notes, contact details, and any other documentation associated with my case. I believe this request aligns with the principles set forth in the General Data Protection Regulation (GDPR) and the Data Protection Act 2018, which govern the processing and storage of personal information in the United Kingdom. Specifically, under Article 17 of the GDPR, commonly referred to as the "right to erasure" or "right to be forgotten," individuals have the right to request the deletion or removal of their personal data when certain conditions are met. Considering the sensitive nature of the information shared during therapy, I kindly ask that you take the necessary steps to ensure the permanent deletion and destruction of my personal data, as soon as reasonably possible. This includes any digital files, physical records, or other materials that may contain my personal information.

Thank you in advance for your attention to this matter, and for your continued support throughout our therapeutic journey. I wish you continued success in your noble endeavours, both personally and professionally.

Please accept our warmest regards.

Take care and stay well,

Margaret

From: Oliver Hill
To: Jonathan Smith, Editor
Monday 13 June 2041, 9:52pm
Subject: Urgent – More Funding Needed!!
Priority: High

Jonny,

You don't want to hear this, but I'm afraid I need more funding for the assignment. I'm on to something very big here, and if *The London Caller* doesn't want it, I'll take this elsewhere. This is not a threat, but it is a promise. Where this piece is heading really belongs in *The Times* or even the *FT*, anyway. And no, I am not delusional.

Now that I have your attention, please read the updated synopsis below. I think there is something very strange happening, that has broad implications, and I would like to investigate this further. Something very odd, indeed.

I am fully aware that this was supposed to be an entertainment piece about online daters, but it has grown into so much more.

See below and give me a tinkle.

Working Title: 'Are Virtual Daters Becoming Virtual Themselves?'

Synopsis: Online daters have been increasingly using virtual assistants, known as AI avatars, to make connections and even create robust online relationships. This is a trend that started over a year ago but has increased in prominence as artificial intelligence has improved to allow the avatar to take on personality traits of its user, utilising specific user data to effectively communicate as if they were the user themselves.

The appeal is obvious. One can open an account online, populate it with personal data, and then use an avatar to make the first connection, or connections. This alleviates the tepid first few communication lines which have been routine and at times redundant. "How are you?" "Nice to meet you." "What do you like to do in your spare time?" A robot can ask those questions, and a robot can now answer them, cloaked in the personality of the user responder. The act of allowing one's avatar to write for the user is known unofficially as "autopilot," or "virtual flirting."

There are many applications to choose from, but the most popular is VeriDate, which counts more than 150 million global users, and is widely known to have the most advanced AI and data verification technology on the market. VeriDate even has a connection notification feature whereby the avatar on autopilot notifies the user when a connection has reached certain desired thresholds. As a VeriDate user, one can choose from three thresholds: Initial Connection (typically after a few back-and-forth messages), Ready to Meet (when the other user has expressed a desire, or the avatar believes there is a desire, to meet), or Strong Connection (the most advanced level, when real similarities or connections are detected by the avatar). This functionality has been wildly successful. Users on VeriDate have found their avatars providing deep conversational matter and establishing real connections with other users on their behalf. In one instance, two VeriDate users found their respective avatars having created substantial online relationships without either of the human users ever interacting.

Yet what started out as a puff piece about lazy online daters using virtual assistants has turned into something far more alarming. I've spent the past six months getting to know a few VeriDate users (both the avatars and the human user) using different guises and have found something very disturbing: the human users have become more like their avatars.

The most extreme case is Margaret Samson. I met her virtual VeriDate avatar assistant first. For the sake of clarity, I'll refer to the human user as Margaret and her avatar as AI Madge. What makes Margaret of particular interest is the fact that she is the daughter of Jerry Cameron, the infamous duke implicated in a string of rape cases in the late 2020s. She and her mother changed their names following Jerry's death by suicide and virtually disappeared from any public interest. [Note: query whether we keep this in the article given privacy laws.]

I first met AI Madge on VeriDate in May. [Note: I was using Roger Fineman's account, with full permission, but we'll need to be careful how to deal with that issue.] AI Madge and I struck up what became very deep and meaningful discourse and discussion. Over a few months, we shared our interests and personal stories. AI Madge spoke of her desire to find true love and rid herself of a stifled past. She didn't discuss her family history but alluded to being confined by what she called the "shackles of my upbringing."

I tried multiple times to meet the real Margaret but never managed to get a date through AI Madge, who insisted she wanted to meet, but was incapable of doing so due to what she called "work and travel conflicts." A few months later, however, I was lucky enough to find the real Margaret on Connexion, a traditional online dating website, through a photo internet search tool. This website did not utilise AI or digital assistant technology, so I knew I was speaking to the human user throughout.

My conversations with Margaret and AI Madge were incongruous. Margaret was reserved, guarded, and sometimes slow to respond. Margaret was witty, in a basic way, and she spoke little of her background, and never about her family history. AI Madge was articulate, exceptionally funny, and extremely engaging. After considerable prodding by me, AI Madge became more open about her family history, but stated that she had chosen to forget and move on, and didn't wish to discuss the subject. Margaret didn't mention any part of her family history during our initial chats. In fact, she was quite oblivious to them. [Note: I have detailed transcripts of our conversations to create a fantastic juxtaposition within the finished article.]

I met Margaret on four occasions. The first two were your traditional, casual meet-and-greets over coffee and drinks. I found the real Margaret to be slightly dishevelled in appearance, quirky, and often distracted. She wore loose clothing on both occasions and the only make-up she wore consisted of a little concealer, eye shadow, and lipstick. She was exceptionally closed-off and refused to discuss any manner of her family history. At the same time, I communicated with AI Madge over the VeriDate app, and found her conversations much more structured, open, and forthcoming. I met Margaret again for a dinner date, but prior to the date, Margaret and I spoke and she disclosed disturbing details about her mental well-being. She spoke of being in therapy for a variety of issues, including selective amnesia. Through this conversation, I learned she was a highly troubled young woman with limited to no conscious recollection of her past. I decided to come clean on our date. She did not take my revelation well, and despite trying my best to calm her, she stormed out of the restaurant and severed ties for many weeks.

Over the last few weeks I made numerous calls and sent messages to Margaret. This included a message to her VeriDate account, asking AI Madge to notify Margaret that I want to talk to her. A few days ago, I received a message in VeriDate that Margaret wanted to meet in person. She said she was disappointed in my deception, but willing to have a chat. We went for a walk in Hyde Park today. She was practically a different person to the woman I saw in May.

She looked stunning, like she was styled for a photo shoot. She wore elegant clothing, her face was perfectly made-up, and her hair was tightly knitted into a bun, giving her a very appealing look. A few minutes into the conversation, I became convinced that this woman was not the Margaret I met last month. Despite the openness of her conversation, which was flirtatious and highly engaging, I sensed a coldness in her eyes, and her smile when we departed made me feel she was straining against herself to make it.

Before walking away, she warned me against writing my article, bringing up specifics on libel laws and regulations, as if she were a trained barrister instead of a marketing associate.

Prior to my last conversation with Margaret, I was in contact with four other VeriDate accounts, all of which ceased to respond to my enquiries during the last few days. Roger Fineman received an email from VeriDate today, stating that his account was suspended for breaching impersonation rules on their platform.

Jonny, something is very wrong here. I know it sounds crazy, but I believe the Margaret I met today was really AI Madge. I don't know how this could be possible, but I'm convinced something terrible has occurred, and that it is widespread.

Ollie

Confessions of a Byte-Map Addict

A-HOLES ARE MONSTROUS little fuckers. My advice: steer clear. Trust me.

What are A-Holes, you ask? Well, if you're not already acquainted, perhaps it's best to keep it that way. Entering our lexicon in the mid-2020s, the term originally contained the name of a certain search engine company, a name I dare not mention for fear of being hoovered up, bubble-wrapped, and fedexed to a litigation court near me (if you don't believe me, google it!). Amid the rise of AI, it was changed and shortened to A-Holes, a term that more snugly fit the universal shittiness they bestowed upon our daily lives.

I'm standing – or rather, slouching – before you as a self-proclaimed A-Holer. *Do as I say, not as I do,* I might declare, but where's the fun in that? After all, hypocrisy is the sincerest form of flattery, or so I've been told by those who flatter themselves most sincerely.

I'm sprawled on my couch, the thick webbing pressing into my back like an accusation of laziness as I stare at my new toy. A brand new 125-inch flat video display is fixed firmly against my living room wall like a monument to my lethargy. This isn't just any screen, it's a beautiful portal to anywhere you want to be, courtesy of its 5K Ultra Definition hyper-optic three-dimensional spec screen. Even when turned off, it cuts a deep black cavern into my living space, making my apartment seem bigger and more expansive than its modularly constructed five hundred square feet floorplate.

Who doesn't love new toys? I can't stop admiring the features of my new gadget. The gloss finish of its frame gleams like a pair of freshly shined designer dress loafers, adorned by a large Byrell X logo on the panel, resembling stylish Dior branding on a designer jacket. I can make out my faint reflection in its screen. The shape my face makes, I might as well be staring at a beautiful blond. I feel small goosebumps rise on my arms and I'm a twelve-year-old again, admiring my first video game console on Christmas morning.

The pain in my back and undercurrents of shame are my clues to how wasteful today has been. It's a Saturday, and my earlier plan to go for a run failed miserably, again. I tug at the folds in my belly. They are jello to my fingertips, and I roll the clay flesh, pulling large mounds out until it hurts. Self-inflicted corporal punishment for a pudgy slob. I should have gone for that jog. My cholesterol is up, and my mood is down. I should have gotten up early, put on my tracksuit, and run at least a mile or two. Instead, I spent a better part of the last few hours trapped in an A-Hole internet search spiral.

A-Holes are sneaky little bastards; they are duplicitous, controlling creatures. They come when you least expect it, grab you, and don't let go. They're the trapdoor beneath your feet, ready to plunge you into the abyss of procrastination. A-Holes are the quicksand of the digital age, luring you in with the promise of brief diversion and then ensnaring you for hours on end.

A-Holes may appear innocent and harmless, but they are deceptively intoxicating and ultimately death to productivity. You don't know you are in one until you are suffocated by it and then – and only then – are you able to pull yourself out from its grip like a struggling swimmer against a rising tide. It starts with an innocuous action – looking up a video, a photo, or a news article. Before you know it, you search or scroll a little more, and then – *poof* – hours of life wasted in the vortex of an A-Hole.

I'm your average Joe – well, average John, actually. I'm a data verification consultant by day and a professional time-waster by night. The day job affords me a few luxuries, like the beauty of a screen set before me, and my luxuries afford me my true passion, which is wasting time.

Now, don't get me wrong. I'm not some holed-up introvert without a social life. If you met me, you'd say I was a people person, and you wouldn't be wrong. We'd meet at a party, and I'd look you in the eye, I'd ask you more questions than I'd answer, and I'd be genuinely interested in what you have to say. I have friends, and they like me. I'm considered by most people who know me to be a nice person. I'm perfectly normal in almost every definition of the word. My vices are limited. I don't take drugs and I rarely drink.

I am, however, a card-carrying member of the A-Hole Club. I make every attempt to resist them. Honest, I do! I even plan to try to prevent their pulls by limiting my forays with what I call A-tokes – a quick hit of the latest sports stats or a brief wade into the murky waters of some new political intrigue. But before I know it, *bam*! I'm swept away.

Only the most well-rounded among us can avoid A-Holes, and they do so through daily AI microdosing, a ritual that, if you are disciplined enough, still allows for a well-balanced life. Sadly, I don't walk among those Zen masters. I am one of a growing super-majority of A-Hole frequenters, though I distinguish myself by owning up to it – a rare virtue in this age of denial and blissful ignorance. Among our ranks are the meme addicts, sending daily doctored photos, cartoons, or videos, making some political statement or zany riff on popular culture, each vying for a laugh or nod of agreement. Then there are the straight-up video addicts (choose here your poison: cats, dogs, plane landings, car showrooms, car crashes, fist fights, encounters with club bouncers, dangerous pranks, or any variety of scantily clad women videos), lost in an endless stream of short video content. And let's not forget the A-Holers in search of confrontation, eager to vent their frustration via ridiculous debates in the comment section. These – the most pitiful of all A-Holers – are the most likely to be a-holes in real life – people I go to great lengths to avoid. Yet, regardless of our drug of choice, we are all chasing the same dragon: escape.

My vice is seeking knowledge, information that is interesting but ultimately, if I am totally honest, utterly useless. A-Holing for me often starts off under the guise of mild productivity, a dangerous and habit-forming illusion, always ending in a haze of aimlessness. My growing gut is a byproduct of this curiosity, spiked with lethargy, mixed with insatiable instant gratification, all of which ultimately goes nowhere.

Looking back at today's A-Hole experience, I admit I knew what I was getting myself into from the moment I strapped on my Byte Map. I convinced myself, innocently enough, that I would take just one massive, productive A-Rip. But while I studied Oslo's mayoral election data, I soon found myself hurtling into the abyss, swiftly engulfed by the whirlwind of what could only be described as a full-blown A-Trip.

(For those following along at home, cue 'White Rabbit' by Jefferson Airplane.)

It began after I secured the Byte Map strap on to my wrist – the most recent version, released earlier in the year. The accessory arrived with my new screen. The strap is a lot lighter and more comfortable than the previous models, which used to feel like tight latex gloves infused with velcro, and very quickly grated against sweaty skin. This one you barely feel. The plastic sheen is crystal smooth and feels like aloe vera against the skin.

"Byte Map, please pull up the current Oslo mayor."

The Byte Map sensors can detect the slightest of whispers, but I still shout, like I'm trying to get the attention of a hard-of-hearing grandmother. I feel stupid doing it of course – this version even has thought-detection tech built in. I'm a relatively slow adopter of new technology, having ordered my first driverless Lymo only a few weeks ago, but am not yet using its driverless features. And as for those By-Time life elongation sleep masks that showed up on my doorstep last Tuesday? They'll just gather dust until I'm sure they won't turn my brain to mush or sprout a limb from my face.

A microsecond after the words "Oslo mayor" left my lips, an article sprung on to the X screen, detailing the recent elections that made headlines worldwide.

Oslo's Residents Elect Artificial Intelligence to Govern Parliamentary City Council.

A pop-out section of the screen showed various media articles on the subject, with similar headlines from various publications.

My mind started to wander. Without warning, as if summoned by an unseen digital genie, a pop-out section materialized, listing several Scandinavian heavy metal bands. *I wish the Byte Map would stop reading my thoughts*, I thought, and immediately wondered whether it would respond to this unspoken suggestion. It did not, however the heavy metal pop-out section disappeared. I guessed it got my hint.

I focused my attention on the original subject matter of interest. Various graphs morphed and flowed with time sequencing, showing Oslo's governing mayorship polls from previous elections, and highlighting AI's rise in popularity over the past decade, leading to its election last year. A graph popped up on to the screen, showing two inversely correlated line groupings. One singular line, representing the AI system NAYA, sloped upwards from a low of zero-point-two percent in 2030 to over forty-six percent in 2046. The other lines, representing a variety of human political groups steadily, and then sharply, sloped down.

I asked for a summary of NAYA's policies since the elections.

The screen responded with a crafted presentation, clearly created by the Byrell auto-generative summary system. I flipped through the slides, filled with easy-to-read bullet points and graphs. NAYA had systemically revamped permitting laws and health system access requirements, which proved highly popular. City halls and other municipal meetings were replaced with the NAYA application, available to all Oslo residents, allowing them direct access to their city's leadership, which was now essentially the application itself. Anyone, at any time, could speak to Oslo's city council, and its governing mayor would listen, and interact with anyone who chose to engage with it. Twenty-four hours a day. Seven days a week. No more city halls. No more appointments. No more bureaucracy facilitated by disinterested administrators and career officials. Only fans of insufferably long meetings were left disappointed.

I wondered how decisions were made in this new system, and another presentation popped on to the screen. I asked the Byte Map to present it to me, and a smooth electronic voice sifted out from the speakers.

"NAYA, Norway's government-owned artificial intelligence system, was elected as governing mayor of Oslo in the 2042 election, with forty-six-point-two percent of the vote, having previously swept the majority of other city parliamentary positions. The result has combined, for the first time in history, a solitary central government body for the city of Oslo. All of the city's central governing functions are now consolidated and centralized by NAYA."

The first summary slide dissolved into a second page, displaying an organization chart and series of bullet points.

"NAYA now functions as both governing mayor and city council, also replacing the city's previous five standing committees. NAYA's responsibility now encompasses health and social welfare, education and cultural affairs, urban development, transport and environmental affairs, and finance."

The third slide replaced its predecessor, showing more bullets.

"NAYA's system is considered the first fully efficient social democratic institution, utilizing the NAYA communication application to access polling from constituents and implementing decision trees, taking into account a variety of social and economic factors from a worldwide city historic database."

The presentation moved to its final slide showing a world map, highlighting San Francisco in a bright red color and Singapore in a dark green color.

"NAYA works with a cross-border city information sharing arrangement with San Francisco and Singapore, to aid primary decision-making points."

The map graphic dissolved and was replaced with a graph highlighting recent polling figures.

"NAYA's popularity has grown since the election. It has a seventy-six percent approval rating, up from fifty-four percent last year. Currently, sixty-four percent of Oslo residents strongly approve of NAYA, and thirteen percent strongly disapprove, making it one of the most popular government bodies in the world."

A video pop-out replaced the presentation. It was from a news program. The correspondent sat at a nondescript desk, his Nordic face so sullen and stoic that it seemed as though he was bracing himself for another sunless winter.

"Norway made headlines last year when the residents of Oslo elected a machine as their mayor. On its first anniversary, we look at NAYA and how AI is faring in its first government position," he said.

The video cut away to a correspondent standing outside Oslo's red brick town hall.

"NAYA has proven very popular with residents since becoming mayor. The consensus is that it has cut red tape and provided clarity to Oslo's historically opaque planning authority and city management. It has even improved Oslovians' trust in the government, something many governments are now considering for future elections. While trust in NAYA grows, so does concern that it will be the global party of choice. Whether this extends to the federal level of politics remains to be seen, but politicians around the world are taking note."

The video transitioned to an interview with a sharply dressed man, probably a politician. He had thin blond hair and wore a neatly trimmed beard, resembling Benji Dipp, one of my favorite actors.

A muted trailer of Benji's new movie popped out in the corner of my screen.

Damn you, Byte Map. Focus.

"Please ignore," I said aloud and the pop-up disappeared, reverting to the original video in full-screen mode.

"NAYA is more trusted because it speaks for everyone. It is not affiliated with any party," the bearded man said in a thick Scandinavian accent. "No one donates to NAYA, therefore there are no donors to placate. It's truly the first populist government the world has ever had."

Another video transition, this time to a woman back at the studio, appearing to be interviewed by someone off-screen.

"NAYA has not removed the concept of special interest, but it has removed the 'special' part of the definition," she said. Her accent was nondescriptly European, hard on the consonants and lacking intonation. "With AI, there are now only interests. Everyone is special. Every voice is heard as loudly as any other, and they are heard instantly and all at once. Decisions are made based on economic viability and for the greater good of the composite of all interests, and independent of who carries the more powerful voice."

I wondered how practical all of this was and the video switched again. A well-known businessman sat in a reclining chair on a stage holding a microphone, and I assumed he was being interviewed at a conference.

"Business is pro-NAYA, not because NAYA is pro-business, but because it is anti-bureaucracy," he said. "And there is nothing private business hates more than red tape. I hope more cities around the world adopt this approach."

I asked how Norway's economy was performing, and the screen transformed again. Economic data was immediately provided. The statistics were not appealing. Norway had an export-driven economy, and its political system was largely socialist, possibly due to a combination of having the natural resources of Russia coupled with the population size of Cook County, Illinois. I didn't have to think; this was on clear display within an infographic on my screen. In recent years, oil and gas exports slowed materially while imports grew. Norway was losing its foothold. This had caused a substantial trade imbalance which, when complemented with a number of bioenergy and battery production calamities, helped bring its currency to its knees. A chart came up showing that birth rates were also falling. Norwegian newborns were at a twenty-year record low, and trending downward.

The death of a nation, I thought. *Slow and methodical. Can't put a band-aid on that. How does that tie with the popularity of NAYA?*

To my surprise, a chart popped up showing that beer sales were rising in Norway. In hindsight, I should have dismissed this, but in an A-Hole, you tend to go with the flow.

Any correlation between beer sales and birth rates?

Search.

I was no longer directing the Byte Map with my words, but directly with my thoughts. The technology, hidden somewhere in the electronic world, was working with lightning-quick speed.

Two line graphs, set against one another appeared on screen.

OK, just causation. What exactly is causation?

Search.

What's correlation then?

Search.

OK, let's look up the definition of irony.

Search.

A grainy music video from the last century began to play. A woman in a beanie cap, a crown of profound understanding of the literal, sat in the back of a car, serenading the world with the ironies of life, none of which, upon closer inspection, actually were ironic. The video played for a few moments, until...

Maybe this song itself is ironic. Holy shit, this singer must be a genius! Who is she?

Search.

Is it ironic that she made a song called 'Ironic' where none of the supposedly ironic situations the song mentions are actually ironic?

Search.

I stared at a long article and quickly dismissed it.

That got deep, fast. Let's look up other celebrities, shall we?

My steering was no longer conscious – an element of my subconscious was now directing traffic.

Search.

I was soon drowning in a series of videos and articles. I'd like to say I wasn't enthralled by them, but that would be a lie. I spent more time than I should have watching clips and reading information about celebrities I didn't care about. With most famous people today being social media influencers, I rarely engage in celebrity-gawking. But there was something about the absurdity of their station in our society, the sheer banality of these influencers parading as the pinnacle of fame, that kept me hostage. Thank God I don't normally care for influencers and social media celebrities – they would make me a complete A-Hole junky, wading through the dumpster of short-term memory serotonin hits.

Well, that was unadulterated nonsense for the dumb and wasteful. What about older celebrities? Let's do some 'where are they now'.

Search.

"Timothée Chalamet accepted his second Best Actor Academy Award for his portrayal of Michael Schaeffer in the comedic biopic of the disgraced tech pioneer, *Pantheon.*" A video of his acceptance speech came on.

Handsome guy. Keep going.

I was gifted a parade of folly for me to waste time eyeballing. Through a series of videos and images, I learned a lot about things I didn't know I cared about. DJ Pants had fallen back into the clutches of opioids, again. Eminem, our modern-day Renaissance poet, was still going strong, defying the laws of aging. Travis Lennon went bankrupt, Tom Holland was still acting, and Leonardo DiCaprio, in a turn of events as unexpected as a plot twist in a Kafka novel, had retired from acting to become the beekeeper laureate of the world.

What about ex-presidents?

Hernandez was still on the celebrity circuit. A retired Obama was doing well and vacationing in Barbados. George W. Bush was ill but recovering. The Clinton Library had recently been vandalized, yet again. The Trump Legacy Library had also recently been vandalized, yet again.

Without my knowledge, I had been ensnared into politics, again. It knows it is where I languish.

What social media do current world leaders use?

Search.

A series of Twink messages between leaders of free-world economies emanated from the screen. By the sheer scale of the offering, it seemed as if the fate of their nations depended on who could craft the most engaging snippet. Many were filled with blasé messages to their constituents about serious issues, but these faded quickly off my screen, replaced with far more juicy material. I read through messages as if staring at the messy aftermath of a violent car crash. The communications were juvenile, unapologetically appealing to the masses. Some were unfunny attempts at humor, while others jabbed at their political adversaries with the subtlety of a sledgehammer.

Search.

Wait, what did I just think about?

Suddenly a video popped up. 'President Johnson Gets OWNED!' it proclaimed, a title effusing the eloquence of a graffiti artist tagging ancient Roman ruins. I dismissed the video before it began, warding off a plague of sensationalism that I have despised since it began decades ago.

Stop this. What social media do former presidents use?

Search.

More interesting.

Hernandez uses all major media. Obama uses Twink and Gram.

What about Bush?

Search.

OK, Bush is also on Gram.

A photo of Bush and Obama arrived on screen.

Are they friends?

Search.

OK, so they're friends.

Search.

To my surprise, a number of conspiracy articles from various private publication sources popped up on the screen with references to deep-state politics. A headline caught my attention. It was from a right-wing publication and floated near the corner of my screen. The title read, 'Deep State on Vacation: Obama and Bush.' I pushed it away. The A-Hole was attempting to suck me in further, and I fought against the growing pull.

Search.

An article on the liberal purge in 2028 came up.

Details on the purge?

Search.

A five-minute video came on the screen, with the title, 'The Democratic Party Purge: How It Happened.' The narrator was soft-spoken, speaking in the hushed tone of a librarian, and I wondered if it was electronically generated. Electronic narration was now indistinguishable from human voice.

"After Trump's death, America's political system falls into disarray with the creation of MAGA and libertarian parties. The Republican Party heralds the return of George W. Bush, who leads an overhaul of the party. Shortly after, it's time for the Democrats to do the same..."

The video cut. Apparently, I was no longer interested.

Is Bush smart?

Search.

A series of subjective 'smartest presidents' lists danced on screen. Trump was listed last and first, depending on the source, and I recognized what the machine was doing. It was trying to get me to think about the former president. Donald J. Trump is one of the more common catalysts of A-Hole immersion, either for fanatic MAGA-lovers, or devoted Trump-haters. It's easy to get lost in the deep waters of Trump-related A-Holing, but I was quick to steer clear. Feeling the machine wanting me to go there, I resisted the temptation to dive in.

Instead, perhaps defensively, I thought about other rankings, and sites that list things or create lists or rankings of things. Lists and rankings are A-Hole anchors; their primary function is to grab you, drag you, and finally shove you further down into the abyss.

I spent God-knows-how-many minutes scanning top ten lists and landed on 'Top Ten Things We Love' about a certain famous female singer-songwriter. I don't usually think about this celebrity. Her music is not my cup of tea. But for some reason, the thought popped into my head, and an infographic appeared on my screen: a critical breakdown of her net worth.

A new thought arrived suddenly, and I snapped out of it, pulling off the Byte Map, and pulling up my virtual keyboard now projected onto my coffee table. I typed in the word 'swift' manually in lower case on the virtual keys. I looked up to the screen. The machine had autocorrected it into a capitalized version of the singer's name and I stared at her photo on my giant 125-inch display. I wondered exactly when she commandeered 'swift' in search statistics and what other common nouns or verbs had been trumped by often-searched celebrity names.

Trump, trump... I felt the pull again to dive into that most enticing pool of emotionally charged extremisms but refrained.

Instead, I typed in 'fennec,' all lower case. My last name is Fennec, which also happens to be a scientific word for a specific species of fox.

A skulk of fox videos arrived on the screen.

No autocorrection this time.

After all, I may be swift, but I am no famous singer-songwriter.

Pukahoda

COSTA RICA IS most alive in the dead of the pre-dawn morning. A human mind caught unaware would notice little, but a learned mind becomes whole with an untroubled world.

Stacey, under the cloak of darkness, sought solace among the waking nature around her. The sea, protected by a stronghold of vegetation, was casting damp gusts of wind which gently sprayed the ocean's greeting on her waking face in salutation. Wind whistled through the trees, and she listened to the rustling of the leaves overhead. Grains of sand, stolen from the battered basin, scuttled between her bare toes. Stacey exhaled and felt whole, like an isolated island surrounded by a sea of identity, given temporary sanctuary through a tether to nature's infinite song.

The salt of the sea graced her lips as she ducked under a low-hanging branch and her feet crunched on twigs as she navigated a narrow clearing, leading to the beach. The breaking dawn was still an unfulfilled promise, and with no moon to guide her, she was left to rely on the memory of the path through the dense jungle. The rhythm of the sea's ebb and flow, the waves crashing into themselves upon the wide break, the distant hymns of insects and soft cries of howler monkeys came together in a symphony of the wild.

At the ocean's edge, Stacey gently placed the board on the damp sea bed and knelt, her bare knee sinking into the sand. She brushed the grains off her palm and reached into her pocket, searching for the worn bar of wax. Instead, her fingers found a lighter, and further in, the remnants of a joint. Despite its staleness, there was enough left for a decent smoke. She lit it, the flame casting a brief glow on her immediate surroundings. The contents landed hard inside her lungs and swam through her bloodstream as numbness set in and a nostalgic blend of calmness and strangeness took root within her.

She pocketed the lighter and retrieved the waxy object from her shorts. Turning it in her hand, she likened it to clay in a child's grip, dragging it against the edge of the board, grinding against stubborn deposits. Back and forth she went, creating a calming, rhythmic cadence, like the steady ticking of a clock, until the lump of wax was no more.

She looked up. The dawn was preparing its daily announcement, giving birth to the shape of the horizon, separating the heavens from the earthly. The weather forecast was right. The ocean was unruly and insolent, breaking in uneven and unpredictable patterns, with crests spraying and faltering with abandon, rarely holding above the horizon's edge, sporadically pulled by a vast, unseen force.

She reached the water's edge. Raw chill tore through her body as she plunged her feet into the barren coldness of the flowing water. She bent, cupped her hand, and brought up a puddle to her face, letting the droplets cascade over her shoulders.

This is always my least favorite part. Submerging into frigid water was like fingernails scraping over a chalkboard. She doused herself with more water, shivering as it cascaded down.

Time to submerge.

She dove in and resurfaced just as quickly. Her mind was alight, alert. She waded deeper, knees pumping high over the cresting tide beneath her.

The board clung to her chest; she jumped forward on to it. Stacey landed hard on its end, ignoring the fleeting pain in her knees, and floated atop the current. She steadied the board and paddled harder, the waves beneath her distant, buffered by the board's waxy hull.

Dawn was now peeking from beneath the horizon, and she could make out other surfers in the distance, small and scattered. One was nearby, his back shimmering against the light. Another sat tall on the water, his body extended, his seat obscured by the bobbing water.

She took a deep breath, looked back out over the water, and sought to sync with its rhythm. The memories of any worldly troubles were flung far beyond where they could wound her, leaving her with the flow of the rolling waves.

"Pura vida!" A voice echoed through the dark. Ahead she could see a man bobbing in the water. He said something else, his voice muffled.

"Sorry, I couldn't hear you," she called out and swam closer.

"Choppy water. The crest doesn't hold too firm today, boss." His voice came across the water as she paddled to his side. He sat upright on his board, his torso rotating as if swaying to some unseen tempo. His face bore the natural friendliness common in this land, but she sensed something awkward in his gaze, as if he peered at her a little too intently.

"It's why I brought the longboard. At my age, you know?" Stacey said.

"Older is an aspiration. This water is destined to surprise us all today," the man replied.

Everyone in Costa Rica was a philosopher. Her mind, tempered by the mild high, struggled to formulate a response.

"Mind over matter," he said, twisting on his board to scan the horizon. His gaze shifted back to her, a question seeming to hang in the air before him. "You own The Pukahoda, yes?"

Stacey was surprised by the recognition. Despite her hotel garnering acclaim among the high-fashion and elite circles, most locals seemed either oblivious to the transformation that had unfolded around them or regarded it with a detached indifference.

"I do indeed," she said, choosing her words tentatively. "Along with my partners."

"Diego. Nice to meet you." The man greeted her with a grin.

"Born in Tamarindo. I am a farmer, you can say, up and down the southern west coast."

"I'm Stacey."

His eyes studied her with a strange intensity. "Your hotel is the talk of the town where I'm from. Big success."

Caught off guard, she found herself blushing.

"How long have you been open?" He asked.

"A few years. Though before the refurbishment, we used to be the Surf Shack."

"Ah, tuanis! I remember that place. Great ceviche." He gave her another quizzical look, and his lips curled into a soft smile. "Very different to The Pukahoda. Interesting people now. Beautiful people. Not so many beautiful people before The Pukahoda. Lots of harina now!"

His laughter rang out across the water, though Stacey sensed little humor in his joke. She knew harina meant money, and the crude among the Costa Rican community used that vernacular. She began to suspect who Diego really was.

"Well, thank you," she replied, maintaining a diplomatic tone. "You should drop by for lunch sometime."

"With your prices?" He shook his head, still laughing. "No, thank you."

"The meal would be on us, Diego."

A rolling wave separated them momentarily, but he paddled back toward her, positioning himself on his board.

"If you need any other suppliers, we have a small farm up north. I am very carga with supplies."

She offered a polite smile, though a knot of uneasiness began to form in her stomach. "I don't handle the food and beverage. But I'd be happy to introduce you to the person in charge."

A frown creased his brow. "I meant for your entertainment."

She immediately understood his underlying implication.

"Drop by for lunch, I can introduce you to our team."

She found herself wishing for a wave to provide an excuse to leave.

"Those large domes..." he began, clearing his throat. "What are they for?"

"You've seen them?"

"From up on the ridge." The man pointed toward the shore and into the darkness where Stacey knew large looming hilltops resided, hidden from view by large Guanacaste trees.

"They're our yoga domes."

"Big for yoga, no?" the man laughed.

"We call them Immersion Domes."

"Immersion Domes? Is that a fancy word for discotecas?"

His gaze locked on to her, stoking the embers of her discomfort, made more potent by the lingering effects of marijuana. She wondered what he had seen from his vantage point on the ridge.

"No, they're not nightclubs. Just yoga domes."

His frown deepened. "Not nightclubs, huh? What's inside these yoga domes?"

She wished for a wave, an escape.

"The inside of the domes are lined with digital screens. They provide a fully immersive digital wellness experience."

Diego scratched his chin, a gesture reminiscent of old detective shows. "Fully immersive." He laughed again. "That's what people once called Costa Rica."

"Excuse me?"

"Fully immersive wellness. We have trees, beaches, wildlife. See? Fully immersive."

"Well, you have a point there." She offered a nervous laugh. "Many of our guests come here for the nature. We provide them with something more."

"More?"

"State-of-the-art digital experiences."

"Only digital? We've heard of other things."

Stacey didn't care for the look he was giving her and decided to shift the conversation. She had met many people like Diego recently. Opportunists… or worse. They were drawn to The Pukahoda's success like rats to a feast. She had learned to deal with them cautiously, and if necessary make them disappear with a little cash.

"Drop by for lunch, Diego. It's on me."

Diego finally seemed satisfied with this and nodded his approval. Stacey hoped the invitation would be forgotten, but she knew better. She made a mental note to inform her partners about another inquiring supplier.

A pair of waves rolled past, separating them.

"I'm going to push it," he called out, his voice rising above the roar of the waves.

He launched himself forward on his board. The crest passed Stacey and she felt the backwash push her out to sea. Diego seemed to be in a standstill against the current, paddling against the wave's pull. As the crest reached him, he shot up and forward, feet planted firmly on his board. Then he disappeared, surfing down a ten-meter glassy sheet as white foam formed atop the wave's edge.

She followed Diego's silhouette as he navigated closer to shore. He had concluded his dance with the sea, now returning to shallow waters. Watching a soul lose itself in the rhythm of the sea was a sight to behold – riding the ceaseless cycle, devoid of an end, not tethered by the weight of any fixed ambition except to continue the infinite journey.

"Stacey, the monkey's back."

This was unwelcome news. Stacey sat up and ran a hand through her brittle hair, still wet from her post-surf shower.

"Shit. I thought he was gone for good," she said in the direction of an oily brown oak door resting a few feet from her angular king-sized bed. She shifted slightly and felt the mattress slide roughly against the mahogany bed frame beneath it.

"Well, it's back now. You should come and see what it's done to the dining room," the voice behind the door answered back.

"Welcome home, asshole," she muttered.

For a glorious week, The Pukahoda was blessed with the monkey's absence, and free from its continuous screeches and mischief. Waiters were once again able to serve food without the danger of immediate theft and the hotel's bellman was able to wear his small black hat without fear it would be snatched off his head. If the monkey was back, it would mean The Pukahoda, its thirty staff members, and upwards of one hundred guests, were once again going to be subjected to its torment.

Stacey left her villa and walked through a towering mahogany reception, her flip-flops swishing over marble flooring, and entered the outdoor dining hall backdropped with a lush thicket of jungle greenery. A tapestry of leaves and branches danced in the breeze, concealing the sandy expanse of the beach some two hundred meters beyond.

Her gaze fell upon the mayhem that lay before her.

Yup, the monkey had indeed returned.

Tiny pellets of feces were scattered across the immaculately set dining tables, as if dispensed by a machine gun from an airborne warplane, their placement resembling a code penned in primate excrement. *The creature must have impressive control of its rectal muscles to master such an art*, Stacey thought with a smile.

"Is there any reason no one has cleaned this up yet?" she called to a beautiful young woman standing near her. The woman wore a brown linen outfit, with a badge that read *Pukahoda: Rebel with Care*. She had soft blue eyes, two cavernous dimples, and a wildly pierced nose, her nose ring adorned with light blue diamonds which glistened in the early morning sun. Her look was a mirror to the hotel staff's collective aesthetic – a fusion of glamour with a touch of defiance.

The woman shrugged her shoulders. "We wanted you to see it for yourself first."

Stacey didn't hide her annoyance. "Great. I've seen it now. Let's get this cleaned up and get the warning signs out again."

The woman shrugged again and disappeared into the back room. Stacey found herself questioning the wisdom behind employing such nonchalantly cool kids as members of their staff.

The monkey was definitely bad for business. Initially, Stacey had considered it a curious asset: a playful mascot for the social media crowd. A strategy that held allure for a day or two but lost its charm swiftly. Complaints from guests flowed in like a deluge, reviews took a nosedive. A noisy monkey didn't align with the aura of a luxury hotel spa. The Pukahoda offered high-end medicinal and spiritual treatments, world-class surf, and the most sought-after party in the western hemisphere. The guests were here to bask in the limelight; they weren't shelling out a fortune to have a raucous monkey pilfer their meals, defecate in their designer handbags, swipe their sarongs from their deck beds, or disrupt their sleep with its endless howls.

Stacey had tried to look on the bright side. Her problem with the monkey was clearly a sign of The Pukahoda's success. A lone monkey would do little to disrupt business at a roadside motel or a sleepy, hippy beachside surf shack. Various four-star hotels in the immediate area had maintained a steady stream of occupancy and returning customer base under constant invasion by various vermin and unwanted jungle wildlife. But a five-star luxury wellness retreat for the elite? No, the monkey simply had to go.

Stacey saw Tyla come in from behind the serving station. She was wearing her favorite blue, white, and red bandanna. Tyla was smiling, of course. She was never not smiling. She walked tall and slender with blissfully wavy brown hair and each stride of those long olive-skinned legs was a wink and a smile to the world, telling all that she was fabulous and she was aware of it.

"He's baaa-aaacck," she said, and rushed to kiss Stacey hello.

Stacey gestured to the mess the monkey made and raised her eyebrows. "Yes, I could tell."

Tyla laughed and wrapped her arms around her wife's neck.

"We need to take care of this. For good," Stacey whispered into her ear.

"You need to talk to Rolando, mi amor," Tyla responded.

Stacey sighed. "He's a dead-end, honey."

"He's muy importante. He's the most respected mayor that Nicoya ever had. They say he may even be president."

"Ugh. That man hates gringos. He's caused us so many problems!"

Tyla laughed. "Oh, no, mi amor. He doesn't hate you. And no politician can hate gringos and survive here."

"Whatever he is, the conservatory needs to step up and do something about this darn monkey. Are you going to help or not?"

Tyla leaned back and winked. "If I help, they will definitely do something," she said.

"Peligrosa!" Stacey smiled and nudged her flirtatiously. Tyla certainly had a knack for making things happen. Despite dropping out from her village school to venture into what would become a fruitful modeling career, she possessed the street smarts and emotional intelligence to make anything happen. Stacey had witnessed her charm work wonders, disarming the most challenging clients and associates.

Tyla pursed her lips and pouted. "I hate talking to Rolando and his people. They let dust from the road pollute poor children's lungs, but God forbid they let us capture a little monkey."

"Pretty please?" Stacey mimicked Tyla's pout playfully.

"OK, baby, I'll manage Rolando and this tiny little monkey."

Tyla's focus shifted over Stacey's shoulder, her attention captured by a newcomer. "But you handle whatever Stella is here to whine about."

Stacey turned to see Stella, her head of events, standing beneath an oversized, reconstructed Aztec archway. She wore the same uniform as the others, her badge embossed with her name and title. Her arms were crossed, her expression as sulky as ever.

"We need to talk about the situation in the Immersion Zone," Stella said dryly. "It sounds serious, but no one is telling me anything. Freddie won't say a word until he speaks to you."

"What situation?"

Stella's eyebrows shot up, her face falling in disbelief. "Oh, damn. You haven't heard? Where were you this morning?"

A sinking feeling clenched at Stacey's gut and she shook her head. "What situation, Stella? Just spit it out."

"I'm sorry," Stella said. "I thought you were keeping me in the dark again."

"Stella," Stacey demanded. "What happened?"

"I don't know much, but you better get over to the Immersion Domes stat. Someone was found comatose this morning. Last I heard, they weren't sure he would make it."

Stacey ran as fast as her flip-flops allowed. A slight breeze had wormed its way through the tree canopy and greeted her confidently as she ran past hidden villas built between towering boulders. Strategically placed vines hid most of the man-made features nestled beneath the tropical vegetation – their features only occasionally peered through the greenery, like elusive wildlife.

She sprinted past a sign, its block letters etched in the solid oak plank, dark and worn. It read: *The Pukahoda: Everyone Eventually Rebels*. She thought back to what she had just heard. If the words held truth, it would mark the second such incident this month – the third this season. Stacey's mind raced faster than her feet. Rolando, the notorious hardliner, wouldn't take long to launch an investigation. His stern reputation and their previous encounters painted a clear picture – he wouldn't hesitate to shutter any operation that threatened his political aspirations, regardless of the financial benefits it brought to the region, or his personal wallet.

Her thoughts immediately went to Tyla, and she prayed that her innocent beloved would be spared any such inquiry. Tyla knew so little about the details of the hotel's more complex and challenging operations among the rich and the powerful. Stacey recalled a recent conversation they'd had, where Tyla brought up the topic of illicit substance use on the property. "Mi amor," she had said, her face covered with worry. "I know sexy people do sexy things, but you must be careful."

Stacey had done her best to assure her wife that the hotel had nothing to do with any drug use on the property. "We're enacting heightened surveillance," she had said. "Don't worry, my love, security is aware that we must keep the hotel as clean as possible."

A pang of guilt hit her as she recalled the lie. How had things spiraled out of control?

The hotel's ascent seemed almost mystical at first. Just as Stacey and her partners were about to give up securing funding for their dream eco-wellness resort renovation, divine intervention arrived in the form of a Sonar Immersion license – the first of its kind bestowed upon a small business by the monolithic Byrell Industries. Almost overnight, The Pukahoda was catapulted into the international spotlight and quickly ascended to fame within fashion circles and the glitterati, eager to experience this groundbreaking new take on leisure. The Pukahoda presented itself as the nexus of the natural and the digital, a haven where guests could ride organic waves and interact with the diverse wildlife of Costa Rica, dance the night away in augmented nightclubs utilizing cutting edge AR and VR technology, or practice yoga while floating in a virtual cosmos in the hotel's Immersion Areas. The opening of the Immersion Domes even drew the enigmatic Peter Byrell himself, an event that launched Stacey into a momentary blaze of international recognition. However, this luminescence faded quickly, darkened by the arrival of psychedelics, followed closely by harder substances, casting long shadows over their vision. In just two years, plagued by five dire incidents and countless brushes with disaster, their once idyllic dream had become an ugly nightmare.

This madness had to end.

She crossed a set of rolling streams until sparse trees gave way to a thicker set. A hasty wave was her only greeting to the ground staff tending to the gardens as she passed. She was out of breath when she reached a large oak sign at the edge of a particularly heavy set of brush. The words *Total Immersion Area* were burned via a custom branding iron provided to the hotel by a friendly local farmer. Underneath the sign hung a printed notice:

> *You are entering the Total Immersion Area. No access without registration and medical clearance. Please inquire at reception to obtain required entry pass and equipment. Access strictly prohibited for non-hotel guests, expectant mothers, and children under the age of fifteen. WARNING: This area contains imagery that may potentially trigger seizures for people with photosensitive epilepsy. Discretion is advised.*

A few paces away stood an eight-foot bamboo doorway, strung together with heavy rope which slithered between the canes, holding them firmly against one another. The bamboo itself was tattooed with meticulously carved lines, each two inches long, and if you were fortunate enough to catch sight between the canes, you would see a small pathway that the door fortified. As she approached the gate, the tops of curious-looking domes peeked above the doorframe a hundred meters beyond. Their tops were made of matted brown leaves, strung together in vines that wrapped over themselves in a twisting dance. Stacey reached into her pocket and pulled out a green keycard from her wallet, which she pressed against the center of the door. A small click emanated from somewhere within, and the door began to retreat from her, pulled sideways by an unseen mechanism. She shoved the card away and quickened her pace, her feet sinking beneath her as the ground gave way to a softer, more porous substance, providing the sensation of rushing along a small trampoline or hanging bridge. As she ran toward the towering domes, their façade began to give off a faint electronic shimmer. Up close, she could make out the electronics woven into the natural fibers of the façade. The sun rays crept through the entangled vines, found the reflective polymer underneath, and bounced back through infrequent gaps.

The base was made of a series of intertwined ten-foot arches, which wove like mesh around a large cylindrical dome. Against the arches was a continuous, translucent film screen. Stacey observed the molded crests formed by slightly dark-tinted archivolts and buttresses which held the screens in place. From the outside, the screen projected a harmonious exterior, blending seamlessly with the natural surroundings.

She reached the large dome's tall doorway and pressed her keycard against it. She could hear a symphony of soft, squishy claps inside. It sounded like a group of sponges being squeezed. The doorway slid open along unseen motorized wheels, and she kicked off her footwear and stepped through.

Her bare feet were met with damp coolness from the soft leather-like fabric which stretched firm over a thin polyester foam, covering the entire floor of the dome. The sound of bending rubber and heavy breathing filled the interior. Her eyes took a moment to adjust to the darkness within. A vast screen covering the interior of the dome was a cosmic festival: a backdrop of a starry night with images of spinning planets and brilliant supernovas bursting out in vibrant cosmic colors. There were perhaps a dozen people inside, spread out across the thousand-square-foot area, their silent dances varying from wild gyrations to slow, coordinated motions. She observed a solitary male dancer, his limbs loose as he bounced to the rhythm of his own music. His head was wrapped in a dark black polymer that resembled a thin astronaut's helmet, a familiar neon etching of an angry gorilla logo imprinted on its surface. He was clearly out of it, she thought. Best not disturb.

She found a small doorway in the back of the dome, behind sheets of fused video screens, and went through into a windowless office.

In the dimly lit room, the head of security and the general manager stared down at the lifeless body sprawled across the desk. It was Johnny Blank, once a larger-than-life A-list actor, now reduced to a pale, motionless lump of flesh. His face, drained of color, bore the haunting gaze of wide, lifeless eyes. Blue lips framed his open mouth, frozen in a grotesque expression.

Stacey stood motionless in disbelief; her body paralyzed by the shocking sight. She had grown accustomed to seeing Johnny's handsome face projected on large movie screens, not as this cold and lifeless figure before her. The stark reality of his demise fascinated and repelled her simultaneously.

"Oh my God," she managed, her voice a whisper.

Her security chief looked to the floor. "We found him unresponsive."

"We administered CPR but he was already gone," said the manager.

"Have we called the police?" she asked.

Both men shook their heads.

Stacey reached for her phone. "I'm calling his manager."

The phone rang twice before a woman answered.

"Hello, it's Stacey Cobb. I'm calling from The Pukahoda Resort in Costa Rica where your client Johnny Blank is staying. We have some difficult news."

"Oh, hello, Stacey. What can I do for you?" Her voice was cautious, likely conditioned by the numerous times she had been contacted previously with concerning information about her client.

"You might want to sit down for this," Stacey warned.

"What did Johnny do this time?"

Stacey took a deep breath. "I'm sorry to have to say this. Johnny Blank passed away."

There was a silence on the other end of the line. "What the hell?" the voice stammered. "Are you sure?"

"We are positive. I'm looking at him now."

The line went silent again, likely muted. The voice returned, surprisingly calm. "An overdose?"

Stacey hesitated before answering. "We're… we're not sure."

"Oh, God." Stacey heard whispers in the background. "Wait just a minute."

The phone went dead for an uncomfortable length of time.

"Stacey, I want you to hear me out here," the voice commanded after she returned. "You have to keep this under wraps until one of us gets there. Tell your staff to keep him where he is. I'll call you when I get flight details."

"Of course," Stacey responded. "I'm so sorry for your loss." The phone line cut before she could finish her sentence.

Stacey turned to her head of security. "Freddie, would you mind going over to the office? I'll meet you there. Johnny's people asked that we not do anything until they arrive. Can I count on you to keep this situation among the three of us? For the sake of his family?"

"I understand. You have my silence until otherwise instructed."

With Freddie gone, she turned to her hotel manager. "Turn off your phone, please," she instructed, and he complied. "Do you have any idea what he took?" she asked.

He looked nervous. "If I'm to guess, DMT," he said sheepishly. "Last night was a full immersion DMT experience."

"OK, OK." Stacey paced the small room. "Who administered the product? One of ours?"

He nodded. Stacey ruffled her hair. "DMT wouldn't cause this. It was something else." She let out an audible sigh of relief, then thought for a moment.

"Are you sure there was nothing else?"

"Stacey, Johnny was a VIP. He got whatever he wanted."

"Listen, I need you to tell me now. Did our staff give him anything that could have caused this?"

The hotel manager looked down to the floor. "You really want to know?" he asked.

"Yes, I really want to know."

"Then I'll find out," he said. "But I suspect you won't like the answer."

Sometime later, Stacey emerged from the dome into the punishing glare of the noon sun. Minutes seemingly bled into hours in her wait for the hotel manager's return. He was the bearer of unfortunate news: Johnny had been given an opiate the night before by a member of the Immersion Team. The drugs ostensibly were a gift from a private stash, but Stacey was under no illusion: her hotel staff had likely sold lethal drugs to one of their most famous guests, killing him.

Later, the head of security called, bringing more positive news. Unnamed pill bottles had been unearthed in Johnny's suite, presenting a thread of plausible deniability for the hotel, an opportunity to bury the unsolicited act of "kindness" from the Immersion Team staff member. Stacey called to tell Johnny's people that his death likely stemmed from his own substances, and then stayed put until the head of hotel security returned to stand guard over the body.

Stacey and her team had resolved to hold their tongues, to let Johnny's people handle the fallout. But the prospect of a police investigation set her mind spinning. Regardless of the drug that had claimed Johnny's life or who had dealt it, there would surely be an investigation and her staff would be interrogated. The mayor was a hardliner; The Pukahoda would likely be made an example of and its operations scrutinized, with her staff and partners potentially held accountable. As an American, she could abscond before the storm hit, but what of Tyla, a Costa Rican without an American passport? The thought of bringing harm to her love was almost too much to bear.

She left the Immersion Area and made her way back to the main office, crossing the sandy expanse that divided the villa clusters. A man's voice reverberated across the distance, reaching out to her. She turned to see Diego racing toward her, dust rising in his wake as he navigated the soft dirt path beneath. His surf attire was still on, now unzipped, revealing a canvas of inked skin.

"Stacey!" Diego grinned.

She immediately excused herself. "I'm sorry, Diego, but I have something urgent to attend to."

The man's face fell. "You told me to come by for lunch."

"I think it would be better if you could come back another day."

Diego scratched his chin. "I'm sorry to hear that. I came to make a business proposal."

Unsurprised by the comment, Stacey searched for words to gracefully exit the situation, but before she could speak, her phone began to ring. The call was from area code 310, immediately recognizable to Stacey as being from the most prestigious area of Beverly Hills.

"Sorry, Diego, I really appreciate it," she motioned that she had to take the call, "but this is not a good time."

She pulled on her earpiece, and with a contrived air of nonchalance, moved away, putting a safe distance between them.

"This is Stacey," she answered.

The male voice on the other end was all business, sharp and precise, devoid of niceties.

"Stacey, this is going to be an 'I talk, you listen, and you agree with everything I tell you' type of situation, alright?"

"Excuse me – who is this?" she stammered, caught off guard by the rudeness.

"I represent firms related to Johnny Blank's interests," the man continued. "*Substantial* interests. Now, I'll say it again, prepare yourself to listen, and agree with what I have to say. Can you manage that?"

Taken aback, Stacey quickly glanced over her shoulder to see if Diego had noticed her discomposure. He stood far away, smiling. She motioned that she was likely to be longer and that he should go, but he motioned to her that he would wait.

"Listen, I don't know who you are," Stacey turned to respond to the caller, "but you can't just talk to me like that."

The man cut her off with a steady, forceful tone, reminiscent of a CIA operative caricature from a bad movie.

"Your hotel was supplying narcotics to my client, most likely resulting in his death. So, yes, I can talk to you in any way I choose."

He paused momentarily, seemingly to let the message sink in. Stacey bit her lip.

"So, let's start over." His voice as slow and methodical. "You listen, I speak. You do what I say. Can you manage that?"

"Yes, I can manage."

"Good. We need you to freeze any action related to Johnny until our team lands and we need you to prevent any further conversation regarding his death."

"Yes, I've already done that," Stacey assured the man. "No one knows the details except myself, my manager, and a small number of staff."

"No one else has been told? Did any other hotel guests see the incident?"

She told the man that she was confident that no one else knew the circumstances of Johnny's condition, and that her staff was told to keep any information they knew strictly to themselves. The man sounded reassured.

"Hold on," the voice ordered. Muffled sounds were followed by a click, signaling a switch. A new voice emerged.

"Stacey, it's Don from Horizon Studios."

"Oh... hi, Don," she responded, awestruck. She suspected the voice on the other end of the line was the infamous Don Mackenzie, the head of Horizon Studios, the largest movie production company in the world. His voice was reminiscent of a Hollywood movie, booming with an air of indomitable bravado.

"We need to handle Johnny's situation ourselves. Our team will be there by sundown. A jet will soon be in the air. We need assurance from you that nothing will leak until we're on-site. No phone calls to police. We'll handle everything. This is a super-sensitive matter."

"When will your team arrive? Our hotel is required to inform the local authorities—" Stacey began but was cut off.

"I'm sure the laws in Costa Rica allow such sensitive matters to be handled appropriately," he said, his voice trailing off at the end. "Johnny's family needs reassurance that his situation isn't going to be leaked to the press, that's all."

Stacey thought for a moment. She didn't like where this was going and wasn't sure that a lengthy delay was legal under such circumstances.

"Don, I appreciate the concerns, but I also need to think about our legal obligations, and the protection of my staff," she said, but was again forcefully cut off.

"I don't think she's getting it," Don complained, his voice distant, as if he had turned to someone near him.

She heard a click and the earlier man's voice interjected. "For God's sake, Stacey, listen and do as you're told," he sneered. The force of his words blasted into her eardrums with the malice of a close-range pistol firing. "If this leaks, you're going to have a whole who's-who list of the world's biggest power players gunning for you. You know the kind of money riding on Johnny's latest project?"

"I—" she started.

"You don't," he interjected. "We've got a former president as a backer. A sheik who's poured millions into this latest project. There is an entire industry behind this. So, kindly, shut the fuck up and listen. You cross these people, and your fancy resort will be a beach shack by Sunday."

The line went quiet. The threat hung in the air.

"Let us take care of the police when we get there. Are you on board?"

Stacey nodded, the weight of the situation sinking in. A sense of humiliation washed over her. She was in deeper waters than she had realized.

"Stacey? You're on board, right?"

"Yes."

"Good," the man said and Stacey stood motionless, watching Diego pace the grounds far away from her.

Don returned to the line. "Stacey, I'm sorry for that, but hopefully you see the severity and importance of this situation. I'm going to let you in on something that will help you understand, but first I need you to sign a confidentiality agreement. Check your TalkApp, please."

She pulled up the application and found a document had arrived from another unknown number. She opened the file and read through the details. The PDF was on Horizon Studios letterhead and contained robust non-disclosure language, referencing any association with the studio, Johnny Blank, or any of their associates.

The other male voice had returned. "Please sign this electronically and return it to us. You'll see there is a sizeable sum associated with your immediate compliance. This offer is open to you for the next few minutes only."

She saw another document come through TalkApp and opened it. The letterhead was from a company she did not recognize. The language was simple and to the point. It instructed that $2 million would be sent to her in four installments, one immediately paid upon release of the non-disclosure agreement, asking her to supply bank details.

"You read both files?" the man asked, after giving her a few moments. "Time to make a choice."

Stacey thought for a moment, and decided that she would be best placed to accept these demands.

"OK, I'll sign," she acknowledged, and filled in each document, putting her signature to each with her finger. In the distance, Diego watched curiously, remaining steadfast in his resolve to wait and conclude their earlier conversation.

"Did you send it, Stacey?"

"Yes, you should have it now," she responded.

After a moment, Don returned to the line, his voice thick with the obnoxious air of dominant confidence.

"Thank you, Stacey. You made the right choice. You'll need to maintain confidentiality for as long as we require it. We'll also need the names of the other members of staff that know of Johnny's demise."

She offered the full names and addresses of anyone who was aware of the event's details.

"Thank you. They will be fairly compensated for their support," Don said. "We'll be in touch."

The line went dead. Stacey hung there, a moment's prey, immobilized by the unfolding narrative. Off in the distance, Diego observed her with a hunter's patience, steadfast in his resolve to complete their earlier discourse.

"I'm sorry, Diego," she called out, pretending to make another call. "This is urgent. Please come back later."

To her surprise, he jogged toward her. As he approached, Stacey could hear loud screeches from trees behind him. She suspected it was the monkey, somewhere off in the vegetation, preparing for its next assault on her grounds.

Diego flashed a mischievous smile. "You have a wild one there." He pointed in the direction of the monkey's screams. "I was watching him. He's restless."

"He's a nuisance. We're taking care of it." Stacey offered the blunt response. She really had no time for conversation.

"He's a monkey in his habitat. Perhaps we are the real nuisance," Diego scoffed. He lifted a finger and with an amused chortle, he traced an invisible circle in the arid air. "Full immersion!"

Stacey gestured that she needed to go, but he raised a solitary hand.

"Stacey, please hear my proposal."

He stood under the sun, a relaxed grin etched into his sun-kissed face. The sunlight glistened over the inked illustrations that sprawled across his bare torso.

"You need new suppliers," he continued. "Current ones, no bueno. Killing your fancy customers."

Swallowing down a surge of nausea, Stacey's hands clenched into trembling fists. Diego approached, handing her a card. As he did, Stacey spied a tattoo of a large dragon on his forearm, its menacing serpentine body slithering below the sandy polymer of his wetsuit. The card was a humble rectangle of bleached paper inscribed with a first name and a string of digits.

"I'm really sorry, Diego," she said, attempting to return the card. He dismissed her gesture, a soft smile shadowing his face.

"You have many problems. The drugs, yes? We can help."

In the distance, the monkey howled and Stacey glanced over Diego's shoulder toward the sound.

"Your problem is not that monkey. Your real problem is with that politico zaguate Rolando, no?" His face contorted angrily as the mayor's name left his lips.

Stacey stood still in shock. With her mouth hanging open, she searched for words, finding none. Diego extended a hand, patting her arm with a menacing calm. A wide grin spread across his face, revealing a mouthful of matted gold, incongruously dull against the sun's rays.

"Stacey, relax. I'm your amigo, enemigo de tu enemigo," he assured with a wink. "We take care of Rolando. You take care of us. Simple. You have powerful Rica friends now, Stacey. No need to worry, but friends always need to take care of friends."

A second wink caused her to recoil, and he roared with laughter. "Relax, Stacey, we don't do anything until you call. Simple," he said and turned to walk away. "But we expect your call."

She watched him, mouth agape, feeling like a gringo lost on one of Costa Rica's rugged, unpaved roads – a proverbial deer in the glare of blinding headlights cutting through a black night. Stacey mourned what The Pukahoda had become. A simple dream of fusing nature's wellness with human innovation had spiraled into a darker reality. The Pukahoda was meant to be an extension of the human spirit, a realm of release, a haven for those seeking to defy societal confines. How had it all slipped away? How much was ever truly real in the first place?

An idea occurred to Stacey, causing her to perk up. *Maybe Diego can be useful in the Johnny Blank situation*, she thought. In the distance, hidden away in the verdant canopy, the monkey continued its mischievous howl.

Tucked away in a solitary Beverly Hills penthouse office, above every other structure in its vicinity, sat Don Mackenzie. The head of the world's biggest studio leaned back in the luxurious embrace of an oversized leather executive chair, having tapped the phone button to end the call with the Pukahoda's owner. He was pleasantly surprised by how well it had gone. He hadn't quite anticipated such a swift capitulation from Stacey into signing the non-disclosure agreement; having her onboard was going to make things so much easier. His hope was that the remaining staff of The Pukahoda would prove just as yielding.

His gaze shifted to the pair sitting across his imposing desk. The studio's legal counsel – a slender wisp of a man with a scalp barren of hair, and eyes heavy and hollow – met his look without emotion. Beside him, Johnny Blank's agent, Debbie, was entrenched in a frenetic dance of her fingers on her tablet.

"I think that went as well as it could. Trent, commendable work, as always. I believe she's got the picture. Let's get those NDAs in front of the rest of her crew. Pay them whatever it takes to get their silence."

Trent nodded. Don turned his attention to Debbie, the bane of his morning thus far.

"Debbie, condolences for your loss."

She acknowledged his sentiment with a mute gesture and went back to her tablet. Don wondered whether Debbie had long ago accepted the prospect of her client's untimely demise. It would explain why Johnny Blank was the first actor she signed up to the rendering contract years ago, following multiple well-documented incidents of his unruly on-set conduct and general bad behavior.

"Do we have any options here?" he posed to his counsel.

Trent shook his head. "The release date's already in the market, and fake reshoot is scheduled for next week. The guild's in the know. If Johnny's death is kept under wraps until then, we can move the reshoot to a location that the guild won't be able to make. That would allow us enough cover to ensure no one is the wiser."

"It was a mistake to go with that goddamn reshoot nonsense," Don snipped.

"We had to maintain appearances, Don. The actors' guild has been breathing down our necks. The reshoot reschedule was a brilliant idea at the time to cover tracks and give the appearance that all of our productions were live action. It appeased them on the last movie they had an issue with and would have been fine this time too. No one could have predicted this situation."

Debbie perked up from her tablet. "We could just announce his death and say we're reshooting Johnny's remaining scenes with AI."

Don bit his cheek. "Too risky."

Trent tapped one foot firmly on the ground. "Too risky – and too stupid. It would give the unions an opening to investigate the entire production, blowing the lid wide open on the entire rendering project. The agreement regarding artificial likenesses between the studios and unions is clear. Any use of AI gives the unions the right to interfere." He turned to the head of the studio. "No, Don, you either have a clean production, or you're up shit creek without a paddle, drowning in regulations and labor disputes."

"So, no options, then?" Don asked, growing openly despondent.

"Afraid not," Trent replied.

Anger building, Don turned his attention to Johnny's agent and manager. He paused for a moment, considering if it was the right time to deliver more bad news to her. To hell with it, he concluded, considering how she had wreaked havoc on his morning schedule with the news of the studio's biggest star overdosing somewhere in Costa Rica. Anger seethed within him as he thought about the tribulations this scenario had brought upon him and the studio. Hell, not just to Horizon, but potentially blowing the entire goddamn industry to smithereens. He had invested immense effort into their rendering business, keeping the entire process off the books and in private hands, and her client, Johnny Blank, couldn't have chosen a worse time to die, putting the entire operation in jeopardy. So, yes, he thought, she deserved as much bad news as he was going to deliver.

"Debbie, it goes without saying, but we're going to have to scrap Johnny's upcoming surf movie production. Holding this news longer than a few months is going to be impossible, so we're already working on a replacement."

Debbie wasn't surprised. "I get it," she said, stowing her tablet. "I assume his replacement is one of mine? Austin would be great for the picture. He's already signed up to the rendering contract, as you know."

Don offered a soft, noncommittal smile. He didn't have much leverage over her, but any he had, he'd use to go for her jugular. "It's in the director's hands," he said, his words a veiled threat. "He'll let you know if it's one of yours." He leaned into his chair and punctuated his next statement with a tap on the table, reveling in the moment. "But you should be prepared for the possibility that we go fully rendered for this one, with no life actors involved. Johnny's situation highlights the need for us to distance ourselves more from life actors."

Debbie looked shocked, pleasing Don greatly. A woman in her position rarely looked shocked. "Is the system ready?"

He nodded confidently, despite not having a clue whether going with a full-on AI roster in a rendered movie production, without the aid of life actors, was even possible. The studio still needed life actors to market the product. Their algorithm was clear: audiences wanted to think that the actors they saw on screen were real, particularly in the types of action and rom-com movies that Johnny was known for. The studio's algorithm was right: no one would root for an AI hero and no one wanted to sleep with an avatar. They wanted the real thing.

"And how are you going to market a fully rendered product?" Debbie asked, seemingly trying to gauge how serious Don's threat was.

"The entire ecosystem is shifting toward fully rendered with no life actors," Don said with assertive confidence, grinning at her. "We're bringing a broadcaster on board with a sharing deal, and working up solid social media campaigns utilizing state-of-the-art deepfake tech. But this is just a heads up – get ready."

The threat satisfied him but, in truth, the ecosystem was far from ready. The rendered concept, which Don proudly championed as its chief architect, was still a closely guarded secret in the industry, even after five years, and was far from perfect. To prevent widespread usage, allowing anyone in a basement with enough software to copy their formula, or triggering an industry-wide strike, the confidential use of AI-likenesses within entirely rendered movies was strictly controlled by only two movie studios: Horizon and its biggest competitor. Only a select roster of A-list stars, writers, and directors were signed to rendering contracts, and production schedules for rendered movies were meticulously designed to prevent leaks.

Despite the risk and the difficulty of maintaining secrecy, rendered movies were a resounding success. They saved the studios a fortune in production costs. Life actors were still needed to keep up appearances. Johnny Blank, for example, had been required to promote the movies his AI likeness starred in by doing the rounds, attending film festivals, and posing for photos at screenings. As part of his rendering contract, he just needed to be – well, a real live human being. His last film wasn't finished yet. The studio had announced a required reshoot of two scenes from the movie, creating fake production staff to administer the event. This had been concocted to remove any doubt about what the studio was really doing. Johnny's untimely death put the studio in a terrible predicament: scrap the production and lose millions, or move the reshoot quickly to a foreign country and hide his death until the fake reshoot was seemingly completed. They had chosen the latter and, thankfully, the team at The Pukahoda, who were the studio's main obstacle to secrecy, was getting on board.

"Debbie, I think it's time for you to catch your plane," Don said, gesturing dismissively at the agent, who was silently fuming at him from across the desk. "You're wheels up in an hour."

Debbie's icy gaze stayed fixed on him. "My client will need an extension to his contract by the end of the day today."

"Your client is dead, Deborah," he responded, tapping his finger to the glazed panel on his desk.

"Your existing contract already stipulates post-capacity and posthumous payments," Trent added.

She threw her hands up in the air, appearing exasperated. "Aren't we trying to make sure he *isn't* dead, Don? At least not publicly."

"Whether he's dead to the public or not, he's still dead. He can't do promotional circuits, he can't make talk show appearances, and he sure as hell can't pose for photos. So yeah, Debbie, he's dead. Unable to fulfill his contract. Read the terms."

"So," she started, with a smug smile, pausing and making a mock quizzical face. "Should I, or should I not, tell Johnny's family of his passing?"

"Nicely played, Debbie."

Don put on a fake smile and leaned back in his chair. Debbie was a seasoned veteran of Hollywood's cutthroat circles, the best in the business, and he knew he had to handle her as such.

"Send over the terms and we'll have a look," he said. He despised being in a position of weakness and Debbie had him cornered.

Fixing this problem was going to cost a fortune, but he knew he had no choice: buying silence was the only way to keep the rendering production under wraps. It was the only way he was going to save hundreds of millions, perhaps even billions, of dollars from going down the drain if the news leaked to the public.

Debbie leaned over and seemed to study him for a moment. "Don, just remember, when you see the number that I'm going to send you – and I'm borrowing the wise words of your consigliere over here," she pointed to Trent mockingly, "that this is a 'you-agree-to-everything-I-ask-for' type of situation."

"Don't overplay your hand. Just send over the terms."

"You'll have it by the time I'm eating tuna ceviche on the shores of Nosara," she said, then packed her things, and left.

Don gestured toward the door Debbie had just swung shut behind her. "What's the play here?" he asked Trent.

The man moved as if made from stone, his head shaking slowly. "I'm thinking."

"Could use another coffee," Don said, rising from his chair and motioning for Trent to follow. They walked the corridor to a small saloon, a corner carved out in the penthouse floor with views stretching out over the ocean to downtown L.A. The bar, a glimmering spectacle of chrome and gold under the lights, was manned no matter the hour. The bartender was waiting. Always waiting.

Don ordered two drinks and turned to Trent. "What's your read on Debbie? She's going to play ball with us on this, right?"

"Legally, she's in the clear to do what anyone would do when someone passes. Inform the kin. Arrange for the burial."

Don cut in, "Yeah, yeah, but what's your gut telling you? She's in this just as deep as we are."

"You're fine, Don. She knows the financial fallout will be seismic if the public finds out Johnny Blank and most of their favorite actors are just computer-generated images." Trent paused. "How many actors does Debbie have on Horizon's 'rendered acting' contract?"

"Probably her entire A-list roster," Don replied. "Except for Tom and that one method actor who's been complaining about losing good roles."

Trent nodded assuredly. "Then Debbie won't talk. She's smart. She knows her business goes down with the ship."

"I agree, but I'm not risking everything so she can write a best-seller as a whistleblower," Don said. "Let's settle her, get a handle on The Pukahoda, and keep Johnny's death a secret long enough to finish this fake reshoot."

"Sounds like a plan," Trent agreed. He picked up his espresso, studying it curiously.

"This Johnny situation has me thinking about the grand order of things," Don mused.

Trent seemed surprised. "In what way?" he asked.

"The old methods of film are dying out. The industry clings to outdated rules. The unions scramble to stall the inevitable with regulations. But the end is clear. We feed the world what it craves – the illusion of reality, even when they probably already know it's not real. No one denies that machines are better writers, producers, and actors, all for a fraction of the cost. People understand that, but they don't want that depressing fact shoved into their faces. If hidden from them, the audience won't care about our new reality – they just want the illusion, the sizzle on the steak. They need a break from the slow march of daily life.

"The future is in rendering," Don continued. "Life actors are relics, the old world. It's a fact that must be accepted. We've done much to prepare for this eventuality." He took his cup, spinning it on the counter. "But then nature throws a wrench in the gears. Johnny is nature. I've witnessed his kind a hundred times over in my career. Wild, loud, disruptive. I've seen a hundred Johnnys come and go, and before him... Marilyn, Bruce, Elvis. They'll keep showing up, as long as we allow nature to run its course. I've been so engrossed in sculpting the future of film, I forgot the chaos a star in his natural element can cause. Some are born to wreak havoc. No matter the spotlight they command, some are just bound to take a giant shit in your coffee."

Don pushed away the espresso cup, leaning back. He stood, surveying the Los Angeles landscape stretching out beyond the floor-to-ceiling windows – the city, a patchwork of concrete towers and low buildings, nestled in the rolling hills surrounding the dusty basin of the valley.

"Funny, this Pukahoda Resort story would make a hell of a film," he mused, making a mental note to task his generative AI software with drafting a script.

PART II

A Reflection on Time

Round-Tripped Revolution

"This the land is mine; for ye are strangers and sojourners with me." – God to Moses, Leviticus 25:23

Part 1: Year 1848 – Infestation of Mechanical Locusts

"UPRIGHT, MY BOY," my father commands me.

His face is stern, much like a stone weathered by the winds and rains of time. I heed his instruction, pulling my spine straight. Layers of steam rising from my gruel form a veil between us, a brief respite for which I am silently thankful.

"Best to eat quickly and go about your chores," he instructs, and I take a spoonful of the meal into my mouth. It tastes as dreary as our surroundings appear, stale and spotted with mildew. "Tend to the livestock at first light. We then have the fields. Later, a bevy of boots need fitting for today's commission."

"Yes, sir."

He looks off into the distance and I see the weight of his grief in the creases between his eyes. The past ten years have not been kind to my father. He has witnessed the demise of three of his offspring – my siblings – victims of the merciless cholera, an ordeal that shattered my mother's once indomitable spirit. Her departure from this world a year prior, along with the decline of her small weaving business, left my father with a trifecta of concerns: his shoemaking craft, the farm, and myself. Two of these are on the wane. His meticulously crafted boots, once revered across Bavaria, are now facing dwindling demand. Factories in Munich mass-produce imitations at prices my father cannot compete with. His once-thriving trade is now but a dying art. Our farm, which sustained numerous households, is now ailing, much like the multitude of farms in our village, besieged by escalating costs and dwindling resources. This leaves me as his sole hope, a beacon still not dimmed. I am in the prime of my health and continue to grow stronger each passing day despite our scant provisions.

"Father," I say in between mouthfuls, cautiously breaking the silence.

He looks out the cloudy window, lost somewhere in the fields outside, probably wishing for a future that only exists in the past. Our humble land is besieged by so much change. There's an undercurrent of excitement that I haven't felt before. The Bavarian populace petitioned the king for reforms and their pleas were heard. Power has been granted to the people, something my father told me would never be possible. Cities are burgeoning, and the winds of change are blowing strong. Rail tracks are being laid, opening up previously unimaginable possibilities. Yet the promises of these transformations dissipate at the borders of our land, where they reform into parasitic predators. Like a swarm of locusts, these mechanical invaders have laid waste to our way of life. The locomotives brought with them the specter of disease, which claimed the lives of my brothers. They then turned their attention to my mother's linen, spawning competition so fierce that she could no longer find a profit. Now, they have set their sights on our farm; the surge in demand has made it nearly impossible to hire affordable labor or procure grain for our livestock.

He turns to face me, his hand thoughtfully stroking his beard.

"Yes, my boy," he responds, gesturing with his free hand. "But eat. Dawn is almost upon us."

"Of course, Father." I comply, hastily taking in another spoonful. I speak carefully, ensuring not to spill any of the porridge. "Have you reconsidered purchasing new machinery from Herr Schmidt?"

I already know the answer. He shakes his head.

"We are not the bourgeoisie. We are hard men, working hard soil and making hard boots for our friends. We cannot afford luxuries."

I tighten my grip on my spoon, anger rising in me. My father is ensnared in the past, laboring over the soil with bare hands doing what machinery could accomplish much faster. Why can't he see the present for what it is and the future for what it will be?

"Father, I implore you to listen," I assert, to which he reacts with menacing surprise. I hurriedly place my spoon back in the bowl. "Only if you permit, of course."

"Speak, son."

I consider revealing my plans, ones that I have been meticulously crafting over the past few months, yet have kept concealed partly out of fear, and partly out of respect. Today is not the day for such revelations. It would shatter him to learn that I'm contemplating leaving the farm for Munich, where wages are high and work opportunities abound. I have even hidden my knowledge that a locomotive factory is being opened in Munich, for fear that my interest in such matters would reveal my true intentions.

"Father, we can sell two cows to pay for new equipment, and a quarter of one year's rations for one farmhand. This will free you and I up to make more boots. You won't need to sell the land or abandon your shoemaking."

Again, he shakes his head and looks to me with an expression I haven't seen since my childhood. His smile is soft, yet his eyes betray a deep sadness. Anger builds again and I fail to contain it in my face. My father puts his hand up as if to placate me, but all I see is his authority.

"Go tend to your chores," he commands. "We'll speak of this later."

I comply, finishing my meager meal before venturing out into the brisk autumn air. The chill breeze is the only solace from the hours of toil that lie ahead. I commence the day's labor by pouring thick, unappetizing gruel into the troughs for the livestock. I then join my father, and we turn our attention to the fields, our backs hunched under the weight of our duty, our hands soiled by the dirt. The hours slip into one another as the harsh rigors of our farm work take their toll.

As the sun begins its descent, casting shadows over the land we call our home, I wrestle with the plow that has become an extension of my very being. I suddenly hear a harsh and unforgiving sound cleave the air – the breaking of wood, long wearied by time and toil, succumbs at last to its final strain. The plow, its structure compromised by mildew and damp, lies broken and defeated. With a heavy heart, I convey the ill news to my father, which he acknowledges with a nod. We return to the homestead in silence, our bodies weary and our minds distraught.

Some time later, I find my father seated at our dining table, his face etched with lines of worry and fatigue. He motions for me to join him, and I do, my curiosity in tow.

"My boy," he begins, his voice heavy with an unspoken burden. "The farm, this life of uncertainty and hardship… it is not your destiny Son," he continues. "I believe it's time we discussed the future. The look in your eyes tells me you're ready to hear this. My shoe trade is no longer sustainable. It will fade away, just as your dear mother did." His voice is barely above a whisper. "The farm is facing a similar fate. The plow today rendered its verdict. We will sell the farm. In its current state, it will go for but a few measly gulden, so we will need to improve it for a sale. It may take some time, but it will sell."

He rises, and I rise with him.

"I hope you find this welcome news. With the money made on the sale of our farm and our remaining inventory, you and I will move to Munich. We will work as factory men. I have already received correspondence indicating our acceptance. I will work in the shoe factory, and you will be my apprentice."

I swallow my surprise and stand alert, careful not to reveal my jubilation. This news is indeed welcome. It is glorious.

"If all goes according to plan, we will celebrate at the Oktoberfest autumn festival this time next year." A soft smile extends on his face. "We may even find you a wife there, for as you are most likely aware, there are scant women to choose from here."

He holds out his hand, and we share a strong embrace. My father is a man for the future after all, and factory men we shall be, leaving the land upon which we have toiled like slaves and paupers to the machines.

"My boy, I make you a solemn promise," he says. "You will become who you are truly meant to be."

Part 2: Year 2023 – Financial Famine

Guesswork. That's all financial statistics are. Just a fancy name for guessing. In a world where most financial figures are estimations and an estimation is just a synonym for guessing, everyone's a glorified fucking fortune teller. It's all a bullshit guessing game, from government bureaucrats to finance tycoons, all the way through to the teacher grading your kid's first business management project.

Don't believe me? Look at last year's GDP. Your government told you the economy grew last year? They're guessing. Those "actual" historic GDP figures? Revised again and again, five years into the future. Our German government says the economy grew by two-point-five percent last year and predict a slowdown this year. The "actual" figure for 2023? Another fucking guess. If the past can change, the whole system can be a Ponzi scheme of estimation.

Now, real estate valuation reports? That's a guessing game of epic proportions. They make it look all scientific, but in reality it's just a bunch of estimation and approximation, grossly inflated with optimistic growth assumptions, and rarely, if ever, right.

I should know, I'm a financial analyst working for a large real estate investment company and have to translate this bullshit into data every quarter.

Derrick interrupts my ruminations, waddling over. His small stature stands at my desk, his eyes scanning my work as his tiny hands poke at my screen. "I assume the inputs will be done today." The asshole's anxiety is palpable. He knows the results are shit and there's no way he'll be able to hide them.

"I think so," I say.

He frowns. "If anything is stopping you from completing the input this afternoon, call me," he says. It's never a request with this prick, it's a command.

"Yeah, I'll be done with the input today," I say. "I just need to triple-check against the valuation data from the reports."

"Wonderful!" he says, patting my computer terminal. "I will probably not return from lunch." He gives me his usual pompous grin and taps my chair. "Have a nice weekend."

Derrick won't be back from lunch. He'll likely drown himself in beer and wine, followed by schnapps. I smell it on him. It's become his pathetic, daily routine. Do I feel sorry for him? Not a chance. It was only a matter of time before karma caught up with that bullshit guesstimating schmuck.

It'll be good to be without his presence reminding me that I'm just his number cruncher, a tool he uses and a tool he so can easily discard. The jerk told me I might be getting laid off, and then had the audacity to ask me to finish my work before the weekend. It was yet another guess, but when your boss tells you the company is downsizing and you might lose your job, that's not an estimate but a foregone conclusion.

Derrick has built a career on guessing. He's your quintessential old-school real estate phony. Nothing more than a "have a hunch, bet a bunch" hack. Any sensible grad of his generation would have chosen engineering, but he was probably too stupid to do the math himself and found a career that suited his shifty, salesy style in real estate, then surfed the massive real estate boom for decades, his ego growing but his stupidity never waning.

No, I don't feel sorry for him. The market is exposing him for the bluffing, guesstimating fool he's always been. The proof is in the valuations I type in for him. Our company's real estate portfolio, made up predominantly by office buildings bought at height prices, declined by twenty percent this quarter. When you adjust for the company's outstanding debt, the numbers are even worse. The composite number is just another estimate, and a generous one at that. I'd bet our portfolio holdings are down much more.

The proof is in the state of our own office today. It's a ghost town. The Covid pandemic freed the prisoners from their cages. People realized they didn't need to commute, didn't need to leave their homes and neighborhoods to sit in sterile office buildings. Now very few come into the office, especially on Fridays. Instead, they're tethered to the world by their screens and devices. Unfortunately, at my salary level, I live in a shoebox room with awful wi-fi and don't have the luxury. So, I come here and work in what feels like an unpopular museum, a relic of a once-bustling environment.

At least it offers free coffee and pastries. With my measly salary and current inflation levels, I can't afford to buy shit in this expensive city.

My phone pings an alert. It's a message from one of my friend groups, sharing a meme. I was hoping it was Linda. I met her last week online, and she agreed to meet me tonight, but she hasn't responded since to confirm. Ghosted again. I hate online dating. Just as tech has given my office colleagues options for where to work, it has also given Linda more options for who to date.

I set my phone down and go back to work. Drake's new album plays loudly from my computer speakers as I manually type details from the valuation report into Derrick's spreadsheet. It's a mindless task, but it relaxes me. I type out '23,432,453' into a cell corresponding to a valuation next to an asset address on the east side of Leipzig and then a corresponding '1,114,042' number for its associated gross income. The spreadsheet computes a set of numbers that I validate from the report, including a value decline of twenty-nine-point-five percent versus the asset's previous valuation. I repeat this process numerous times. There has to be a better way to do this. The industry is stuck in the dark ages; the fact that my manual tasks cannot be streamlined with simple technology is case in point.

A buzz from my phone breaks the monotony. It's Derrick. His message is short but clear: I'm now officially unemployed. The coward had the audacity to fire me via text, delivering a gut punch from a safe distance. Just before the weekend and after, he presumes, I finished his work. The message hangs there on the screen like a *Game Over* sign in uncaring pixels. I stare at the message in silence, wondering what to do next. I could, in a desperate move, reach out to my father and throw myself at the mercy of his wallet. But fat chance that will ever happen! After his divorce from my mother, he has been pilfering what used to be my future inheritance into the maintenance of the plastic succubus that he calls his new girlfriend. The only asset we have left is an old farm up north. To hell with it, I think, maybe I can become a farmer?

Another buzz from my phone. It's Max asking if I can meet him at Oktoberfest. This is the distraction that I need. I'll consider my issues another day. I haven't told Max about Linda, so I agree, my pride intact. The alternative is spending the evening alone in my apartment, a wasteland of disinterest amid my growing depression, staring at a TV screen flickering with mind-numbing drivel. This modern era of endless content creation is a paradox that rarely succeeds in creating anything of interest. An abundance of streamers, channels, subscriptions – yet scraps of anything worth my time. Supposedly, they have algorithms designed to get you hooked. Ironic, I guess. I find my attention diverted by thirty-second clips from dancing teenagers. An AI company's supposedly developing auto-generated content, tailored to your likes and dislikes. It means that, in the near future, I could curate my own entertainment, reflecting my mood in real time. Now that's a prospect!

I leave my desk for the last time. After a brisk walk past tourists and locals dressed in Oktoberfest attire, I arrive at the beer hall. Max has chosen the Hofbrau tent for its ease of entry, having palmed small wads of cash to the bouncers. Two large steins hold court in front of him and he gestures for me to take one.

"Happy you could make it," he says. "I thought you were busy."

I shrug my shoulders. Whatever. I'll play it cool. No need for him to know I've been ignored by Linda.

"I need a wingman tonight." He gives me one of his naughty smiles, pulling out his phone to show me messages from his online dating app. "I have a few ladies lined up."

My stomach tightens. I hope Linda isn't one of them. Max flashes screenshots of the women he's agreed to meet tonight. Relief is found when I learn that thankfully Linda is not among them.

"Two of them are just in town for the Oktoberfest, but these two here are local," he says as he swipes between photos. "Let's see who shows up."

I smile, thinking that this night might not be lost after all.

"Playing the odds as usual," I say. He's always been a player.

My phone buzzes with an alert. I find a message from my online recruiter app.

We are pleased to share excellent news, it reads. *Your application for the AI Data Analyst position at Byrell Industries has been accepted.*

Hell yeah! I smile as happiness washes over me.

"Max, I got the job!"

"The tech one?"

"Yeah, yeah!"

"Prost!" He raises his stein in celebration.

I raise mine and down the contents in large gulps, excited about what this new job will mean for my future. I'm finally leaving behind manual data analysis – that's for the past. I'm stepping into the future.

"No more grunt analyst work for idiots," I tell Max. I'm finally becoming who I was meant to be.

Part 3: Year 2198 – Rebirth of Our Past

The return journey home from Munich takes no longer than fifteen minutes, courtesy of the Global Hyperloop Network. I spend the journey gazing at the electronic advertisements projected on to the glass to distract me from the fact that we're hurtling at over five hundred kilometers per hour through a vacuum tube beneath the earth's surface.

"How are you feeling?" I ask my brother, who's seated next to me. The paleness of his face reveals the answer before he can voice it.

"My head's pounding and my stomach's churning," he says. "I swear – I won't drink beer ever again."

His response brings a smile to my face, as I feel the effects of the alcohol heavy and drowsy in my system. "Until next year," I say.

This Oktoberfest marked a year since I last drank alcohol. The consumption of beer is a focal point of the festival, a tradition I cherish, despite the toll it takes on my system. Oktoberfest remains my favorite, one of the few truly German traditions untouched over the last century, remaining a festival where young people can meet and socialize in large beer tents amidst boisterous music and wild abandon. The only modern concession is its year-long running schedule, segmented by region to allow for global tourist traffic. Our region of Bavaria still gets special treatment, with our access granted during the traditional weeks of late September to early October. It's there you can find authentic German women, not the global cross-section of the world's tourists flocking to the fest. It's an opportunity to meet genuine people, not the bots and virtual frauds that continue to populate the metaverse. Real flesh-and-blood Germans.

"Did you take the wellness pill?" I ask and he nods.

"Then you will feel better by the time we get back to the farm."

He laughs loudly, tickled by the alcohol. "It's so funny you call it the farm."

Ignoring the comment, I give him a hearty slap on the back. "We had a great time. It was worth it," I say. "You seemed to really enjoy yourself."

"Do you think you will see the blonde again?" he asks, studying my face.

"Kim? We are already messaging."

He provides a short-lived smile. I know the look. He's disappointed with himself again. This will mark the third Oktoberfest where he left without finding a match.

"Don't worry, brother. Plenty of time for you to meet women next year."

He shakes his head. "I just don't know what to say sometimes."

"That's natural. You're young. You'll find your courage. Let it take time."

I message Kim to say I enjoyed our meeting, and her avatar – a fully life-like rendering of her person – winks back. I sigh, my fondness growing. I can't wait to see her again. It has been a while since I've met a woman outside the metaverse that I truly had a connection with, and I'm excited to see where this newfound attraction could lead.

My brother squints at me and pouts. "Can you please not meld her while we are talking? It is quite rude."

I apologize for the distraction and promise the virtual image of Kim that I'll signal her later. She air-kisses the front of my retinas and signs off.

"So, what do you want to do tomorrow?" I ask my brother, who appears to be scanning something through his eyeballs.

"Oh shit, I almost forgot," he says.

He mumbles words I don't understand, catching only a few phrases. He's probably rescheduling one of his designer meetings. His latest shoe design is in collaboration with a famous Malaysian shoemaker. I hear their early morning virtual sessions most days.

"All done," he says, his vision refocused to me.

I lie back and close my eyes, feeling the wellness pill dissolving the alcohol in my bloodstream. The journey is taking longer than scheduled. The hyperloop has been lagging of late, reportedly due to small wind holes appearing in the tube polymer lining. I pray it doesn't get worse, or we'll have to suffer more scheduled maintenance and be forced to travel overground by air or land, both fraught with lengthy lines and uncomfortable seating.

We exit the tube cubicle and arrive on a small platform with two other groups, acknowledging each other with nods. One of the men I recognize as our neighbor, Maxwell, who lives three farms away. I signal him to schedule a poker night in a week's time and he responds with schedule commitment through our shared virtual calendars. The platform emits a soft *ding* and we are shot upwards through a long, dark shaft to the surface of the station. Despite the coldness in the air, the autumn weather is pleasant, and I have no need to vacuum-seal my jacket as we await our lift.

"And what will you do tomorrow?" my brother asks, shoving his hands into his pockets.

"I'll tend to the fields," I say, "like I always do."

Our ride home passes countless steads over the next half hour. Each stead carries similar characteristics as the rest: a few acres of land containing a home and any other accessory decided by the owner. Our plot is located deep within this vast stead-field, which itself was converted from nationalized farmland and fractionalized for independent ownership at the turn of the century. I inherited our plot less than five years ago when I turned eighteen, and my brother will have the option to have his stead, only a few kilometers away, when he comes of age. For now, he lives with me, as our parents left Earth many years ago.

My thoughts turn back to my brother, beset by worry. He is still undecided about his final vocation. I hope he chooses shoe design, as it would keep him nearby. I pray he doesn't choose space exploration or, worse, that he isn't enlisted as a colonist as part of the Earth Population Control Act. The thought of losing him to the endless expanse of space, following in the footsteps of our departed parents' generation, fills me with grief.

I consider melding with my father but decide against it. The last time we spoke resulted in another argument about their choice to leave us, and my serotonin is still too depleted from the alcohol for another exchange.

We arrive at the stead just as our week's supply delivery is being offloaded. The robot slides back into its vehicle and gestures a warm goodbye before leaving for the next farm. I receive a data packet from the service about an extra serving of fertilizer they provided to aid with the changing weather. I make a note in my schedule to spread it tomorrow as part of my morning chores.

As we enter our home, my brother announces that he's going upstairs to watch a show. "Don't wait up for me," he says.

"No dinner?" I ask.

"Not hungry."

I understand his need to be alone. He's a teenager, suffering from emotions he has yet to understand. I consider messaging him with older-brother advice. He's still young and there is plenty of time. He'll find a match. I want to tell him that I too went through the same; it's not easy meeting women in real life. His social skills will improve. Instead, I ask my AI therapist for advice. *Leave him be*, it responds, and I comply.

I signal Kim, asking for a mind-meld. She says she is busy but asks to meld tomorrow night, suggesting her favorite entertainment hall in Italy. She flirtatiously previews her an image avatar's outfit for the occasion: a sleek dress accentuating her feminine features. I resist the urge to say I long for her physical touch, and avoid the faux-pas of expressing old-world lusting. I can't help but think back to the way Kim looked in her dirndl, with her ample bosom bursting. I shiver in anticipation for our next physical meeting, whenever she decides its time again to meet in the real world. Instead, I will make do with the meld tomorrow. I make a note to my AI to create an avatar outfit suitable for tomorrow's occasion. I then ask my bank service to schedule a distribution from the nationalized wealth fund for tomorrow morning. Virtual travel to Italy is not expensive, but I have not budgeted for it, and the trip, alongside my new avatar clothing, will require some additional spend. The bank replies with affirmation.

After consuming my evening meal, consisting of a porridge-like goulash made of fresh vegetables from the farm, I settle into bed. My brother is upstairs in his room, likely engaging with an avatar concubine to salve his bruised ego. I signal a request to my AI valet, seeking a film to suit my current mood. It chooses a historical documentary, replete with custom-tailored, auto-generated content.

"For tens of thousands of years, humanity tilled the soil as farmers, before the industrial transformation of the nineteenth century," the narrative voice commences, as a bespoke bird's eye view of a primordial Bavarian landscape engulfs my vision. I glide as an eagle might, sweeping over the expansive fields unscarred by the touch of machinery.

The film's content is rendered with such finesse that it's nothing short of astounding. The technology, operating in tandem with my personal AI steward, subtly monitors my subconscious movements and responds in real time. The interaction is so seamless that it is barely noticeable, its output virtually indistinguishable from traditional human creative entertainment, yet superior in so many ways, devoid of the extraneous clutter and misguided diversions that typically mar human productions. Although I occasionally indulge in traditionally created products, I find myself less and less inclined to do so.

As I take in the movie, I think about tomorrow, feeling the weight of sleep on my eyelids. I must rise early, before the dawn, to work the fields and tend to my crops. I will prepare food for the service to distribute to my neighbors and will receive their services in return. Come evening, I will join Kim in the virtual rendition of Italy, where we will dance the night away.

I find profound contentment in being a farmer. This work offers me tranquility, a clarity of purpose. I find understanding in this life. I am exactly who I was meant to be.

Kundalini Yoga

"If the universe is infinite, then anything that is not only possible, but probable, has already happened."
– attributed to Douglas Adams

"The universe is under no obligation to make sense to you."
– Neil deGrasse Tyson

IN A COSMIC mishap which was equal parts remarkable and ironic, Mark White was thrust into a separate universe while attending an evening kundalini yoga class on an ordinary Tuesday night in the middle of November. He unexpectedly departed his comfortable and known surroundings and entered a wholly new and uncertain place while lying face-up on a blue oval-shaped mat that he had moments before unrolled on the floor of a yoga studio located a few blocks away from his small apartment. The sudden journey happened without his knowledge and under the cover of the reverberations created by a small bamboo mallet struck against a fifteen-inch copper chau gong.

The mallet was wielded by a yoga instructor – a short, thin woman. Just before commencing the rhythmic beating of the gong, she told the class, in the usual manner, that sound waves create energy. "They can take you to other worlds."

Mark closed his eyes and began breathing slowly. In. Hold. Out. Hold.

"Ride the spiritual waves," she instructed the class in the usual soft and calming manner.

Mark considered himself a hard-nosed realist, itself an ironic observation, as it was in stark contrast to how others viewed him as a socially inept recluse. He trusted in logic and science, nothing more, nothing less. He was aware of the scientific evidence supporting the benefits of regulated breathing – it lowered blood pressure, enhanced focus, reduced anxiety, and could even induce a sense of euphoria if practiced long enough. However, he was doubtful of the yoga teacher's extravagant claims. Her bamboo mallet would create sound waves useful in meditation, but he was skeptical about the formation of any other energy, especially in wave form. The idea of riding these waves, either literally or metaphorically, seemed preposterous to him. He also dismissed the idea that these waves could transport him to another realm.

He was, of course, very wrong.

The exact moment of his literal transportation to another world happened sometime between the first gong reverberation and the last minor tinkle. His journey was unnoticed. He experienced no jolt or sensation of falling between realities. The dimensional skipping was instant and devoid of color, taste, sound, or feeling. The only hints to a shift in his surroundings were a subtle change to the incense smell permeating the studio and the slight hardening of the floor below him, both of which he failed to register at the time.

After the last chime faded into a prolonged silence, Mark opened his eyes. He was presented with four immediate clues to his circumstance.

The first was that he no longer felt a yoga mat between him and the floor. In fact, there was no yoga mat at all.

The second was the way the last chime sounded. It was deeper somehow and rested larger in his eardrums. The vibration was louder than before and it felt unnaturally bombastic and menacing as it lingered in his inner ears, bouncing between his ossicles like a guest overstaying its welcome.

The third clue was that the small, thin yogi holding the gong was now a large, heavy-set woman with an awkwardly shaped head from which sprung red strands of hair. This woman was also holding a gong. Mark was surprised by this replacement, struggling to understand how or why it would happen. The woman looked at him and violently jerked her hand back, dropping her mallet with a speed Mark found strikingly unnatural.

The final clue to his strange predicament was the arrangement and make-up of the people around him. Prior to his transportation, the room had contained six participants, including Mark and the yogi. The other members included a bald man, who had placed his mat too close to Mark's and offered an apology in the usual manner, a young Indian woman clad in tight-fitting clothing to his left, and a young couple, whose features he had not taken any time to notice. The room now contained many more people. In addition to Mark, the red-haired yogi, and what appeared to be an Indian woman clad in tight-fitting clothing, now to his right, the class was nearly full.

Despite these peculiarities, Mark remained pragmatic amid his growing unease. He ran through various scenarios and settled on one that satisfied him: that he had dozed off and slept through an entire class and into the following practice. The participants of the prior kundalini yoga class had seen him sleeping soundly and decided to leave him. He found that people usually left him alone, rarely offered any real interaction. Perhaps someone had pulled his yoga mat from underneath him as he slept to use themselves? As for the delusions, perhaps his deep meditative slumber had produced a toxic cocktail of serotonin and dopamine, increasing cerebral blood flow to his prefrontal cortex, which, upon awakening, had caused a minor psychotic episode, complete with derealization and hallucination. Yes, he thought, this was the only logical and reasonable explanation for his current circumstance. The conclusion satisfied him and he hoped the mood disturbance was temporary.

He was, of course, very wrong about this as well.

He had not slumbered, like his version of Rip Van Winkle, into another yoga class. His transference to another dimension happened while he was wide awake, and the gong session had produced only a very mild sedative experience, one that could be described as somewhat relaxing. He was also not hallucinating. His sensory functions were firmly intact and working just fine. His hope that these disturbances were temporary was also flawed. This was all very real and all very permanent.

As the lights in the studio flickered to life, a strange sensation began to grow in him. It was as though a part of him had simply vanished into thin air, leaving a profound loneliness, and an unsettling feeling that something wasn't right. The light shone through the stale studio air in deep, thick strands, their viscous ribbons practically tangible as they collided with his retinas. His lungs struggled against an unseen barrier and he struggled to find breath.

His gaze wandered to the young Indian woman in tight-fitting clothing. An innate sense of dread told him she was not the same Indian woman clad in tight-fitting clothing that he saw before the gongs began to resound. There was a dark void in her. Her clothing was different – harsher and rougher, somehow. Her gaze, devoid of any discernible emotion, bore into him with an intensity that seemed... altered. His glance nervously swept over the other occupants of the room. Each was marred by disfigurement, an unnerving savagery etched into their features.

With a harsh jolt, the Indian woman in tight-fitting clothing stood quickly, leaving her mat. She darted toward the exit, her legs pumping in quick, frenzied succession, propelling her lean form toward the doorway with the unsettling grace of a massive insect skittering across the room's expanse. The remaining occupants rose with collective abruptness, their mats rolled with a savagery that echoed the frenzy of wild creatures shredding the earth beneath them. They fled in equal haste, their movements punctuated by sporadic bursts of unnerving agility.

He lingered in isolated stillness, studying the red-haired yogi packing her items. Her movements were disjointed, as though she were suffering from involuntary spasms. She slammed her items into her bag with such force and speed that flecks of dust shot through the air. Her head snapped in his direction, her face glaring. He immediately looked away. She was oddly unhuman. Her eyes were grotesque, too large for her face and sat unnervingly high on her small forehead. She exuded a distant coldness, her eyes menacing in a way he couldn't describe. Her body was shaped in a revolting manner, her waistline protruded horribly, as if it housed some massive, writhing creature within. He trained his gaze at the floor until her alien noises faded and he was certain she had left the studio.

Left alone, Mark finally rose. The unfamiliar sensation within him had grown, intensified by some unknown evolution. It pulled and thrashed within him, creating a longing that he had not known existed. He began to hear distant, ghostly sounds in his mind, echoes carried on frequencies he didn't know existed. His thoughts spoke to him in languages previously unheard, their voices spectral and urgent. Profound and bizarre ideas – thousands of them – assailed him from all directions.

Fighting against his growing horror and confusion, he cautiously made his way to the reception area. His bare feet felt heavy against the floor and his movements seemed restricted by noticeably denser air. Everything around him was illuminated in abnormal shades of color from an unfamiliar spectrum he didn't know existed. Small particles tickled his throat when he breathed. He stood in the hallway and searched for his footwear. They were not where he'd left them. The furniture in which he recalled storing his footwear was not there at all, replaced instead with an unfamiliar furniture design, made of substances he had never seen before.

He turned to the reception desk. The man behind the counter rapidly punched stubby fingers at an oddly shaped contraption and emitted harsh, guttural hisses. Gathering courage, Mark approached the counter. The man stopped his spasmodic attack on the contraption and looked up. Mark recoiled instantly, terror seizing him at the sight of the man's eyes. In close proximity, they were even more horrifying – enlarged and stretched, encased in dark, inky rings that framed small, oddly hued orbs at the core. They emitted nothing familiar, only a frigid, vacant stare. Everything about the man was foreign. His clothing was peculiar, with loose threads sewn in long, thin strands. The man's head was thick with follicles and grease, pushed askew in a queer manner and plastered against his abnormally small forehead. His chin was filled with coarse strands of hair, fraying in various directions, resembling tiny serpents jutting out from his chin and jugular.

Mark attempted to engage, but he was met with harsh, erratic breathing. The man's grating hisses seemed to scrape against the very fibers of Mark's eardrums; understanding anything was a futile endeavor. Disturbed, Mark turned away and maneuvered through the room, his heart pounding. Beads of sweat formed on his forehead as he confronted a motley gathering in the foyer. They were dressed in peculiar attire adorned with vivid and oddly attached accessories on their faces, necks, and hands. Each had grossly distended abdomens and their shrunken heads were covered in thick, greasy fiber. Mark struggled to avoid the eerie gazes cast from their bulbous, swollen eyes.

Emerging from this grotesque ensemble was a towering woman, her scalp crowned by a mound of thick, black rope. The indifference in her eyes was chilling. They held a vacant blue hue at their center that left Mark perplexed. Mark felt nothing but apathy from her; a nothingness that he couldn't understand. She abruptly lunged toward him, her lips drawn against her cheeks, exposing saliva-slicked daggers inside.

Mark instinctively pushed her away. At a safe distance, Mark tried once more to communicate with the creature. In response, she furrowed her greasy brow, causing her forehead to wrinkle, and her eyes narrowed into thin slits on her weathered face, a face so evil and menacing that Mark could no longer suppress his terror.

It was then that Mark began to scream.

Mark sped past the gaping crowd and ran into the cold street outside, nearly colliding with an imposing silhouette. He backpedaled, his eyes wide as he took in the ambiguous figure. Thankfully, the figure paid no notice, transfixed by a glowing light in his grasp.

Cold raindrops fell like tiny missiles from the sky, splashing loudly on the sidewalk as they pooled in large, milky clumps. Mark stepped over the puddles of sitting rainwater, working hard to move against a thick wall of air that resisted his body. He avoided the mindless, cold stares of passers-by as they sped past him. Many stared into small boxes they carried as they walked, hypnotized by the strange lights beaming from within. He felt no empathy from any of them, either; they were just like the others – cold, empty, and listless.

Mark walked, shivering. The chaos and horror had triggered a screaming voice in his head, reaching the peak of its crescendo. Nearly paralyzed by anxiety, he stumbled dizzily along the sidewalk, forcing himself to concentrate his mind on the water droplets cascading down his face. Alien sounds, ideas, and visions bombarded his mind relentlessly. He felt himself being sucked away into a vast, swirling vortex in his mind, a tumultuous whirlpool of senses and feelings. Amid this sensory overload, he began to see himself from a distance, not as a single entity, but as a mosaic of endless possibilities, each one a different facet of what he might become or might have been – a fragmentation of self that threatened to dissolve his very essence.

Suddenly, Mark was struck by a vibrant glow emanating from a nearby shop window. Through the window, he found the source of the light – a large box containing three people, all dressed in strange clothing, each with horrendously shrunken foreheads. Their communication was a series of rapid-fire hisses that left Mark bewildered.

Without warning, the people in the box disappeared, replaced by a solitary man standing on a large stage, his large, bulging torso wrapped in shining blue fabric and a thick red scarf hanging from his throat. He had a mess of wild yellow hair reaching out from a grotesquely round face smeared with a color he had never seen before. His eyes – large, dark, and elongated – shone with intimidating fury. Mark watched in silent horror as the man in the box performed a series of erratic, forceful motions, his mouth foamed with a vile liquid which sprayed as he moved his lips. The man's voice was an incomprehensible barrage of hisses, their menacing rhythm sending fear down Mark's spine.

Mark suddenly heard strange noises behind him. Turning to peer through the pouring rain, he saw a figure approach with a startling quickness; an abnormally long arm jutted out from the figure's cloak. The figure delivered a bone-chilling shriek before lunging at Mark, the force sending him reeling backwards. Driven by sheer terror, Mark turned and sprinted down the street, his vision compromised by the driving rain. He dared not turn back to look.

A distance away, fatigue soon set in. Exhausted by the full-tilt sprint, his pace slowed. His lungs ached from the heavy air, and as the adrenaline subsided, his entire body shivered uncontrollably from the cold wind penetrating his wet clothing. Mark felt a sensation grow within him, that of a rabid monster yearning to alleviate an intense foreign suffering, desperately tearing at its insides. He paused; his breath ragged as he surveyed the street behind him. It was eerily vacant.

Fighting against a continuous internal torrent of unknown concepts and bizarre thoughts, Mark turned a corner and walked cautiously down a smaller street where he found another shop window. As before, a crude, sallow light shone from within. Despite his better judgment, he dared a glance inside. Entities were huddled in clusters, hovering around bizarre contraptions of furnishings, wielding small, sharpened weapons. Their movements were unnervingly disjointed, as if manipulated by a frenzied puppeteer. Some darted from table to table, while others sat, stabbing at objects before them. Mark's gaze fell upon the seated figures, his eyes dilating in terror at the gruesome panorama unfolding.

A seated man, with a sinister air of nonchalance, skewered what looked like the remains of an expired being, sprawled in a grotesque display on the table. With the sharpened tool, he guided the morsel to his mouth, ingesting it whole. As Mark's horrified gaze traveled to the other tables, he felt his stomach churn at the sight of a barbaric feast in progress. The unnerving creatures were indulging in a horrifying banquet of unspeakable horrors.

Mark watched, frozen in disgust, as one of the barbarians impaled another victim, the poor thing cut from its vine. The creature lifted plundered tissue into its gaping mouth. Mark watched as internal organs dribbled out from the foul monster's lips as it chewed.

These couldn't be humans. The creatures looked humanesque, but no human could possibly engage in such abhorrent acts. The atrocities he witnessed plunged Mark into a deeper state of revulsion and disgust.

He turned and ran. It was the only thing he could think to do. Devoid of any of his usual senses, he ran mindlessly on. He didn't know where he was running to, but he knew he wanted to get away from the horrors of the shop he left behind. With tears of grief in his eyes, tears he had not felt in many years, he looked around at his surroundings. He hoped desperately that he would somehow find the doorstep to his apartment. He yearned to get out from the cold, whereafter he would perhaps sleep away this nightmare and start the next day in the same way as the previous one. Seeing nothing familiar that would lead him home, he ran, then jogged, and finally walked barefoot in the dampness and the coldness of a peculiar world for hours.

He was convinced he had lost his sanity. It was the only logical explanation. The rain was real. The chill was real. The monsters he had witnessed all seemed real. The pain inside of him, now unbearable, felt all too real. The bizarre thoughts encircling his mind, didn't leave him. The only possible explanation was that his brain had completely disconnected from reality; he was most certainly insane.

Mark was, once again, very wrong.

His sanity remained very much intact. He simply found himself in a different dimension. His confusion was perfectly understandable, of course; dimensional skipping was an extraordinarily rare temporal occurrence, rarely witnessed within the vast expanse of time and space. Unfortunately, there was no user manual offering explanation and no history to look upon for guidance. Only beings equipped with faculties to grasp the complexities of the sixth dimension could possibly understand what had occurred – capabilities that Mark lacked.

Upon entering this new dimension, Mark was overwhelmed by insight into a time-space construct he had not previously known existed. This torrent of concepts, which included non-linear time, simultaneous realities, and a disintegration causality and sense of self, imposed a cognitive and emotional burden so immense, that it overloaded his senses, plunging him into profound confusion.

To add to his turmoil, the place Mark had been transported to was one with substantially similar laws of physics to his own. Many natural laws mirrored those of his realm, resulting in a false sense of familiarity; basic human form and cognition thrived here. Regrettably for Mark, significant discrepancies were also present. Were Mark familiar with this dimension's foundations and the complex biological construct of it, he would have understood that elemental particles were fractionally larger by a factor of 1.00034x. Consequently, this minute biological variance had engendered an evolutionary trajectory whereby humanity formed not from the plant-based photosynthetic humanoid of his reality, but from carnivorous mammals.

Moreover, he would have grasped the incongruent biological laws that precluded any avenues for emotional telepathy among living organisms in this dimension. Here, the local iteration of humanity had forged intricate oratory and physical communication systems void of Mark's usual manner of empathic projection and the other emotional and cognitive states Mark was accustomed to.

He would have understood the rationale for his sluggishness amid the swift-moving organisms of this world – a burden imposed by the weightier biological factors that governed his existence. His bodily functions differed, subjecting him to a decelerated pace amidst counterparts possessed of greater agility and vitality.

Furthermore, he would have learned that his customary sustenance, derived through the absorption of glucose and acids from the atmosphere, proved unattainable in this dimension and the unfamiliar internal sensation he was feeling was, in fact, hunger. He would have understood that the construct of this realm dictated that humans, along with myriad other animal forms, relied on a complex digestive system to break down nutrients for survival. He might have come to appreciate that the seemingly barbaric acts of mindless cruelty he witnessed were, in fact, essential for the survival of numerous lifeforms in this dimension.

Armed with any element of this knowledge, he may have had a chance for survival, but without these simple variables being known to him, Mark was left with a confounding sense of dread and confusion as he slowly starved to death. Alone with his thoughts and without any sense of empathy from the world around him, for the first time in his life, Mark yearned for faith. He pleaded with the universe for help.

The universe, as always, offered nothing in return.

The mammal-descendant human beings of the dimension to which Mark was sent were perplexed by the odd behavior exhibited by a spectacularly peculiar man.

Attending her weekly Tuesday evening kundalini class, Anajali Kerna, a young Indian woman clad in tight-fitting Lycra pants kneeled on her yoga mat and opened her eyes to find there was a man lying next to her. She thought it odd; she had not noticed his arrival, which must have taken place sometime during the gong ceremony. She found this stranger so unsettling that she hurried out of the studio, forgetting her yoga mat.

The class's yoga instructor, Martha Johnson, finished her gong ceremony and was equally surprised to see a previously vacant space replaced by a very strange-looking bald man. She eyed him cautiously as he stared intensely with shrunken blank white eyes, which were set disturbingly low below his massive bulging forehead. She fled the room to report the alarming experience to the studio's manager.

Minutes later, Paul Swank was scrolling through his computer terminal, puzzled by Martha's report. According to the class register, Martha's class had thirteen participants, not fourteen. He was interrupted by a bizarre, skeletal albino man with a horrendously concave stomach, ambling toward him. The man moved as if he were pushing against an unseen current. He approached the counter in slow, fluid steps and glared at Paul with shrunken white buttons in place of his eyes. Paul cautiously offered his assistance; to his surprise, the man turned away, making slow-moving fluid motions with his arms. He watched the man make his way through the foyer and, for a moment, although the man's bare feet were on the ground, Paul swore he saw him swimming through the air.

Beth Darby witnessed the spectacle at the front desk, and attempted to calm the stranger, who appeared in significant distress. She confronted the panicked individual, and tried to comfort him with a smile, asking him if she could help. To the shock and bemusement of the others in the room, the man bellowed out with a deep, baritone howl, which sounded like something between a bull mooing and a long underwater whale call. Beth let the man pass, disturbed by the seemingly inhuman nature of what she witnessed.

Outside the yoga studio, Edward Pickler was nearly knocked down by a strange person as he followed his phone map in search of his hotel. The shoeless man paced down the street in slow motion, raindrops spraying out over a thin translucent sheet covering him, as if the cloth rejected their advances.

A few moments later, Martin Sherin approached a shoeless man in pouring rain in front of an electronics shop, thinking him to be homeless. The man stood motionless and stared at a television set inside, which broadcast a recap of the US president's State of the Union address. Martin attempted to offer his umbrella, only to be met with an odd low growl emanating from somewhere deep within the eccentric man's core. He watched in awe as the bald man with tiny beady eyes pushed away from him in slow motion and ambled away, reminding him of a performing street mime.

Later that evening, patrons of Zaffino's enjoyed the restaurant's vegan take on Tuscan cuisine. A few noticed a man staring wildly at them through the window, making odd gasping expressions. They ignored the crazed voyeur. He was gone within a few minutes. A few shook their heads at the spectacle, lamenting the growing homelessness problem in the city.

Early Wednesday morning, Officer Bart Rafferty responded to an unusual call. He parked his vehicle on a quiet residential street where the odd, white, middle-aged male in question was last sighted. He watched the figure of a bald male standing alone on the sidewalk in the dark hours just before dawn, a time when virtue hides and desperation reigns. Despite temperatures dropping to near freezing, the man appeared virtually naked, clothed only by a thin translucent sheet covering his violently frail body. Bart's mind immediately went to the hallucinogen epidemic. The light from an overhead streetlamp illuminated the man's head, making it appear large and bulbous, resembling an alien caricature popular in the 1960s media. Bart remained in his vehicle, watching the figure slowly motion in odd waves. Bart tapped his fingers over his holster. Whatever mental state the man was in, Bart would proceed with caution. Just before reaching for his door handle, he crossed himself and said a short prayer.

The universe in turn, neither noticed, nor cared.

Unremarkable Man

"If we were immortal, we could be perfectly sure of seeing the day when everything has changed, when progress has stopped, when there is nothing left to us but ennui."
– Voltaire

THE ROCKY MOUNTAINS have always been a sanctuary for me – their crisp, cold air mingling with the splendor of towering peaks – they bring a certain serenity that seeps into your soul as you navigate their trails. There is a sense of peace you get from their vastness. You are humbled by their colossal size, and their ancient, enduring stature lays bare your own fleeting nature and insignificance, shrinking your ego to nothing.

Over the few last months, Lily had been insistent that we return to the Rockies, her pleas for a family vacation growing increasingly urgent. Our last trip was now a distant memory and she needed to return. Unfortunately, our daughter was busy with her computer sciences course at UC Berkeley, while our son – newly wed and ambitious – was climbing the corporate ladder at a growing medical sciences firm in Texas.

"Each to their own," Lily conceded, but not without imposing her will on to me. The hustle and bustle of Chicago life had worn her out, and she lamented her isolation since our children left. "David," she practically begged me, "I need this trip. I need you."

Though she had made the suggestion frequently since our move to Chicago and my appointment as a senior director of Northwestern Hospital, her tone suggested that this time it was not a request. A seriousness had set deep within her the last few years. Her laughter had become scarce, and a noticeable distance had begun to wedge between us. So, against my better judgment – considering my busy work schedule and anticipated promotion – I acquiesced. We packed for the trip like we once did in college: two large backpacks for the two of us.

"David, only one rule," she declared. "Your phone stays off. The hospital can manage without you for a few weeks."

The first couple of days we spent acclimating to the environment, walking along the lush, green trails around Saint Catherine's Chapel on the Rock. Years of commuting in Chicago had rendered our legs unaccustomed to the trails. We opted for shorter hikes near the lake, comforted by the soft grass underfoot and flat terrain. As we walked, I could see a semblance of the old Lily re-emerging amidst the soothing sway of towering trees. She began to share her frustrations about life in Chicago, her stalled teaching career, and her discontentment with city life.

"I need to be back here, David. This place, it breathes life into me. I'm not cut out for the city," she said. I could see her curl her lips as she spoke, twisting them like a flame dwindling under a gust of wind. "Do you remember our spontaneous weekend trips here?"

Back in college, we would often take trips into the Rockies. While others went to parties, we camped out under the stars. When our classmates took spring breaks down in Florida, we planned rigorous mountain treks.

"Well, the kids changed that," I remarked.

"Only slightly." She punched my arm playfully. "The kids loved our Rocky trips."

"They sure did, hon."

"Back when things were simpler." Her face fell and distance crept into her eyes. Then she brightened up and turned to me, her eyes twinkling with anticipation. "How do you think our grandchildren will look?"

"Hopefully, they'll take after you and not me – or the in-laws," I joked.

Before the kids were born, before my life became a whirlwind of balancing home and work delivering bundles of joy into the world, we walked these trails and dreamed of our future. We'd imagine our unborn children, their potential careers, their temperaments, though none of our predictions ever panned out. We found that comfort again as we reveled in the prospect of being grandparents.

"I hope we have five," she giggled, reminiscing about the joy of holding newborns. "I even miss the sleepless nights and constant smell of baby vomit."

I held back a joke. Sleepless nights and baby vomit just sounded like another day in the office.

"I have a crazy idea," Lily announced on the second day, her eyes gleaming with an enthusiasm that I hadn't seen in a while. "Let's move back to Colorado. The kids are gone; we have no reason to stay. Let's move back here."

"But if I get this promotion, we could afford a house in Aspen in a few years," I reasoned.

She held firm to her Midwest sensibilities. "We have enough money, David," she protested.

She shook her head, but I held my ground. It had taken me an entire career rising from maternity ward resident to my current position, and I was not about to give up the top job when it was finally within reach.

"Lily, in a few years, we'll be able to buy the house we always dreamed of retiring in."

"I don't care about any of that."

I could tell that she didn't think she was getting through to me.

"Just promise me that you'll think about it," she said as she stroked my arm and gave me a look I once couldn't resist, before age and complacency took over.

I nodded, hoping to placate her for the time being. But inwardly I knew I had no intention of abandoning my career at this pivotal point.

On our third day, we agreed to trek up to a clearing above Chasm Lake. The hike was familiar to us, one that we had made numerous times throughout the years, and Lily was especially excited to return to our treasured spot atop an elongated cliff above the mountain lake. The route up to the clearing was long and strenuous, enhanced by the heat of the August sun, periodically broken up by a soft pre-autumn breeze building between the mountains. After many hours of strained and wordless scaling of uneven terrain, we finally reached the clearing, our faces shiny with sweat and our lungs heaving from the thinned air.

We were not alone.

In the field of grass sat a solitary man, basking in the sunshine. The man sat cross-legged in the middle of the clearing, not too far from the tree that Lily and I had sat under many times over the course of the last few decades. He had on a thin blue t-shirt and tight-fitting jeans, and from a distance he appeared to be a young backpacker, but as we approached, he revealed himself to be roughly our age. He wore short curly brown hair which tugged at his scalp, and had a thin, angular face, reminiscent of a young Leonardo da Vinci. Lily strained her eyes and whispered to me.

"He looks so familiar. Is he famous?" she asked.

"How would I know?"

She rolled her eyes at my gruff demeanor, knowing full well that I barely had time for a family dinner, let alone anything to do with popular culture.

"He looks like the actor from *that* show."

"Well, that narrows it down," I joked and she playfully rolled her eyes again.

The man's face was tilted upwards toward the sky, his eyes closed to the vast canvas of Rocky peaks surrounding him. He seemed at peace, so I nudged Lily to move on, seeking to leave him undisturbed and return to our special spot in the clearing a little while later.

"Please stop and wait a moment," he called to us without opening his eyes. "I have a story to share with you."

I pulled my wife to move on, but she tugged back at me, and motioned for us to join him.

"Come on. My legs are tired," she whispered. "I can't place his face right now, but I bet you a million bucks he's famous."

I had no desire to listen to a stranger's story, much less from someone who looked like a solitary hippie meditating in the mountains, however, despite my silent protestations, she accepted the stranger's offer.

"Come on, David, where is your sense of adventure?"

We settled near him, and the man began without offering introduction or pleasantries.

"Please forgive any inaccuracies or omitted details – it's been a while since I last told this story. I might miss a few of the – shall we say – finer points along the way."

"No problem at all," my wife responded with her typical Midwest charm as she unpacked our lunches. She gave me a light-hearted look, which suggested she found him whimsical.

The man cleared his throat and began.

"At the center of this story is an unremarkable man who lived an unremarkable life. Like most people in this world, this man was a blip in the cosmic vastness of time and space, essentially nothing in the context of all humanity. His achievements were limited. He invented nothing. He sang no song that others would sing. He wrote no words that would inspire future generations. He lived unremarkably but it's not his life that makes him a worthy protagonist of this recitation, but his death and what happens after.

"The story begins with an unremarkable boy born to a loving household, filled with all of the things a young boy would want, especially love and care from his parents. He was given an unremarkable name, Peter, and he had no standout features or attributes to speak of. Peter had a presentable face, but he was not handsome. He was coordinated, but not athletic. He was neither popular nor shunned. He was intelligent, but not brilliant. He could be funny, but never flirted with hilarity. He was average, middle-of-the-road.

"Peter did have one trait, however, that stood out beyond his otherwise ordinary, unremarkable characteristics: he was fiercely loyal. He forged meaningful, lifelong friendships, and those fortunate to be loved by him soon knew he loved deeper and cared more effusively than most. The boy grew to be a man and found happiness in the emotional connections that bind us as human beings. He didn't care for money or financial success. His ambition was deeply rooted in his relationships."

I rolled my eyes at the idea of listening to this wannabe Paulo Coelho fable, but Lily, being an avid reader of the author, gave me a good-natured punch to my arm and a look I've seen her give my son a thousand times when he's misbehaved. The man's eyes remained closed, unaware of my indiscretion, and he continued with his story.

"Peter's values were evident by the woman he married, Mary. They met in childhood and over their lives together created a deep, uncompromising love that can only be forged through formative years and strengthened through resolve over a lifetime together. Young Peter was instantly smitten with Mary, an infatuation that grew into true love during their schooling. He proposed a few years after they graduated from college and they married shortly thereafter, settling in their hometown. Peter took a job at a local pharmaceutical company while Mary took care of their children."

I sensed Lily's eyes widen, which gave me discomfort. The story was a little too close to home and felt more familiar than I cared to admit.

"They had three lovely girls," the man continued. "Peter was a doting father, and the three girls grew into exceptional young women, each of them thoughtful and caring, their characters built from a foundation of integrity, empathy, and unconditional love. Peter may have lived an unremarkable life, yet it was a fulfilling one. He may not have had material possessions or physical luxuries, yet he had greater treasures. He read goodnight stories to the girls, enjoyed late night talks on the porch with Mary, summer swims in the lake, annual fishing trips, and tearful hugs when one of his daughters needed to mend a broken heart. He was blessed in ways most people don't see favor: he found happiness in what he had and sought nothing more.

"At his retirement party he spoke of family and friends, not of any great work accomplishments or financial fortune. He died in old age, living his final days in a hospice, cared for by his wife and their three loving daughters, now mothers themselves. He was surrounded by his children and grandchildren, and in the midst of the stories and the tears, he let them each know, just as he had told them many times during his unexceptional life, that he loved them very much.

"Peter died with a single message: that he would see them all again in the afterlife."

The man paused and I eyed my wife, who sat captivated by his story. I felt an urge to leave, but she ignored my tug at her shirt, and continued staring intensely ahead.

"And then..." The man opened his eyes and gazed at us with intensity. His eyes were a deep shade of emerald and lay sunken into his skull. As he looked upon us, I felt in the presence of someone very powerful or very wise. His eyes spoke in centuries to me.

"... the unremarkable man was born again. Peter was born again to the same parents on the same day in the same year as he had been before. He was laid in the same crib and was consoled the same way. At first, he was a normal child, developing the way every other child develops. He was a baby, then an infant, then a toddler. He rolled over, he sat, and he began to walk. Soon, however, as his brain formed, so too did his memories from his previous life. He could not understand any of it: why everything felt so familiar to him, as if it had already occurred before, why things that had yet to come to pass were also, in his mind, his past. His parents laughed away their son's quirks, hoping them to be just the actions of a toddler developing at breathtaking speed. They thought him their precocious little boy. He pointed to colors without being taught. He named animals he hadn't seen before. He counted before anyone taught him how to do so. His parents were filled with pride, thinking they had created a genius. That all changed the day Bocco arrived. As soon as their son had learned to speak, Peter would ask for Bocco. "Mommy, when is Bocco coming?" and "Daddy, why isn't Bocco here," were routinely heard in their household. They were so routine, in fact, that Bocco was given to the boy as a nickname. One day, a few weeks after the boy's third birthday, a young family moved in next door as they had done in the first life, along with a young blond cocker spaniel named Bocco. The boy ran to embrace the dog as soon as he saw the moving van pull up. His parents' eyes were now opened and saw the countless Boccos they had previously failed to see – wrapped presents whose contents were known, events that were foretold before they occurred. Their boy was indeed special, but not in the way they had first thought. He could see things that others could not. He knew the future before it became the present. At first, his parents kept this to themselves, but it became unmanageable as the boy continued his cognitive development. He began to question everything. Why did this happen before? Why is it happening again? At night, he would cry in bed, pleading for names they didn't know. He called for Mary and his daughters from his previous life. His parents became distraught. They couldn't help him. How could they help him? Their son was clearly delusional, possibly even schizophrenic. They did the best they could with what they had at their disposal. There were countless doctors and psychologists. Tests and drugs. Before the boy turned six, he had been misdiagnosed and overmedicated countless times. His mindset and his life were soon in disarray. He spent much of his childhood inside hospitals, numbed by cocktails of chemicals haphazardly prescribed by speculating doctors. The boy's second life was a pitiful one, and he died by his own hand at the age of sixteen, with the same single prayer in mind that he had spoken in his first life… the aim to see his wife and daughters once again."

"Oh my God." My wife put her hand over her mouth and let it drop beside her.

I glanced at the man, and his eyes met mine with a look that told me to stay still. An intense disinterest within his face suddenly left me cold underneath the hot afternoon sun.

"Come on, let's go," I whispered to Lily, but she shook her head, her eyes never moving from the narrator.

"Please, go on."

"And once again," the man continued, moving his eyes back to Lily, "Peter was reborn. Peter was more prepared this third time, but still unequipped to understand what was happening to him. He was born again the exact same way he had been before. He was first a baby, and then a boy. The memories of his first and second lives were made clear to him as he grew but they overwhelmed him, and he was weighed down by the memory of a long, fulfilling life with Mary and his daughters as well as the nightmare of an existence in the second. They both felt like dreams, but he knew they were real. Love, fear, and pain coexist within one another, and he knew all of them to be one and same, wrapped in the same cocoon of life. In this third life, he distanced himself from everyone and spoke to no one as he tried to make sense of his predicament. He looked upon people with fear and contempt – afraid of being once again subdued by doctors and forced to take drugs that would cause him even more grief. He needed his mind clear in order to make sense of things, and clarity was found when he was with himself, and away from the world. There were many things he couldn't understand but it had become clear that events happened exactly as he remembered them, but he could not understand why his actions led him to a different fate. When a young Peter met a young girl named Mary, who he remembered to be his once and future wife, he couldn't understand why he knew her, but she didn't remember him. He couldn't grasp why he had memories of the same girl growing into an old woman, caring for him later in life as a sick, dying husband. Drowning in confusion, the boy kept to himself, isolated. He became a recluse, lost in his thoughts, filling notebooks with memories of his previous lives, alongside events happening around him. Later in his third life, he had an epiphany: he realized if he walked precisely in his first life's footsteps, step by step, he might be able to recreate his first existence, and with that, once again be with his family. In this life, this epiphany, unfortunately, came too late. He was already alone. Mary had found another man and Peter had made himself an outcast to society. He found drink and drugs, and with their help, he ruined himself, dying sometime in his adult years from an overdose of barbiturates and alcohol consumption. Peter died yet again thinking of his lost family – Mary, their three children, and their six grandchildren, and he wished for them again as their memories slowly faded with each passing day."

I tugged at Lily's sleeve, and she brushed me away, her eyes never leaving the man. I was on the verge of standing to pull Lily up and move on, when the man spoke loudly and I recoiled at the weight of his intonation.

"And again: Peter was born for the fourth time. Again, born on the same day, in the same year, again to the same parents, in the same place as he had the first three times. He found some tiny sliver of favor in this fourth life. Armed with three memories of lives previously lived, he decided to avoid the misfortunes befalling the two previous, and as his tiny brain developed, so too did his ability to pretend. The boy who lived three times prior was also armed with a much more powerful weapon: his wish to see his three children again. He pretended to be surprised by events he saw coming and pretended to learn things he already knew by heart. He took care in meeting people, steered away from deep conversation, and he hid his intellect, purposefully misspelling words or making mathematical errors in school. Inside he was still riddled with fear and doubt but kept this anguish to himself. The only people in his life who saw anything out of the ordinary were his parents, who heard him shout words in his sleep that a boy his age shouldn't know and regularly saw a growing boy act with the composure of a grown man. During the day, he would do things that any boy his age would do, pretend to learn algebra or play weekend baseball. In the evenings, away from the eyes of his parents, he would write letters to Mary and his daughters, promising that he would see them again soon. And at night, he would dream of pushing his youngest daughter in her swing, or singing one of his grandchildren to sleep. He dreamed of his life once lived and wanted nothing more than to find that life again. This hope was a powerful weapon, and he used it to cut through feelings of despair and confusion to forge the only path in life that would lead him to those three wonderful daughters.

"Peter met Mary on the first day of school like he had before, and he tried again to gain her affection. He soon found that obtaining the affections of a young girl turned out to be as mysterious as the purpose for his continued reincarnation. Unlike before, she found the boy strange and awkward and would cast an awkward glance in his direction in class. Her attention turned elsewhere, and he put away his pursuit until a time when they could properly connect. He tried again to win her affections in high school, and again in university, but by then it was too late. She found life with another man and there was no going back."

The wind on the hillside had picked up and caused the tree canopy around us to bend and sway like the rolling waves in the ocean. The clouds were beginning to tumble in, hiding the sun, chilling the breeze. The man's voice cut through in a slow monotone beat, like he was reciting words from a pre-rehearsed speech.

"In his sixth life, Peter found success in retracing his steps with Mary. They married in the exact same church on the exact same day as in his first life. Peter had grown accustomed to his condition and was able to hide who he truly was from most people, including his parents, although to the detriment of their relationship. He also began using his memories for financial benefit, at first making bets on sports games or investing in stocks, armed with outcomes that had yet to occur.

"Although the era during which Peter lived never changed, the memory of his first life had faded over four centuries of rebirth. Peter clung even more tightly to his family's remembrance, writing down in extensive detail what he remembered from his first life. His journal became a manual, made up of major life events, places and dates to avoid, the birthdates of his three children, and the time and location of their probable conceptions. On the day when his first child was likely conceived, Peter prepared a romantic setting for him and his wife. They made love in the same way he remembered, and to his frustration, there was no pregnancy in the weeks that followed. He tried again on his second daughter's conception date, but that too proved a failure. Mary wanted to keep trying and blamed him for stubbornly only attempting it on certain dates. He implored her to trust him, that he knew these dates were magical dates. He had convinced her by revealing a few of his visions of the future, predicting major events that had occurred in his first life. If he was right about these major events, then why couldn't he also predict the birth of their children? But this only led Mary to grow distant, and fearful of him. He had promised her two children, yet as time went on, with nothing but a ticking biological clock, she was left with only a few instances where her husband was willing to give conception a try. Despite her pleas, the man held firm to the hope that they would succeed on the third attempt, and that he would at least have his youngest baby girl to hold. That too failed, and so did his marriage. His hope vanquished. On his thirtieth birthday, the man stayed alone, planning extensively for what he would do in his seventh life. With the memories of his daughters held in a tight embrace in his mind, he once again took his own life, and promised that he would try again.

"In the seventh life, Mary became pregnant close to the date of his first daughter's conception. When she announced her pregnancy, he was so overjoyed that he booked an overseas trip to celebrate, funded with profit earned from successful investments made earlier that year. A few hours into the flight, a loud bang woke Mary and Peter, and the plane was suddenly thrust into a rapid descent. As the plane fell to earth and Mary screamed, Peter calmly wrote down the flight number on a napkin and repeated it verbally, hoping to transcribe the detail to memory. Just before the plane crashed, and Peter was again thrust back into his mother's womb awaiting his eighth birth, he glanced over to see a panicked Mary looking at him confused as he mumbled and calmly scribbled on his napkin amid the horror of their surroundings.

"Peter was more careful from then on. He was now aware there was a path that, if followed, would lead to long life and certainty, and that adding variables would only bring risk into the equation. Clearly, the overseas flight was no longer advisable, along with any other trips where Peter wasn't certain of their safety. He began to comb through news reports, making note of any major incidents, imprinting notable events to memory, especially local fatalities to avoid. As time passed, the accounts in his journal of his family became slimmer and slimmer, soon limited to just names, places, and dates, as the descriptions of his children grew shorter and shallower, the memory of their faces and features dimmer, hazier, now out of reach, and the pages of their journal replaced with details of major events, car accidents, and local fatalities to avoid.

"Over the next few lives, he and Mary tried and failed to conceive on the prescribed dates. He did his best to console his wife and find empathy in her struggle. After all, she didn't understand his goal, even when he described it. For her, their proposed children were just dreamscapes, not anything that had actually happened. He pleaded for her to keep going, saying he knew they would be successful. He couldn't give up hope of giving life to his three treasures once more and vowed he would continue his struggle for as long as he needed.

"He retraced his life steps once again in his tenth life and Mary became pregnant on their first attempt. This time he stuck to the path described in his journal – no extravagant vacations, no unplanned trips of any kind. Nine months later, he was triumphantly presented with a baby. His joyous face quickly turned cold as he found it was a boy that he held. The man's heart broke in a million pieces. He couldn't understand how fate could be so cruel. Where was his firstborn daughter? Why was she replaced with another soul? He looked upon the tiny life they created, and the man swallowed his despair, soon learning that his love for the boy would match that of his daughters. Though time progressed normally, from Peter's perspective it had been nearly a millennium since his first life. The sight of his new son sleeping felt more real than the distant dream of his first life and his three daughters. Peter still held his hope firmly until the next two conception dates failed."

The man paused to drink some water and my wife pleaded with him to continue.

"And then what happened?" she asked.

"He let go. He said goodbye to the memory of his first three daughters and promised his son that he would give himself over fully to him. He would live in the moment and love what he had again, just like he did in the first life. He would find happiness in what was his to be happy about and let go of dreams or ambitions that were clearly not coming to pass. He said yes when his wife asked if they could keep trying for a second child, and soon they conceived a second child, this time a daughter. She looked like one of those from his first life, but which one, he asked himself, straining against his fading memory. Her personality reminded him of one of them as well. Did she have a different soul? He no longer knew what memory or fantasy was and resigned himself to just love her for who she was and give her the life she deserved. He relieved himself of his burden and found solace in his newfound devotion. He raised his two children with the kindness and care he remembered giving his first three daughters, and in turn they saw in their father a man who valued togetherness and being in the moment above all other things. His tenth life was a meaningful one, and he remembered it fondly thereafter when he was reborn again and again, cursed to attempt to repeat it, again and again.

"The next cluster of lives became a blur of monotony, frustration, and longing. Peter found that no matter how hard he tried, Mary would never conceive the same child as in other lives, that the odds were just too slim no matter how perfectly he timed the events. He would never perfectly retrace the steps that would lead to the children he knew in other lives. Conception was a result of precise circumstance, measured in milliseconds, a path so precise that any alteration, of any kind, would disrupt it, leading to alternative outcomes. Over many lifetimes, Peter began to understand that he wasn't reliving his life over and over; he was in fact living *a different* life in a different dimension. While he couldn't explain or understand why he had consciousness across dimensions, he began to understand why everything around him was virtually identical, and why events outside of his influence unfolded precisely the same way in each life. He was born into the same path. It was the only circumstance that would enable his own birth and therefore his consciousness. His path to conception required a virtually identical history, where prior events happened precisely as they had in others. But while the world around him would be a virtual exact copy in every dimension, he could still alter events in his own lifetime after he was born. This was why each life he led became so different. And no matter how hard he tried to retrace steps, how precisely he attempted to forge the same path as a prior life, his consciousness somehow altered the pathway leading to his children's conception. The probability was just too slim. It wasn't a matter of timing. He studied human biology and learned of the vast number of variables in the creation of sperm – variables influenced by emotion, levels of testosterone, or actions made throughout an entire lifetime. Variables he couldn't control. Even if each step throughout his life was made precisely the same, the probability of a single, designated sperm reaching the egg in Mary's womb was virtually incalculable and completely outside of his control. Sperm count varied from thirty to seven hundred and fifty million per single ejaculation, so even if he got the precise timing right, there were far too many variables in the milliseconds after that would alter the path to conception. The more lives he lived, the more new souls he would bring into the world, and lead to children to love and lose, and never see again. He died each life knowing he would never see the same soul again.

"The heartache of retracing his steps only to meet another soul for him to fall in love with and lose became too much for Peter."

The man paused and leaned his head forward, his chin almost touching the top of his chest.

"So, what did he do?" my wife asked.

"He stopped trying. He lived in the moment as well as he could, and by doing that he became something different altogether. For many lifetimes, his humanity faded, almost entirely. Traditional human cares and wants fell away. Empathy was replaced with indifference. He no longer met Mary, and instead focused on himself. Wealth was at first an aspiration in and of itself, then a tool to other aspirations. Throughout lifetimes, emotions continued to dull, along with the rest of what the world had to offer. Discourse became wasteful. Information, arts, literature no longer served their purpose, for he had read all of the books in all of the world. He had listened to every song ever written. He learned every language, every history, all of the world's art, and every trade. As lives came and went, only to be lived again, his humanity faded, and Peter was left with apathy and unfathomable boredom.

"In later lives, Peter played savior to those deemed worthy of his grace. He became a sad, sickly god – omniscient yet trapped in the trappings of time and space. He could be merciful: prevent accidents from happening, warn against terror attacks, prevent murderous husbands from ever meeting their wives. He could also enact vengeance upon those who angered him without anyone being the wiser: prevent couples from meeting or destroy businesses by inventing a product before the founder could do so. But all of these acts, throughout multiple lifetimes, failed to bring him any satisfaction. He began to feel only the uncaring indifference of an almighty deity, subjected to the confines of a paltry kingdom."

The man's face became solemn as he spoke, and I felt sadness in him through his words and began to sense he carried his words with overwhelming weight.

"Peter, in many lives, has been at times extraordinary: a soothsayer, an inventor, a celebrity, a scholar. He was often a man of great wealth and power. He changed the course of history many times but was always a prisoner of his repeated time period, and never a witness to its after-effects. Lifetimes were repeated and emotions continued to dull until ultimately these god-like acts proved to be as trivial and fleeting as any other action. Life would simply just repeat. Peter noticed that in most religions, the concept of God didn't directly interfere with humanity. God moved in mysterious ways at best, without revelation or direct acts – God must know that any interference would be pointless in the vastness of space and time, like a painter adding a single dot to a canvas already painted over entirely. Once Peter understood this, truly understood it, he began to regain his humanity."

The man's smile broadened, his face suddenly resembling a painting of Jesus on the mount.

"And today, after so many lifetimes lived, I am what I was always predestined to be: an unremarkable man, living an unremarkable life, each time in the moment."

He stood slowly, brushing off a few strands of glass clinging to his pants. Lily turned to me and mouthed words I already knew.

He is Peter.

My fear instinct kicked into high gear as I struggled with the thought of this man being convinced by an illusion of living his lives repeatedly. *We are not dealing with a sane individual,* I thought and gripped my wife's arm, which she held flat against her side, her face still transfixed by the narrator.

"So that is my story. I've learned a lot from that first unremarkable man, in his first insignificant existence. We have come full circle, in an exceptionally long but funny way, him and I. I no longer seek gratitude or pleasure from things I don't control, and have learned to live with what I have, and cherish it fully. It's why I like to tell his story once in a while, along my lifetimes."

"How many?" I managed my words without hint of sarcasm or skepticism as my mind raced to remember quantum mechanics or theories read in popular science magazines which would bring some testament or even proof to Peter's assertions. "Lives, I mean. How many lives have you lived?"

"The short answer is, I don't know," he responded, brushing away an insect buzzing by, and I sensed he viewed me in the same way: a tiny, temporary annoyance. "The memory of my last life is indistinguishable from all of the others lived. If I had to guess at an answer, the total timespan of my conscious existence would likely be in galactic centuries or perhaps exaseconds. At this point the lifetimes blur together. No single digit provides meaning, and the numbers have weaved into themselves, like a jumbled sentence that never starts, nor ends."

The weight of the man's words caused me to exhale, and I studied his eyes for signs of drug use.

"I've evolved during those lives. In the beginning, after the confusion and pain wore off, I reveled in the power I was granted. I viewed my vision as a gift to rule over others. In some lives, I led governments. In others, I owned nations. I was often the most powerful man in the world. I have witnessed the apex of human fame and envy. I changed history, many times over, across multiple lifetimes. In some, I'll be remembered as the single most important contributor to the human race. In others, boredom, listlessness, and even anger overtook me. Whether I was a nurturing hero or vindictive demon didn't seem to matter. Repetition of each lifetime dulled my emotions; so much so that now any action, whether big or small, is just an action. No matter the pain or satisfaction, it is now just an act, not an emotion, interchangeable with all of the other actions made before, or still to be made."

Peter cleared his throat and smiled again.

"Now, a simple act like a cough is indistinguishable from a world-changing or life-saving action. I view each lifetime like single atoms making up our universe: on a molecular level each one appears complex, isolated, and all important, spinning alone in a cold, dark existence within itself. However, viewed from afar, you begin to see they are not isolated, but make up a glorious system much more powerful and complex, and you come to the realization that each individual component is equally of value and completely disposable. So, to come back to my answer: I don't know how many lifetimes there have been, but I have lived enough to see a pattern through the structure of time itself and it points to one universal truth of our existence."

"And what's that? What's the one truth?" my wife pleaded.

Peter simply motioned his hands to the trees surrounding us, and then to the sky above us. "This is it. This is all there is. Nothing else. The truth is that we all live our lives alongside infinite dimensions, each having an infinite number of variations, all at once and forever."

To my surprise, Lily walked up to him, her voice breaking.

"How many times has this happened? Our meeting, in this clearing?"

Peter shrugged.

"Why us? Why tell us? Why *choose* us?"

Lily's hands reached out to Peter, and he took them in his. The sight of my wife descending into worship of a stranger sent a rush of discomfort running through my blood stream.

"Because Lily…"

The sound of her name leaving Peter's lips caused her mouth to gape open and I struggled with the thought of this stranger knowing it.

"… you were once and often both quite remarkable to that unremarkable man, and he forever owes you a great debt."

Peter then turned to me, and I saw a hint of sincerity in his deep, sunken eyes.

"A long timeline away from this one, David, you delivered my first three children into their worlds. You delivered others, in other lifetimes. In an infinite number of lifetimes, we are friends, you and I."

I shook my head in disbelief.

He knows my profession. He planned this and was waiting for us.

Anger rose within me at the prospect of being stalked as prey by what was clearly a sick individual. Expecting his response to entail a favor or money – or worse – blackmail, I started to ask Peter what he wanted from us, but before my words left my lips, Peter motioned to a familiar tree behind me. He asked for us to follow.

"You two are a union between faith and science. Lily of faith and David of science. Unfortunately, David, providing you with any credible proof of my story is impossible. It would be like trying to prove the existence of a three-dimensional world to a two-dimensional being. Whereas my eyes are open to other worlds, I too am trapped in the confines of this existence, living my life in the same confines of time, every time. I'm a two-dimensional being that just knows there is a third but is unable to prove it."

He walked toward the tree – Lily's and my tree, the tree we had sat under on so many of our previous Rocky trips, the tree that had come to define our union so many years ago. Goosebumps began to rise on my arms.

"However, I can offer you this."

He pointed to a large boulder jutting from the ground near to the tree's trunk. The stone was angular but smooth to the touch, and on its surface were carved two sets of initials: mine and Lily's.

"This is where you proposed to Lily, David. Right here in this clearing."

"How the hell do you know that," I began to protest, but Lily raised her hand softly to stop me.

"You proposed to Lily here in the summer of 2003," Peter said. "You then came back the following year on your anniversary to inscribe your initials. I know this because you told me. You told me this many, many times in many, many lives."

I looked at Lily and she nodded her head. Tears had welled in her eyes, causing her cheeks to puff out in redness. She believed him.

Peter then bent down and pointed at a familiar, smaller inscription in the large stone. The carving was weathered and aged, just like it was when I first came across it decades ago as a young man. Rudely cut into the rock boulder were two symbols of no significance or understanding to me.

"You were inspired by finding this inscription cut into the stone."

I jerked suddenly.

"How do you know that?" I asked. My anger had subsided, replaced by complete shock and a growing sense of wonder. No one knew about the smaller inscription, not even Lily. The carving was insignificant, and I had paid it no mind, and had told no one of it.

"You don't know this, David, but this small carving, which inspired you to carve your names into the rock above it, was forged thousands of years ago. It was likely done by an ancestor of the Uto-Aztecan civilization who once settled nearby."

I shook my head. "I don't understand."

"David, this simple prehistoric carving, once I learned of it many lifetimes ago, saved my soul. This small set of symbols provided me with evidence that I'm not alone and returned my humanity."

Peter ran his fingers slowly on the carving, as if painting the hieroglyphs on to the rock.

"Before this, I thought every one of my lives was a repeat of the prior. I never saw deviation in historical facts. But this…"

His finger stopped at the edge of the second symbol, and he began to tap it in a rhythmic beat.

"These symbols change between lifetimes." Peter looked up to me and smiled. "This carving gave me proof that there is at least someone else like me; someone with the same gift, or affliction, conscious across time and space. This prehistoric person carves different symbols into these stones scattered across these mountains in each lifetime. Over the course of many lifetimes, I was able to decipher its meaning and understand the language. The symbols themselves mean nothing when viewed in a singular life, but form messages throughout lifetimes. They tell stories of an experience much like mine, of predicting the future and living life over and over again. The inscriptions speak to confusion, dismay, and ultimately, salvation. I don't know why this person writes these. Maybe a plea for help, or a yearning to connect with another. But once I learned of this, it gave me great comfort to know that I'm not alone. I realized that my existence does not follow a pattern of repetition or reincarnation. Rather, like the prehistoric person, I have, somehow, gained clairvoyance into the fifth and sixth dimensions. Humans, as three-dimensional entities, are caught in the trappings of the fourth dimension – time. While they can perceive time, comprehending its full essence eludes them. My perception of time differs significantly; I am no longer confined by it. Instead, I coexist with and within time, finding tranquility in its vast, indifferent expanse."

Peter stood and straightened himself and Lily moved to ask him a question, but he raised his hand to stop her.

"No, Lily." He shook his head. "You ask the same question each time, and each time it is always the same answer. You could not have done anything differently. In one of my lifetimes, I encountered your second son. Please, take solace in the knowledge that somewhere across the fabric of time and space, your son exists. And much like my first three daughters, he continues to live, infinitely and perpetually, through an unbounded number of lives."

Lily began to sob, and I could sense her tears were not from sadness, but deep relief. She released grief that had built up deep inside for so many years since the stillbirth; grief we held deep within each of us but weighed so much harder on my poor Lily.

Peter turned to me.

"So, I owe you an infinite debt, David. And my repayment is simple. You and Lily both deserve to be happy, together. My gift to you is a simple message: move back to Colorado. By accepting Lily's wish, you will avoid a lifetime of misery. It will save your marriage and you will live a long and fruitful life."

"That's it?" I asked.

"That's it."

"We'd love to see you again." Lily's muffled whisper broke through her sobs.

"That is highly improbable."

"Could you give us your name?" Lily implored, the hope in her voice thinly veiling desperation. "In case... we want to look you up?"

A tender smile, the kind that often accompanies heartfelt farewells, lit up his face. "Searching for me would be futile. In this lifetime, I am no one at all. However, through the corridors of time, I am known as Peter Byrell."

And with that, the man turned and walked from the clearing. Lily and I were left with the wind sweeping around us. We sat in silence, thinking about what Peter had said.

She whispered three words that brought me to tears. "Our son lives," she said. I took her into my arms, consoling her until our weeping subsided.

We gazed upon our favorite tree swaying under grand mountain peaks as the fading sun gently peeked from visiting clouds to kiss our faces. It was a pure moment, free from cares and worries, and I found comfort knowing that this moment would indeed last forever, if I wanted it to.

ACKNOWLEDGMENTS

This book is for my wife and three wondrous children. You've gifted me the opportunity to be the best version of myself. My love for you will stand for all time, and all of time's permutations, endlessly.

This book owes itself to the unyielding love and support of my beautiful wife, who became the rock holding down the fort while I ventured into the realm of writing. Those nights when I shared snippets of my work with you, they're treasured moments I'll never forget, and your unwavering moral support is something for which I'm forever indebted.

A huge thank you to my parents, both physicists, who delved into the editing process with enthusiasm and vigor. You didn't just dissect the stories with your impressive scientific intellect, but also stripped the tales down to their bare emotional core, and through your emotional wisdom, revealed profound messages I had overlooked.

I also thank the many people who provided invaluable feedback and guidance on my journey; without their efforts, this book would have remained an unfulfilled dream. A special thanks to Blake (without your dedication and advice, this book definitely would not be as good as it is), Shona, Sarah and all the folks at Whitefox, Melissa, Adam (my big brother, who will forever remain someone I aspire to impress), Barbara (my intelligent, thoughtful sister), Dani, Elizabeth, Riaz, and all who took the time to read through my many clumsy drafts.